Wishing Quilt

Jodi Thomas
Lori Wilde
and Patience Griffin
The
Wishing Quilt

ZEBRA BOOKS
Kensington Publishing Corp.
kensingtonbooks.com

ZEBRA BOOKS are published by

Kensington Publishing Corp.
900 Third Avenue
New York, NY 10022

ZEBRA BOOKS and the Zebra logo Reg. U.S. Pat. & TM Off.

First Kensington Books trade paperback printing: September 2022
First Zebra Books mass market paperback printing: February 2025

ISBN-13: 978-1-4201-5375-0
ISBN-13: 978-1-4201-5376-7 (eBook)

10 9 8 7 6 5 4 3 2 1

Printed in the United States of America

Contents

The Secret Wish

JODI THOMAS

A special thanks to all my friends who are quilters. Thanks for the hours of conversations that helped make this story come alive.

Chapter 1
Stormy Tuesday

Late Fall in Texas

Avery Cleveland inched her rusty, red Mustang off the highway as icy rain blasted against her cracked windshield. Gripping the wheel, she yelled at the car she'd had since high school, "Hang on, boy. I don't want to go this way either, but it's our only option."

After fifteen years the car still refused to answer.

She made two lazy curves before the road narrowed and lightning flashed, revealing the black outline of a small town. The place looked abandoned, forgotten, slowly corroding.

Worthless, she thought, then sighed. The place looked pretty much how she felt right now.

Avery headed toward the buildings with only a line of blinking stoplights reflecting on a blacktop ribbon winding between stores and huddled homes.

They should have named this place Nowhere, Texas, she decided. While-a-Way, Texas, didn't fit.

But this was her last chance. Her one refuge in a world that had finally broken her spirit. The name didn't matter. It was a place to stay until she figured out how to restart her life.

As always Avery refused to let one tear fall. She'd been down before and she'd learned no matter what life threw at her, she could always tumble lower. She'd danced when her feet bled onto the stage floor. She'd given up meals so she could pay for lessons, and she'd learned to walk again when she'd fallen into hell. She was a survivor, and she'd survive here.

One red light blinked at her just after she passed a city limit sign. The electricity must be out all over town if only the traffic lights worked. That, or all the people of While-a-Way had moved on.

The second stoplight blinked, shining only far enough to reveal last summer's dead plants still hanging in weathered baskets from the lamp pole. Avery pushed on through the rain.

The corner of the town square loomed before her with trees shaking their bony, bare branches toward the sky. It was almost December but there was no sign of Christmas here.

Third stoplight in town and she saw her great-grandmother's old storefront. The quilt shop was dark and huddled between two bigger buildings. Avery fought the urge to turn around. Her last place to run to wasn't welcoming her, but she didn't have enough gas to make it back to Austin.

She parked and cut the engine in front of a tilted sign with several letters missing. This was the end of her journey. The bottom of the barrel. Her last place to hide from a world that no longer wanted her.

Pulling her poncho around her thin body as the Mustang engine rattled to a stop, Avery grabbed the chain of keys from the glove box.

With icy rain pelting her, she ran one more time toward the unknown.

A few seconds later, three locks blocked the door. One was broken, the second opened with the first key she tried and the third lock was jammed.

Avery pushed hard, breaking the rotted frame that held the bolt. What did it matter if she broke into her own property? The shop probably didn't want her any more than she wanted to be here. Austin, Texas, had always had a heartbeat full of life, but this place was silent. "Where the dead go to sleep," she whispered.

Her world had stopped fifteen months ago when a stumble on stage had put an end to life as she knew it; and now the silence, the shadows of this place were her last sanctuary.

In a blink she was inside the shop. Standing in the stillness of total darkness. She didn't even breathe. Damp air weighed down the thick layer of dust.

Fear won out for a moment before she turned and pulled the heavy paper off the windows. Lightning raged, showing off a huge space with rubble scattered around. Ornate shelves and staircases bookended both sides of the chamber.

Her life had finally melted down to one room.

Slowly, a memory of this place drifted into focus. Her mother had brought her here once when she was four or five. The room had been covered with patch-work quilts and bright bolts of material and shelves of books and notions.

Avery remembered thinking the shop looked like a fairyland of color. While her mother had talked to an old woman, Avery had pulled off her coat, fluffed her tutu, and begun to twirl across the polished floor.

Her mother yelled, but the music was too clear in Avery's head. She had to dance. Up the stairs she'd gone, leaning over the railing as if posing for a picture. Onto the wide landing she pirouetted like the great ballerina she knew she would someday be. The huge lights two stories high spotlighted her dance, and she could almost hear the crowds cheering.

Now, on this gloomy night, Avery let her poncho hit the floor and slowly began to dance as she had years ago. Her life might have crumbled, but she still needed to move. In a strange way she understood why Nero fiddled while Rome burned. It was all that was left to do.

Her legs were no longer strong, but they held as she moved across the dusty floor. Arms wide, she whirled with the grace of an artist and the joy of a five-year-old child. Lightning was her footlights and thunder played bass. Rain tapped a melody as she danced.

No one could stop her midnight performance this time. She was alone. She owned this room. No critics around to see her imperfections. No one to care.

Avery felt a moment of peace as she moved, light as a butterfly through sleeping air. Dance, the one thing she'd always understood and loved.

The unlocked front door tapped open against the wall. For a moment the sound was merely a crescendo to the orchestra playing in her mind.

Then, she turned and saw a man framed in the doorway. The ghost of a cowboy from another era, maybe. His shoulders almost touched both sides of the frame and a gun belt circled his waist. His hat was worn low. A rifle fisted at his side.

The moment she saw the weapon, Avery hesitated and missed her footing. She wilted into a tangle of arms and legs still spinning. Her body swirled out of control on the floor like a bottle twirling in a game.

"Stop!" the stranger yelled as if he could halt chaos in flight.

Avery's head hit the stairs hard. She closed her eyes, no longer wanting to even breathe. Her last dance was over.

Chapter 2
Winter's Shadows

Sheriff Daniel Solis stood stone still as he stared inside the abandoned building in one of a dozen dying towns scattered across his county. In the lightning's blink he'd thought he'd seen a woman dancing in the dark. She'd seemed featherlight, almost as if she'd take flight. Her movements were so graceful, for a moment he didn't believe she was real.

A broken lock said break-in, but why would anyone bother with this place?

Pulling his flashlight from his belt, he panned the room. On his third sweep of the empty store, he spotted the dancer lying at the bottom of the stairs like a marionette with broken strings.

Without hesitating he stormed toward her. Boots hammered, echoing off the empty room. He fought not to raise his weapon. He'd found drifters and druggies in these abandoned buildings before. They came in out of the rain like rats. But this woman hadn't looked like a vagrant and the Mustang outside had to belong to her. After being the county sheriff for five years, he pretty much knew every car and person around.

The vision he'd seen in the lightning's flash couldn't have been real, but the body at the bottom of the stairs was.

"Hello?" he called, worried that he might have startled her into a faint. "Ma'am, you all right?"

Dan set the flashlight down on the first step and knelt beside her. The long, thin body still didn't move. With two fingers he slowly pushed light brown hair away from her face. "Lady . . ." he tried again.

Something wet dripped over his fingers as bright red blood trickled along her temple.

He grabbed the flashlight and saw a tiny cut on her forehead, no wider than a fingerprint. Slowly he moved the light down her body. She wore jeans and a loose sweater that stopped a few inches above her waist. No more cuts. No red spots of blood on her sweater, only dust.

As he moved back up to her face, ice-blue eyes stared at him. More angry than frightened.

"Are you all right, miss? I'm sorry if I scared you." When she just stared, he added, "This is private property. You're not supposed to be in this building. Want to tell me why you broke in?"

Dan didn't want to arrest her. After all, breaking into a building to dance didn't seem much of a crime. Maybe he'd just warn her and suggest she get back on the interstate. Nothing in this town was open this late.

To his relief she sat up and rubbed her head. "I own this place," she whispered.

Dan offered his hand. "I'm Sheriff Daniel Solis. As far as I know no one owns this place. It has been empty for years."

"Great, you can go ahead and shoot me then. Right now, I don't really care." She slowly unfolded as if testing her strength before she stood.

He gave up waiting for her to take his hand. Dan moved to her elbow and lightly touched her arm to steady her. She was almost as tall as him, and when another bolt of lightning reflected in her blue eyes all he saw was anger.

The lady was beautiful in a fragile, fine china kind of way, but she definitely wasn't friendly.

He tried again. "I'll need your name and some ID. I'm the sheriff of this county." He attempted a smile, but he was too out of practice to make it look believable.

She limped to a shelf by the door and grabbed her purse. "Here." She shoved her driver's license and a legal-size envelope toward him. "I've got a letter from a lawyer that says my great-grandmother left her place to any relative who would move to this town, live here a year, and open the quilt shop again. The only relative desperate enough to take the bait is me."

The woman's head injury must have affected her brain because she kept rattling. "Granny Dorothy Dawn had only one daughter, my grandmother, who died before I was born. My grandmother had one daughter and one son. The son died twenty years ago without leaving any children and my mother died three years ago. I guess longevity doesn't run in my family. Which leaves me and my sister in line to inherit this nightmare."

When he just kept staring, she kept talking.

"My sister says she'd die in a small town, so that left me. She also said the only thing the big hall of a room was good for was hosting the town's Christmas party, and the town stopped renting it two years ago. Which means the shop is worthless."

Dan held the letter to the light. "This note from the lawyer is dated five years ago."

The intruder, named Avery Cleveland according to her license, shrugged. "It took me a while to make up my mind. What do you care, Sheriff? I've paid the taxes on the place for years."

The lady had plenty of sass, but for tonight she had enough proof to stake her claim. He was used to people saying "yes, sir" to him, but she seemed to be staring him down with those cold blue eyes. He had a strong feeling she never backed down or took any lip from anyone, including a sheriff.

"Welcome to While-a-Way, Miss Cleveland." He almost added his condolences for being the relative who had to take the place. "You're a great dancer from what I saw."

"I'm not a dancer, Sheriff. I was once, but now I'm nothing."

"No, miss, you're a quilt shop owner." He handed back the letter and her license, then surprised himself by brushing a layer of dust from her cheek. There was something about her that was sexy as hell even if she reminded him of an alley cat ready to bite him as he tried to help her.

He'd never seen a woman like her. So thin the wind would blow her away, yet graceful. Fine china. Deep beauty age would never take away.

"I really don't see myself as an owner of anything much," she snapped without moving away from him. "Owning this place and wanting it are two different things."

Dan tapped his hat with two fingers and thought about asking her if she wanted to go down the road a few miles for a cup of coffee at the truck stop. He'd kind of like to see her in the light. But she had that big-city edge that worried him. City girls talk too fast and shoot questions as quick as bullets. He was way out of practice in the dating game to last a meal with her.

"Good night, miss." He decided to run. "There's a motel north on the interstate if you're looking for a place to stay."

"No, I've got a house somewhere around here that comes with the store, but I think I'll camp out here tonight. This place might whisper to me in the night. Maybe it'll tell me what to do with this shop."

"Suit yourself." He handed her the flashlight. "I'll pick this up the next time I come through town. If the room tells you to go away, leave the flashlight by the door."

"Thanks." She almost sounded like she meant it.

With nothing more to say, he walked back to his cruiser. It was still raining, but before he started his car he watched her run to her Mustang and pull out what looked like a backpack and a blanket.

Dan frowned. Old car. No real luggage in sight. Not staying in a hotel. He'd bet a week's pay she was homeless and broke. One other thing. The lady was probably meaner and crazier than any rats in the shop, so he guessed she'd be safe enough.

Only she'd danced with such grace she'd probably haunt his sleep.

Chapter 3

Silent Wednesday Before Dawn

After midnight Avery crawled into one of the wide shelves made to hold bolts of material. She needed sleep before she could solve her mounting problems. The deep square shelf was low enough for her to slip out easily and too high for any rats to reach. Thanks to the sheriff's flashlight, she'd found a working bathroom under the stairs and an old quilt packed away inside a glass cabinet.

She used her backpack for a pillow and an old picnic blanket for her mattress and the quilt as her covers. With her knees folded she just fit in the space. After two days without sleep, even a shelf felt comfortable. Her body relaxed in dreams of dancing. She probably needed a shower, but she was too tired and too cold to take off her clothes.

Hours later she thought the silence must have awakened her. The rain had stopped and a blue moon spread an eerie glow from the now bare windows. Dawn was just starting to blink its way between the buildings across the street.

A sound came from the second floor open balcony. Not whispering or music, but movement. Then, she swore she heard someone walking down the stairs. Slow steps, as each level creaked with age.

She glanced at the flashlight by the windows four feet away. Whoever was in the shop would see her if she moved toward it. She'd be safer where she was. Stone still in the dark.

Avery slid farther back on the shelf. Unless the intruder came very close, the layers of shadows would hide her.

The steps stopped creaking, but now she heard the floor groaning with someone moving toward her.

Avery stopped breathing. She'd traveled halfway across Texas to be killed.

The slight sound of someone walking past her toward the windows, then a man's dark frame stood in the pale moonlight and seemed to be staring outside as if there was nothing unusual about him watching the main street at dawn.

For a while he didn't move. He was studying something on Main.

She tried to memorize every feature of him. Tall, maybe six one or two. Slim, in an athletic way. Not the body of a man who lived on the streets. He was dressed in black from his cap to his boots. A short dark beard covered the lower half of his face.

When he turned, she thought she saw binoculars in

his hand. Then, before she could see his face clearly, he was moving toward the door and away from the dawn's first light.

The shadow man knelt three feet from the front door and pulled something from his pocket.

There was just enough light for Avery to see what looked like a pet door low on the wall. Only this one had been painted to look just like the front door in miniature.

The stranger opened a small tin and set it by the tiny door, then vanished back into the darkness.

He traveled faster now, suddenly in a hurry.

Halfway across the room, he disappeared completely but she listened as his steps tapped up the staircase. Then the slight sound of a latch clicking and the shop was completely silent once more.

Avery remained still as morning spread across the floor. The beauty of the mahogany wood welcomed her. Even with its shroud of dirt and cobwebs, the workmanship shone through.

Slowly, like a bear waking from a winter's sleep, she crawled out of her shelf. Her legs were stiff from lingering echoes of being broken but she began to stretch, pushing muscles to work.

The old quilt she'd found slipped off her shoulders. In the early light she thought it looked like the one her great-grandmother had been piecing the day they'd visited. The old woman had said it was a wishing quilt because with each stitch she wished Avery a full life.

As she moved in a routine she'd learned long ago, her silhouette looked like she was dancing. Avery smiled watching her black outline sway in beauty with twin shadows along the walls. Graceful carbon copies of her form stretched in rhythm even when all she felt was pain.

A new day, she thought. A new challenge.

A fat tabby cat banged his way through the pet door and began to eat from the tin the man in black had left. The cat glanced at her once but showed little interest.

"Morning, Euthyphro." She smiled, remembering Plato's play. Her big sister once made fun of her for not being able to pronounce Euthyphro. Karen had been nineteen, in college, and Avery had been thirteen. Always the dumb little sister.

The cat didn't seem to mind the name or that she was talking to him.

"I never read the play, but I did learn to say the name. It seems a pompous title for you, cat. But after all, you can't have a plain name. You have your own door and a ghost who brings you meals."

Deep down she knew she should be afraid of the man in black, but she wasn't scared of him or the sheriff last night. In fact, she decided she'd give up fear. She'd lived with it too long. Besides, any robber who breaks in to rob an empty store and takes time to feed the cat couldn't be too dangerous or too bright.

As she moved through her stretches she took inventory. She had one relative, a sister who wouldn't answer her calls. Avery owned a quilt shop without anything to sell. Sad fact, she didn't know how to quilt or run any kind of store. Her car was teetering on worthless. And, somewhere just outside of the city limits, she owned a house. Which was probably a shack.

Oh, one last fact. She apparently had a cat who would probably never answer to his name.

Using the flashlight the sheriff loaned her, Avery moved to a bathroom beneath the stairs. She combed her hair and brushed her teeth, then said a prayer of thanks that no one had turned off the water.

First thing on her list today: Go see how rundown the house was, then eat breakfast and plan. If she could manage to live here a year, the land and this shop would be hers and she could sell them. A few thousand might be enough to make a start. Maybe the house would have something worth selling to give her pocket money. Then she could move back to Austin, find an apartment, and look for a job.

Only problem was how to pay the bills, food, and gas for a year when she had nothing to sell in the shop she owned.

When lights began to come on in the apartments over the shops across the street, Avery saw another pressing problem. Electricity. Mentally she changed her plans. First the house, then call about lights, and last breakfast.

She didn't bother to lock the door as she walked out ready to face whatever came.

As she drove north toward her house, she glanced at the directions scribbled on a yellowed piece of paper. *Drive down Main heading north, first right turn after the big billboard, one mile then take the left fork, about a half mile later take first dirt road. If you turn the wrong way you'll end up at the interstate. Turn around, go back to town and try again.*

"You have got to be kidding," Avery said to no one.

She pushed her sister's number. When the "leave a message" speech came on she shouted, "Call me back, Karen!"

Avery pulled off the road and waited. Karen always went to work early, but that didn't mean she'd answer her phone.

Every five minutes Avery left the same message. Karen hadn't flown to Paris a year ago when Avery had been hurt, but she had met her in Dallas months later and driven her to Austin for the second surgery on her legs. She'd made a big deal about letting her stay in their guest room for a few weeks while she was recovering, even though Karen's new husband hadn't liked the idea.

When Avery was on painkillers, she didn't do everything right, or fast enough. She left her wheelchair in the hall because the bathroom door was too small, and she couldn't pick up things she dropped, so clothes and towels littered her room. According to Karen, Avery slept too much and didn't eat meals at the right time.

Karen complained she wasn't a nurse. She hated it when Avery made any noise and acted bothered when Avery asked her to pick up things like medicine. When she fell in the bathroom, Karen called nursing homes until one finally came and picked Avery up, walkers, wheelchairs, and all.

The new place was noisy, the food was terrible, the staff indifferent, but the physical therapist, Sarge, was great. He'd been in the army and Avery felt like she'd gone through boot camp before she finished his workouts. She might have lost her dream of dancing on stages around the world, but when she'd walked out of the nursing home, she'd made it to the cab without limping.

Avery smiled wryly, knowing she'd hear the old guy yelling in her head every day for the rest of her life. "One more step," he'd shout like a drill sergeant. "Straighten that skinny body up and march. Ain't nobody goin' carry you through this life, girl."

As she held the phone waiting for Karen to call back, Avery decided there had been blessings scattered among the rubble of her life this past year. Unfortunately, she just couldn't find many. But Sarge was one.

Finally, Karen returned her call, pulling Avery back to the present.

"What do you need?" Karen yelled. "We're busy with work." Apparently, she really loved the boss since she'd divorced husband number two to marry the workaholic lawyer. When Avery pointed out his faults, one being he married her so he wouldn't have to pay her, Karen got mad at her sister and not the bum named Ron.

Avery jumped in before Karen remembered she was not speaking to her. "You know anything about the house that comes with the shop? I'm having a little trouble finding it."

"Yeah, Mom said it was a little farm at the end of a dirt road. When Great-grandmother left for the nursing home a few months before she died, she rented it to some farmer. Mom said she never got a rent check so he probably skipped out. The house is long gone for taxes so don't waste your time. Mom said it was a dump."

"That's all you know?"

"Yeah, and Avery, don't bother me about your problems again. I signed that problem over to you. I'm allergic to small towns. You're crazy for even thinking you can live there, and you'll never survive in a nothing town for a year. Sell anything you can fast and get on with your life. Ron says places like that with strings attached are nothing but money pits."

The line went dead.

Avery stared at the phone. They'd never gotten along. Karen was six years older and had always seen Avery as a bother. Now Avery was moving into her thirties and nothing had changed. Karen's last text read, **Don't bother asking me if you can stay with us again when you get out of rehab in a few months. We no longer have the room. Ron needed the guest room for workout equipment.**

Pulling back on the road, Avery took the first right turn then clocked off a mile and took the first left fork. Suddenly she was on a dirt road rough enough to swallow her Mustang.

When the house came into view, she was sure she'd made a wrong turn somewhere. The little blue house with a white porch was cute enough to be on a postcard. To one side was a garden bedded down for winter and on the other side was a barn. There was a chicken coop that matched the house.

This place was occupied, which meant it had probably been sold for taxes years ago and was no longer part of her inheritance. One more might-have-been in Avery's life.

She'd wasted her time driving out. Now all she had to do was figure out where to turn around.

When she tried to back up into wet grass just off the road, her back tire fell into a mud hole. Avery didn't even bother to cuss. Bad luck was all she'd had to hang on to lately.

A man stepped out onto the porch. "You lost?" he yelled.

"Probably," she yelled back. "I seem to be planted out here. You think there's any chance this Mustang might grow into an all-terrain Land Rover?"

Avery heard a woman's laughter drifting from inside the house, as the man stepped off the porch and started toward the road.

Avery watched as a woman in a wheelchair came out on the porch and shouted, "If you're stuck, my Ben will help you."

When he was within twenty feet he stopped and smiled. "How can I help? If you're selling something, I'm not buying. If you're preaching, I've already been washed in the blood. If you're looking for someone, I'm not him."

She laughed. "You don't get many visitors, do you?"

"You're our first this year and it's almost December." He moved closer and offered his hand. "I'm Ben Tucker and that lovely lady on the porch is my wife, Mattie. I've farmed this place for years."

"I'm Avery Cleveland." She liked the man's smile, honest and open, and she liked the way he introduced his wife.

Only he didn't turn loose of her hand as he grinned. "You're Dorothy Dawn's great-granddaughter. She told

me you or your sister might be coming around one day.
I'd about given up on seeing you."

"When did she tell you about me?"

He thought for a while. "I don't know. Six years
ago, maybe. She hired me to fix up this place when she
said she needed to move to the nursing home. I called
your mother when Dorothy died, but she said it was too
far to come to the funeral and one daughter was on her
third honeymoon and you were in New York. She told
me I'd have to take care of the arrangements for
Dorothy."

Avery wasn't aware her mother had kept up with anyone in town. She hadn't even called Avery until she got
the will.

"You knew my great-grandmother well, Mr. Tucker?"

"I did. My wife often visited with her and even
painted a few scenes of your great-grandmother's flowers, while I worked on Dorothy's house. She told us her
only granddaughter, your mother, wrote her a nice letter every Christmas. Dorothy Dawn didn't live a year
after she left this place, but she always said the great-
grands were coming to take over her shop one day.
Once I got this place all ready for you, she asked me if
I wanted to rent the farm and the house. We jumped at
the chance, even though we knew we'd have to give it
up once her kin inherited."

Ben removed his hat. "I've been putting the rent
checks in the bank ever since. Just over five years. The
deal was, I pay five hundred for the house and a thousand a month for the little farm, plus I keep up repairs
and make sure the taxes were paid from the rent account. When my Mattie had her accident, I skipped two

rent payments to pay for supplies and built onto the house so she could move around in the chair. I didn't think anyone would mind. Almost doubled the square feet of the house."

Avery climbed out of her car. "Are you telling me this place is still mine?"

"It is. If you like I'll try to be out within a month. It'll take time to move the stock and find a place big enough for the horses." His smile seemed sad. "I was career navy so we're used to moving, but I have to tell you we'll miss this place."

Avery was trying to process the idea that somehow she had fifteen hundred going in a bank account every month. She'd been broke for so long it was hard to fathom what that meant.

Ben straightened slightly with pride and kept talking. "I fixed everything around here so you wouldn't have any problems. This far out the electricity goes out anytime a storm comes along, but I could leave you a generator. Don't have cell service but there's well water."

"You get the internet or cable?"

He shook his head. "Never needed it." He glanced at his wife. "If you'll come up to the house, Mattie can tell you how long it will take us to pack. We've lived a lot of places but we kind of grew roots here. Leaving won't be easy, but it was nice to have for a while."

Avery folded her arms. "Well, that settles it."

Ben leaned his head toward his left shoulder. "Settles what?"

She looked at him directly. "I'd like to make you a deal if you're interested. I'll continue to rent you this place for the same price if you'll help me fix up the quilt shop. A month's work and I promise you won't have to move. In a year, if I sell out and move away, you'll have first option to buy the house." She glanced back at the road. "You're probably the only person for miles around who can navigate that road, I'm guessing."

They talked as they walked to the house. He told her what he'd done over the years to improve the place.

Avery asked questions just to make conversation.

When he finished, Ben added, "Dorothy told us you are a great ballerina."

"Was," she answered. "I took a fall in Paris." When she didn't add more, Ben was kind enough not to ask questions.

Avery had no doubt this house was far more the Tuckers' home than it would ever be hers. She wasn't sure she could live for a year in a small town, much less survive out here with the wild animals and snakes.

Ben's wife, Mattie, was shy but her art filled the house. Running the length of the back of the house, was a wide studio with the walls covered in paintings of wildflowers.

Ben said that his bride wanted to paint a mural on the barn, and come spring he'd build her a ramp and a swing so she could.

Avery no longer even noticed the wheelchair as Mattie maneuvered about the kitchen and served coffee and apple bread. By the time the bread was gone, Avery had told the Tuckers the story of her career in dance and the accident that had ended it. She'd traveled the world dancing until one night, on a stage smaller than most, she'd fallen, breaking both legs. It had taken her five months to get back to the States and then months before she left rehab the first time. More surgery. More rehab.

She understood the challenges of a wheelchair and crutches. Even when she started walking, she always hesitated when she stood, counting the steps, wondering if she could handle the distance before her legs failed her.

By the time she left the Tuckers' home, Avery had a plan. She'd find a cheap place to rent that was close to downtown and use the rest of Ben's rent for food and supplies for the shop. Maybe she'd even try to live in the quilt shop.

Her great-grandmother was way off the market price as far as renting farms, but Avery couldn't charge the Tuckers more, and the thousand for the land rental made up for the loss.

Ben pulled her car out of the mud and followed her into town, promising to see if he could get the electricity on at the shop. Then they'd figure what he needed to do to get the shop in shape.

On the drive back to town she thought over their conversation. There was so much to do.

When Dorothy Dawn had become so very frail, her quilters had run the shop for one week and sold everything for ten cents on the dollar. Everything went out the door, but they talked Ben and a few other men into dragging some of the stands and frames to the basement.

Ben had pointed out to Avery that it was lucky winter was coming on. "I've got plenty of time to help you get started."

"You might want to take a look," Avery had said. "The place has been sleeping for years. It might even have a ghost . . . who feeds the cat. And to be perfectly honest, I have no idea how to run a quilt shop."

Ben had looked over at her and said, "Maybe you could open a dance school? Dorothy told me once that you'd studied dance since you were tiny. She said you were so talented she didn't know what to say when she saw you dance."

"Sure." She laughed, thinking that a broken ballerina teaching dance was almost as crazy as a non-quilter running a quilt shop.

Then, for some reason she remembered the old woman who had been standing with her mother, watching her dance among the quilts all those years ago.

The old woman who hadn't said a word to her that day. But Dorothy had wrapped her in the quilt she'd been working on when Avery tumbled. The same quilt that kept her warm last night. The wishing quilt.

Chapter 4
Thursday Hope

In the hours before dawn Avery awoke in her shelf bed and began to think of what-ifs, knowing she was just dreaming. Could she teach dance? Could she run a quilt shop? Could she last in this place for a year on only Tucker's rent money?

Impossible, she decided. The fifteen hundred might pay her basic living expenses, but it wouldn't buy what she needed to open a shop or a school of dance.

She was almost back to sleep when the shadow man tapped his way down the stairs. He was still dressed in black, but he had something over one shoulder. Too flat to be a body. Too flowing to be a weapon.

From her hideout on the shelf, Avery watched him move toward the windows. As before he watched until the first light of dawn. The only sign of life on the square was the blink of the coffee place opening.

Slowly she could hear the town waking. The sound

of a car door closing. A light blast of laughter from someone rushing past. A child's footsteps, whirling on the sidewalk that sounded like she was tap dancing her way.

Something had caught the intruder's attention as he stayed a few minutes more than he had last time.

Avery leaned out slightly, trying to figure out what drew him. There was a young woman sweeping the sidewalk outside the coffee shop. A car pulling into a space beside the mailbox. A window opening in an apartment above the hardware store.

Nothing unusual, Avery decided.

Then, as if he suddenly remembered time, the shadow man knelt and opened a tin of cat food. The big butterball of a yellow cat was waiting this morning and politely meowed a thank-you.

When the shadow stood and turned, Avery shrank back and closed her eyes as if he wouldn't see her if she couldn't see him. Frozen, she listened for the steps so she'd know when he was gone.

Something seemed to float over her body. Then a moment later she heard the rhythmic groan of the stairs and knew he'd vanished.

Slowly she opened her eyes. There was another navy-colored blanket on the bottom step of the stairs.

The intruder knew she was there and he hadn't killed her. She looked at the cat and whispered, "I should marry this guy, Euthyphro. I haven't even said a word to him and he's already nicer than any guy I've dated in ten years."

The cat looked back at her, and Avery was sure she saw agreement in its eyes.

Avery cuddled into the warmth of the wishing quilt and went back to sleep. In a few more hours she'd go over and get a coffee at the place across the street and then she'd decide whether to start her new life.

If she stayed, she'd use the blanket the ghost gave her to pad her bed.

Half an hour later the doorknob rattled. As she stumbled out of her shelf, she noticed the sheriff blocking most of the light from the door. There was no mistaking Daniel Solis. Not much taller than her, five feet ten maybe, dark hair and gray eyes. He might even be handsome if he didn't look like he was irritated and tired.

On the bright side, he wasn't carrying his rifle this time.

As she walked to the door, she straightened her clothes and hand combed her hair. She really wasn't ready for company.

"You sleeping in here, Avery Dawn?"

She gave him her best dirty look. "My last name is not Dawn, Sheriff, and it is none of your business where I sleep." Sheriff Solis was definitely not one of those people who grew on most folks.

"You're right. It's not. You got a shower in the back room, so I guess you could turn this place into a ground floor loft apartment. I'd suggest putting up blinds though."

"Why? You afraid someone would see my body?" Small-town people were definitely prudes. "I'm thin, flat-chested, and scarred. Not much worth seeing."

Dan took one step inside like she'd put an "open" sign up. "No. I was more worried about them seeing that wild hair. You might scare someone." He managed a lopsided grin. "Of course, if you want to show me that thin, flat, scarred body, I might vote on whether it's worth seeing."

"Not a chance. I'm not your problem, remember, Sheriff?" She reached for her brush.

"I know. I know. Let's start over." He pulled off his hat. "I just stopped by to see if I could take you to breakfast, Miss Cleveland. Kind of a welcome-to-town thing. Think of it as part of my job."

She studied him. "This is not a professional call?"

"Right. I'm off duty as of one minute ago."

"So"—she thought of shaking her head to wake up, but that would just send her hair flying—"this a date?"

"No, this is breakfast. I figure I'll wait until you've had a shower before I ask for a date."

The sheriff looked like he was in his thirties, probably a few years older than she was, but she swore that was the worst line she'd ever heard. "Any chance you'll give me time to change clothes?" She looked at the jeans and sweater she'd been wearing for three days and slept in two nights.

"I was hoping you'd say that." He showed no sign of kidding.

Avery frowned and asked, "You have a lot of first dates, Sheriff?"

"I don't date much. And never since I put on the badge. It's hard to ask a woman out when you're giving her a ticket or frisking her for drugs." He grinned. "I did have an almost date last year while I was on vacation in Vegas. Halfway through the evening I told her I was a cop and she disappeared."

Avery laughed. "But I already know what you are,

so you figure you might have a chance with me? Maybe you figured if I'm sleeping here I might need a meal."

"Do you?" he asked.

"No, I can take care of myself, Sheriff."

He stared at her for a moment, then shrugged. "Look, you're a beautiful woman, a little wrinkled and muddy, but so am I most mornings. I'd just like to have a chance to get to know you, Avery."

She smiled. "I'd love to eat breakfast with you, Daniel."

Ten minutes later in clean clothes, hair in a long braid, and face scrubbed, she walked across the street with the sheriff. He held the door open for her and announced, "They serve breakfast burritos till ten. Almost as good as my *madre* makes. That okay for breakfast?"

"*Madre?*"

He smiled. "My mother. My folks live down near San Antonio and I do miss her cooking."

She brushed his arm as she passed through the door. He'd shared something personal. Who knows, they might become friends if she stayed around.

It was early but the coffee shop was busy. The blonde behind the counter was polite, but not overly friendly. Her nametag said "Sunny" and Avery guessed she missed little. She took the order for coffees and breakfast burritos, then pointed toward one of the tiny tables by the window.

If there was a book on what not to do on a date, Sheriff Daniel Solis probably wrote it. He introduced her to everyone who stopped by their table and filled each one in on all her story. When they were alone, he gave a lecture on the town and informed her the coffee shop owner was a recluse who rarely came downstairs. Some folks believe he left months ago.

When Sunny brought their order, she nodded once at Dan. Not friendly, more just acknowledging him. "Sheriff," she said as she turned to Avery.

The sheriff did his duty and introduced Sunny with no details, which told Avery that he had finally run into someone in town he didn't know very well.

The blonde nodded once and rushed back to her line of customers. She did her job, but Sunny wasn't very friendly.

Halfway through the best breakfast she could remember having in months, Avery accidentally bumped Dan's leg. A few minutes passed and he bumped her leg. The game was on. Conversation might be boring and broken from one topic to another, but below the table they were having fun.

His gray eyes showed no emotion as he stared straight at her while he straightened his napkin and accidentally brushed her knee with his fingertips. She moved her foot against his boot, letting her calf brush against his. Avery felt like they were in junior high, but there was nothing PG about what she was thinking.

He set his coffee cup so close to hers that his knuckles brushed her wrist now and then. Again, no emotion in his gray eyes, but she felt like her whole body was reacting. All she had to do was move an inch away and the game would be over, but she was having too much fun. It had been so long since she'd flirted with a man.

When Daniel wasn't frowning at her he looked younger. Slowly she was learning the man behind the badge, and she had a feeling Dan let very few people close. Beneath this strong, handsome sheriff was a shy man who didn't know how to flirt. She might be wary of the sheriff, but the man fascinated her.

They were on their second cup of coffee when Ben Tucker came in wearing his tool belt. Avery jumped up and thanked the sheriff for breakfast. Daniel stood but didn't move toward her. He was all formal now, making her wonder if she'd read too much into their touches. After all, they were both long legged and the table was tiny.

While Ben got a coffee to go, she and Daniel stepped outside. He'd saved his one real smile for the blonde behind the counter. Avery decided she probably had imagined the whole footsy game.

Something was wrong with her. She hadn't kissed a man since the accident and now she was fantasizing about a sheriff who was just doing his job, getting to know the newcomer in town.

For a few moments she stood on the walk. She'd already thanked him for breakfast twice. His hat blocked his eyes, so she had no idea if he was even looking at her.

Finally, he broke the silence. "I read about your fall off a stage in France. The account was written up in *The New York Times*. You must have been some dancer. The paper said you might never walk again. It said you twirled like a feather in the wind, barely touching ground."

She didn't look at him as she whispered, "That part of my life is over. Thanks for not including my inheritance in my résumé you told everyone who passed."

He studied her for a minute. "Folks want to know

who you are. You'll be welcome just because you're
Dorothy Dawn's kin. They'll help you settle in if they
think they know you."

She stared over at the dark shop crowded between
buildings. "I don't know if I can do this."

The sheriff pushed his hat back and looked worried.
"Hell, I saw you dance in the dark and you say you
can't do that anymore. If you can twirl all over Europe,
you can do this."

Avery looked up at him as Ben Tucker came out
with his coffee and a bag of donuts.

"Ready, Avery," Ben said. "Let's go to work."

As she walked away with Ben, she looked back at
Daniel. He might be growing on her. He thought she
could dance.

An hour later while Ben was redoing the plumbing,
Avery walked into the tiny branch bank three doors
down from her store. Two clerks and a branch manager
all welcomed her.

After she showed ID, they presented her with Dorothy Dawn's financial records. First, one small checking
account with three hundred dollars in it.

Avery was impressed.

The banker explained that twelve dollars was pulled
from it every year to pay for a safety deposit box.

The box held only one piece of paper. A copy of the
will leaving the shop, the house, and the farm to any
direct relative who would run the quilt shop for a year.
At the bottom of the will was a short list: the names of
Avery's mother, Avery's sister, and Avery. Any one of

the three who had the keys could claim the store and the house. After one year the properties would be legally transferred.

The keys had been mailed to Avery's mother before Dorothy Dawn died. Her mother gave the keys to Karen first because she was the oldest. Karen opened her hand as if they burned her fingers and dropped the keys. Avery picked them up, thinking someday she might visit the place. Over the next few years she'd tried to give the keys back to both of them.

During her recovery, she'd found the keys in her jewelry box as she looked for something to sell. Somehow the keys, the shop, became her last-resort plan.

The banker standing beside her smiled a rather sad smile and whispered, "Since you are the only one to show up in five years, looks like it's yours, dear."

Avery showed him her mother's death certificate and a notarized document Karen had signed saying she was not entitled to anything and was not responsible for any bills.

Finally, the banker handed Avery the last piece of paper. The savings account statement. "We'll be changing this account to your name today. She'd want you to have it to make your start."

Avery put the pieces together. When Dorothy Dawn died, she'd had less than four hundred dollars. For the next five years there had been one payment each month to the savings account. Ben Tucker had kept his word. He'd paid rent for the house and the land.

Counting interest and subtracting taxes, Avery now inherited almost ninety-two thousand dollars.

A fortune, she almost said aloud. When she lowered

her head and covered her eyes, the banker stood. "I'll give you some time, Miss Cleveland. Dorothy made it plain to me that you were to have access to all her accounts. If you leave today, you won't get the land or the shop, but the money is yours."

Avery closed her eyes and thought back to when she was five. She only had bits of memory of Dorothy Dawn. The old lady had frowned when Avery had danced through her shop. The wrinkled woman had barely talked to Avery, hadn't even hugged her except to put the quilt around her when she cried, but today she was giving her a chance to start over. No more deciding which bill to not pay this month. No more putting back food from her grocery basket to save for gas money.

Avery picked up the phone to call her sister. Then, she saw the notarized statement and her sister's signature. The bum of a husband, Ron the lawyer, had drawn it up. "If our old grannie owes anything, even for her funeral, Ron and I are not paying a dime," Karen had said. "You go check it out, Avery, but you'll just fall into another hole. That's all you've been doing lately, and you are not dragging me into anymore of your problems."

When Avery said she wasn't sure she even had enough gas to get to While-a-Way, Karen had added, "That's not my problem either, is it?"

Avery put her phone back in her pocket and stood. Win or lose, Avery was in this alone.

The banker was talking to the teller when she walked out of his office. "How can I help you, Miss Cleveland? We're very sorry for your loss."

"Thank you," she said. "Can I use some of her savings to fix the shop up?"

He straightened to his official stance. "If you take the money and walk away today, both properties will revert to the town. If you reopen the store, all properties pass to you in one year. Do whatever you wish."

There was that word again. Wish. She would have never wished for this shop in this town, but she had wished for a place to stay . . . a place to belong, a place to rest. Maybe, right now in her life, that was worth wishing for.

"Thank you for explaining everything. I'm staying." Her last-chance place to run to had just become her new address.

The teller clapped her hands. "Oh, we were so hoping you would. I've missed my quilting group that used to meet every Monday night. Maybe you'll be starting that up again."

"I might do that as soon as I get the shop up and running." Avery smiled at her. "I'd like checks printed with Dorothy Dawn's Quilt Shop on top and my name beneath. I'd also like five hundred dollars cash."

The teller squealed. "You're really going to open the store again! I can't wait to tell the girls."

"Yep." Avery grinned. "And I have no idea what I'm doing."

"Oh, don't worry. We'll all help you if we can. Half the women in town quilt."

"Thanks," Avery managed to say as the clerk handed her an envelope with five hundred dollars in twenties.

An hour later while Ben worked on the electricity, Avery started cleaning. Twice, she had to run back to her purse to look at her money. Two years ago, five hundred dollars would have just been pocket money for a weekend, but since the accident, her savings had dripped away.

She found cleaning supplies tucked away under the stairs and a file cabinet with inventory lists and names of suppliers. A place to start. The newly polished landing halfway up to the balcony became her office as she spread out files on a floor shining in sunlight.

When all the lights finally came on, Avery saw the true beauty of the place. Ben promised to return tomorrow and told her to make a list of what she wanted done.

"If you don't mind, I thought I'd bring my Mattie with me tomorrow. Her folks used to run a hardware store; she said she'd volunteer to help you set up the books."

"I'd love that. Tell her I'll buy her lunch if she comes."

Ben smiled. "Sounds like a deal."

When he stepped out of the door, she was whirling across the newly polished floor and laughing. A tiny part of her was starting to believe in possibilities.

As she moved, she noticed a tiny face pressed against the window.

Avery waved the little girl in along with her mother.

"Hello." Avery offered her hand to the child.

The child giggled. "You dance too. Would you show me how to do it like you do?"

The mother stepped forward. "No, Lily, don't bother the lady." The mother took the child's hand.

Avery knelt to Lily's level. "I would love to show

you. Was that you tapping along the sidewalk yesterday?"

The mother smiled as Avery moved slowly around the empty room with a tiny dancer following every step.

"Thank you," the mother said when they stopped.

"You are welcome." Avery touched the child's head. "Come back any time, Lily."

"We will. Thank you." The mother laughed. "My girl was born to dance and I'm afraid I have two left feet."

As Avery watched them walk away, she smiled. That was the first time she'd danced with someone since the accident. She'd forgotten how fun it could be. As she gazed out at the town, she noticed someone had taken down the dead hanging plants from the light poles and replaced them with huge Christmas bows, but she felt Christmas had already come early.

She'd meant to look for a place to live, but it was dark before she'd thought of it. So, alone, eating the cheese crackers she'd bought next door at the hardware counter, Avery studied the catalogs until her eyes were blurry. She left one light burning beneath the stairs as she crawled into her shelf to sleep another night. Her backpack for her pillow. One picnic blanket and a warm wool navy blanket for padding, and her great-grandmother's quilt to keep her warm.

For the first time in a year, she felt that she was a dancer—not on a stage in Europe or a grand hall, but in a quilt shop soon to be surrounded with bright colors. Her world seemed to have more light in it.

Hours later she heard the click of a window latch upstairs, then soft footsteps on the stairs. It occurred to her that this might be her dawn wake-up alarm every morning if she didn't find an apartment.

The man in black crossed the empty store as before and moved to the windows. In the shadows, he watched, but this morning Avery noticed he stared only at the coffee shop, the first lights to blink on around the small town square. Then, just as silently as he'd come, he fed the cat and turned to leave.

When he passed her, Avery closed her eyes and remained still until she heard a click and knew he'd closed the window he seemed to think was his private door.

Maybe he was homeless, watching the town sleeping, or maybe he was a time traveler simply passing close to her space in this world. But one thing she knew. He meant her no harm.

Chapter 5
Sunny Friday

Dan walked into Avery's shop a little after dawn. He'd seen her unlock the door and go back and forth to her car and knew this new resident of While-a-Way was up and apparently moving in. The lights were on and so was the water, because her hair looked still damp from a shower.

"Morning," he said as he handed her a paper cup. "I forgot how you liked your coffee so I brought cream and sugar."

"Thanks, Sheriff. I thought you might be coming by to collect your flashlight. I forgot to give it back to you yesterday."

"I do need it back. Government property, you know." He tried to smile. For some reason this woman made him nervous. She probably didn't need coffee, but it was the only reason he could think of for dropping by.

"I hear you're staying and reopening the store. That true?" he asked before she had time to hand him the flashlight and say goodbye.

"I am staying. You know where I can pick up used furniture? I could use a desk or a counter. A few chairs. A bed. Maybe a dresser."

She was unpacking as she talked. Her movements were fluid, as if her whole body was blowing gently in a breeze. Dan could see the dancer in her, the grace, the beauty.

He cleared his throat and tried to get his mind anywhere but on her body. "Sure. There's a flea market down by the rodeo ground every Saturday, except when they have a rodeo. You wouldn't believe what the locals haul out there to sell. Get there early and you'll have your pick of pretty much everything. Come after noon and the junk is half price."

He couldn't think of anything else to say. The last thing he wanted to do was have her think he was flirting with her. He was still officially on duty for five more minutes.

Thinking about work, he asked, "Any chance you've seen a stranger around here? Tall man dressed in black."

"No," she said slowly and for once she stilled. "Why?"

"Oh, nothing. I don't want to scare you, but some teenagers claimed they saw a man standing at your window before dawn."

She took a drink of her coffee. "Maybe he was just walking by."

"The kids said he was inside the store looking out."

This time he thought she hesitated a blink too long.

Those blue eyes were cold again, giving nothing away. There were few people he couldn't read and she was one of them.

She turned away. "That's impossible. I keep the door locked."

Another clue she might be lying, he thought. Not meeting his eyes when she answered. Or maybe not? She could be just getting back to work.

Dan nodded once and said he'd let her know if he noticed anything and asked if she'd do the same. She agreed, but something about her behavior bothered him. He'd been in law enforcement for ten years and he swore he could smell a lie even in a woman with true blue eyes.

Only problem was, why would Avery lie? He'd run a check on her and the lady didn't even have a speeding ticket.

He checked his watch. He was officially off duty. "I didn't come by just to get the flashlight. I thought I might ask you for a date, that is if you're free some night. I clock in at eleven, so I can't keep you out late." He should have asked if she had a boyfriend. Too bad that wasn't on her record.

Daniel frowned. The boyfriend question should have been first. She could be involved with someone back in Austin. Or she could be newly married, or separated. He was out of practice. She'd probably say no just because he was an idiot.

She laughed. "You don't look too happy about asking me out, Sheriff. You sure you don't want to think about it first?"

Daniel walked a few feet into the empty shop. It had

been so long since he asked a woman out, he didn't remember the rules. His track record with women was simple. They usually lasted three dates. One to calm down enough to talk without sounding like his next question would be, "May I see your license please?" Second date, they'd talk, maybe kiss good night. Then, date three. He'd spend the date listing what was wrong with her, or worse, he'd figure out why he'd never be the man she wanted.

He'd been crushed in college by his first love and been left gun-shy.

Dan knew Ben Tucker would probably be coming into work soon, so he didn't have much time. "Look, Avery, I'm not good at this kind of thing."

She looked like she felt sorry for him as she joined him in the shadows. "How can I help you, Sheriff?"

Great, now she felt sorry for him.

She was one foot away but it felt like a mile. The memory of her dancing that first night drifted through his mind. He straightened as if facing trouble. "First, call me Daniel or Dan when I'm off duty, and I don't need help asking you out." He took a deep breath and added exactly what he wanted. "I really want to kiss you, lady, and if I have to take you to dinner and spend a few hours trying to think of something to talk about, then I will."

She laughed. "After you get past kissing me, then what?"

"I have no idea." Daniel fought down anger. He never got things like this right. "You've been in my head since I saw you that first night."

To his surprise, she moved closer. "You want to kiss me, Sheriff. Why?"

There was that smart big-city attitude. He felt like he was at the O.K. Corral and forgot to bring a weapon.

"Hell if I know." He thought about what his mother used to say, and the words just came out. "*La magia del corazón*." But he felt more of a need inside to touch her than any magic in his heart. "I think you should know I've never said that to a woman."

He froze as she cupped his jaw with her hand. She rose slightly and pressed her lips against his.

When he didn't react, she moved away. "Sheriff, if you want a kiss, it would help if you participated in the process."

He slid his arm around her waist and pulled her against him. "Avery, don't call me Sheriff when I'm off duty."

Before she could answer, he participated.

Chapter 6
Saturday Dreaming

Even wide-awake at dawn Avery couldn't get the sheriff's kiss out of her mind. It had been a hard kiss, almost bruising her lips at first, then he'd softened slightly and, like a man remembering how to kiss, he practiced. She'd rarely taken the time to study people. Her career had always been more important than relationships. But she guessed there was something broken in the strong sheriff. He might not have scars on the outside but he was far too guarded, too unpolished with women, not to have been hurt in his past.

He'd held her with one strong arm and she'd made no effort to touch him, but with her body held against his chest, she'd felt him breathe. Like a man facing danger, his heart had pounded. Saying he was attracted to her was an understatement. She might have been a bit frightened if she hadn't felt the same way.

As fast as he'd held her, he stepped back. He'd just

stared at her as if he was as surprised about the kiss as she was. When he ran his thumb along his bottom lip, she fought down the need to attack him, again.

He nodded once. "You okay with this?"

"I'm okay." She couldn't complain when she'd kissed him first and then dared him to take action.

He turned and walked out the door as if nothing had happened between them. But the man's kiss kept drifting in her brain. She had no idea if it was the beginning of something or the ending, and Dan seemed to have forgotten about the date he'd been asking about. When she'd answered that she was okay with this, that seemed to be all he needed to know.

She decided she didn't have time to worry about the sheriff when she noticed three little faces at the window and one was Lily.

Her heart lightened. She'd prepared just in case the little girl came back. Turning on music, she invited the girls in, and they began to dance in the open space. Avery handed each a long silk scarf she'd bought from street vendors in Paris. The tiny dancers laughed as the silk followed them.

In what seemed five minutes the mothers had slipped in and were watching. Their little darlings were willow trees circling Avery.

Then, giggling, the girls were rushed off to school. Alone, with the music still playing, Avery slowly moved. She knew she'd never dance on a grand stage again, but the love of the movement was still there, if only for a short time. Even if she never grew stronger, she could dance for a few moments. Heaven in small doses.

As the sun brightened the store, reality finally pulled her back to her life. Ben was working while Mattie gave her a lesson in bookkeeping. Folks stopped by to say hello and tell her stories of her great-grandmother. Dorothy Dawn may have been a wild child, but all those who could have testified were now dead, so her pranks were now simply funny legends. To Avery's surprise, she learned Dorothy outlived three husbands who were now buried in a row. Dorothy Dawn had been cremated and sprinkled evenly across all three graves.

Strangers wandered in to tell of her laughter and how she'd thought people who didn't pick up a needle now and then were lower life forms.

Avery tried to work as she greeted every guest with "We're not open yet." But they came in anyway.

One lady dressed in black rushed inside and said she was there to have an important chat. Avery was too interested to turn her away. Ben and Mattie took a break while Miss May sat down on a box to talk. The little lady began her life story.

She said she and Dorothy Dawn had been friends all their lives and she'd left a box for Avery, but Miss May couldn't remember exactly where she put it. "Dorothy had meant to mail it to you but your sister never sent the address. I'll start looking for the box since all I have to do is bring it to you."

Then Miss May asked questions in rapid fire about Avery's life and got excited over every fact she learned. Avery loved her tenacity. She told stories of the town and of hard times over the years. Avery decided when she turned eighty she was going to be just like Miss May. Put it all out there. Say what she meant.

Live life on her terms. "You're not the first to come back home," Miss May said. "An old friend from my school days came by to stay a while. I do love catching up with folks."

Avery thought of reminding Miss May that she wasn't "coming back." But then, she decided she wouldn't mind belonging somewhere for a change.

When Avery mentioned the sheriff, the old woman frowned and looked directly at her. "You like country music, girl?"

Avery had to say yes. She wasn't sure what Miss May would do if she'd said no.

"Well, our sheriff has a Humpty Dumpty heart. He's broke and there ain't nobody who can fix him, just like that old song by Hank Thompson. He grew up with a girl, they started dating in high school and through college. He bought a nice place west of here and asked her to marry him. She said yes, then left to travel that summer and never came back. Sent his engagement ring back without a note."

"Maybe someday . . ."

Miss May stopped her with a shake of her head. "He's a great sheriff but he ain't never going to be any woman's man." A tear wiggled down her wrinkled face. "I've seen that kind of broken before. I've lived it."

As the old woman stood she added, "I have to go, dear. I've got a coffee date across the street."

Avery helped her walk out. "You come back anytime, Miss May."

The old woman smiled.

As Avery walked back into her shop, she realized

that Miss May was one of the side dishes of the banquet of life. No one noticed her. No one loved her. Few would miss her when she was gone.

One tear drifted down Avery's flawless cheek as she realized she and Miss May were the same.

Avery worked hard all afternoon thinking of only what had to be done. If the folks stayed too long, Ben Tucker put them to work. Carrying up display stands from the basement was his favorite job. After a few trips the visitors said their goodbyes.

Avery worked late, knowing the sheriff's kiss would keep her awake even if she tried to sleep. It worried her that she hadn't told Dan the truth about the shadow man who looked out her window at night. He could be a stalker or a drug dealer. After all, this nowhere town could be a drop-off for trafficking. Or the shadow man could be a serial killer, going from town to town in alphabetical order and he finally reached the W's.

But somehow she couldn't believe a serial killer would feed cats or bring along an extra blanket to a killing. He'd smiled when the light went on at the coffee shop as if all was well.

When Avery finally crawled into her shelf, she swore that tomorrow she'd find an apartment or at least a bed. The storage room next to the bathroom could double as a bedroom once they got it cleaned out. Ben, as he'd worked all morning on leveling the floor, had mentioned that under the stairs could have been a living quarters, maybe fifty or sixty years ago.

Only Avery couldn't work and sleep in the same place. It didn't seem right.

She laughed. She was doing that now. "Tomorrow I'm buying a pillow," she whispered as she fluffed her backpack.

As she slept, she made lists of all that had to be done. It was almost dawn when she woke, still mentally making lists.

When she rolled over she saw the shadow man by the window. She knew he was waiting for the light to come on at the coffee house. Maybe it was a signal or maybe it just marked his day beginning.

Silently she watched him. When he finally bent to feed the cat, she swung her legs out of the shelf. "You want to tell me what you're doing in my shop?" Her words came low, asking for an answer, not demanding.

If he planned to kill her, he might as well get it over with before she moved furniture in.

Avery sensed him tighten, but he didn't panic. He just turned his back to the window. "I mean you no harm, Avery Cleveland. If you want to play 'Elf on the Shelf' I won't even tell anyone." He had an honest smile and a bit of mischief in his grin.

Avery let out the breath she'd been holding. "I figured I was in no danger or I would be double dead by now. You know, for a shadow, you make too much noise. I'm guessing you've got your reasons for breaking in."

She thought she heard a muffled laugh. His words came low, calm. "I don't guess you'd settle for the answer that I just dropped by to feed the cat?"

"Not a chance. I've traveled the world, Shadow Man, and you are not from Texas, probably not even from the South." His black clothes were heavy, almost with a military cut, but there was a touch of a big-city look about him. Or maybe it was in the way he moved, his personal space pulled in like New Yorkers do on subways.

He fanned his hands out in surrender. "Chicago born, but I've lived the last few years in D.C."

Avery kept staring, just in case he attacked. Of course, she had no weapon, so it wouldn't be much of a fight. Might want to add "weapon" to the pillow and bed list. Only this guy was talking to her as casually as if they'd met on the sidewalk.

Avery could play along. "So, Chicago, you breaking into every store on Main, or just my place?"

He looked back at the dark coffee house before he answered, "Until three days ago this was an abandoned building. I've been here longer than you, so maybe I got squatter rights. And I didn't break in, the window latch is broken."

Why not argue with the stranger, she decided. "I saw that window, even went around back to look at it. It's twenty feet straight up from alley dirt. Want to tell me how you climbed up? Nothing to stand on and you don't look like Spider-Man."

He gazed back at the square as first light moved between the buildings. "I didn't climb up. I swung down from the roof."

"Oh," she managed to say as if his explanation made sense. "And why?"

The light blinked on at the coffee shop. He watched for a moment. The dawn offered just enough light to allow her to see his face. He was smiling as he watched the barista pulling open the shutters.

"She's pretty," Avery said, following his stare.

"She is," he answered, then straightened and turned back to Avery. "Look, Miss Cleveland, I'm just doing a job here and I mean you no harm. I've got equipment up in your attic that I'll have cleared out in a few days. I can see the roads from up there but I can't see the coffee shop, so I need this vantage point a few times a day."

"Good guy or bad guy?" Avery waited, guessing if he was a "bad guy" he'd lie. So, dumb question.

"I'm investigating for the marshal's office. Just observing. I don't suppose you'd keep my secret. I'll be out of here in a day or two, and you'll never be bothered again."

She could see his face now. Twenty-four or maybe as young as twenty-three. Hair combed straight back, Chicago style. Beard trimmed close, just long enough to hide his jawline. This was probably his first case, and if she told anyone it would blow the stakeout. "Does the sheriff know about you?"

"No. We'll let him know when the time is right. In this kind of surveillance there is always a chance the local law is involved or being paid to turn a blind eye."

"Then, why trust me?"

"You're not from around here. Believe me, Miss Cleveland, we know all about you. And before you ask, I think Daniel Solis is clean too. It's just a precaution to keep him out of danger until we know there is no threat."

"So, you investigated him too."

The kid smiled as if he knew she and the sheriff had kissed. "Yes, I did, but maybe not as close as you did.

Would you believe both sides of his family have roots in Texas back to the first settlers? He's got ancestors who fought on both sides of the Alamo." The shadow took a step toward her. "You sweet on him, Miss Cleveland?"

She swung her foot and almost hit him. "You sweet on the blond barista?"

"No comment," he answered.

"No comment," she echoed.

And that was it. Almost like kids on a playground, they were friends. Avery spent her life keeping her distance from men. Never getting too close to people was her mantra. She didn't even know this guy's name, but there was something about him. An honesty in his eyes, maybe, or the fact he fed a stray cat.

"So, what are you looking for?"

"I can't tell you."

She tried another question. "What's your name?"

"I can't tell you."

She groaned. "Then I'll call you Mikey. He's my dumb cousin who's about your age. He's fat and going bald in his twenties, but he thinks he's handsome. He was my dad's brother's only son. My sister and I hated him because he bugged us at every family gathering. He even called me Stork because of my long legs."

The shadow man actually looked offended. "You think I look like him?"

"No. You look nothing like him, but if you're going to hang around here, you might as well be kin to me. I would say you could be my boyfriend, but I'm too old for you and I've kind of got this thing going with the sheriff."

"Yeah, I saw. You'd think if two people in their thirties got together that at least one of you would have
learned to kiss."

"Shut up, Mikey." Shadow Man was looking more
like her cousin by the minute.

"You know, Avery, this might work. It's way off the
books but I've been getting nowhere for two weeks. I'll
play your cousin, even help out around here, come out
in the sunshine for a change, but you got to swear that
if any trouble comes, you will not get involved."

The mood grew serious. "In most investigations I
can't interact with any locals, but I might get away with
being your cousin. You could even act like you hate
me. I'm a bother. That way folks might feel sorry for
me and talk to me."

"Then you'll fill me in on a bit of what you're doing?" This seemed more like a game than real, but she
was interested.

"Not a chance, Stork, but when this cover is over,
I'll take the time to teach you to kiss."

"You will not."

He laughed. "Well, I'm sure not teaching the sheriff, so you two will have to experiment on your own."

"Not likely. I'm not sure he's even attracted to me.
That kiss was a onetime thing."

"I can help you with that," her pretend cousin said.
"He may not like you, but he's hot for you. He works
all night, but he doesn't go home to bed. He drives over
here and buys you breakfast or coffee. The man wants
to see you before he sleeps." The shadow man checked
his watch. "Which reminds me, I've got to get out of
here. I'll go find some Mikey clothes and be right back.

The sheriff will probably be here by then and you can introduce me."

The investigator seemed almost to be a kid playing a game. He was watching someone or something. Avery couldn't help but wonder if he might be in danger. If so, maybe pretending to be a relative might offer him more of a cover.

"One more thing, Mikey," she added as he headed up the stairs. "You're buying me breakfast. Be back in an hour. Whether the sheriff shows up or not, I'll be hungry by then."

"Will do. One burrito with hot sauce and coffee with two sugars."

Avery watched him go, thinking the shadow knew her better than the sheriff did.

Chapter 7
Saturday Morning

A little after nine, Sheriff Solis walked into the coffee shop and waved at her like she was someone he almost knew.

Avery had watched him check her shop's door and then turn toward the coffee house. In a town this size there were not that many places she could be, and she had no doubt he was looking for her. There seemed an invisible pull, like two magnets drawing toward one another.

She'd recognized his build first. Everywhere he went the man walked like he was storming a castle. For once he wasn't in uniform. Daniel Solis was dressed in western clothes, with a white, pearl snap shirt and a leather vest. His jeans were boot cut and his boots were worn just enough to look comfortable. His dark skin and solid build made him look like a cowboy stepping out of the Wild West.

Avery closed her hand as a need to touch him came over her. She told herself all she wanted to do was brush her fingers along his white shirt from collar to belt buckle. Maybe push the vest aside. Maybe unsnap one of those pearl buttons.

Unbelievable! This small-town sheriff was becoming a need. Men in her life had always been distractions, never a need.

She cleared her mind. If she went any farther with that fantasy, she'd be into R-rated.

The fact that he was frowning at her did little to cool her thoughts.

To her surprise, no one in the coffee shop seemed to notice how sexy he was. They just waved their familiar greeting and he gave them a smile he hadn't offered her.

Sheriff Daniel Solis glanced from her to Mikey, sitting at a table by the window, then turned to the counter.

She still stared, wishing she could read the man's mind. Avery watched him let Miss May cut in line in front of him. He must have asked her to join him because she shook her head and pointed to the last table in the back. Three people about her age had left a seat for her.

When Daniel finally had his coffee in hand, he walked toward Avery. He still wasn't smiling, but at least the frown was gone.

"Morning," he said as he stood in front of her.

"Morning." She saw the question in his gray eyes. "Sheriff, I'd like you to meet my cousin."

She looked over at the shadow man, who now looked

like a country bumpkin. Baggy jeans. His black hair hanging almost to his nose, cheap glasses a bit lopsided, shirt buttoned up, one button off.

"Mikey, meet Sheriff Solis," she said, her words slow as if her kin needed time to think.

Mikey did his part. He jumped up and pumped Daniel's hand, almost spilling the sheriff's coffee. "Glad to meet you, sir. You want to sit down with us? We got room."

Dan smiled. "Sure. Nice to meet you, Mikey. Cleveland is it?"

"Yep."

Avery could almost see Dan making a mental note to research Mikey Cleveland. She laughed. The name would check out. The real Mike Cleveland lived just north of Austin and had been taking one class at a time at Austin Community College for three years.

Somehow the polished guy she'd thought of as big-city slick at dawn now looked clueless. No conversation. Just a grin.

Dan took a drink of his coffee and smiled at her. "We still have a date to the flea market this morning?"

She nodded like she remembered being asked, then looked at Shadow Man. "You want to come along, Mikey?"

"No, thanks. I plan to hang around here. The girl behind the counter gave me a free refill, so I'm thinking she's sweet on me. I'll rest up and be ready to help you move in furniture by the time you get back, cuz."

Dan stood and offered his hand to Avery. "You ready? We probably need to get there early."

"Sure." She thought he'd turn loose of her fingers after she stood, but Dan just tucked them on the bend of his arm like she'd given them to him and he had no intention of giving her hand back.

She wasn't surprised he drove a huge pickup on weekends. As she climbed in he said, "Your cousin seems like a nice guy."

"He is. I think my sister sent him over to bug me, but in truth he might be some help. He works construction now and then, and Ben Tucker said yesterday he could use an assistant in putting together the balcony workout room."

"I didn't know quilters had to work out."

She laughed. "No. I want to work out. Ben said he'd put up a few bars along the wall and if I have any money left, I'd like to buy a bit of equipment to help me stretch out. I might not be able to dance, but the workouts have been part of my life for as long as I can remember."

The sheriff frowned. "I kind of like you the way you are. You don't need to be stretched." He took the time to look her over, then it was back to business. "You want to tell me how long your cousin's staying?" The sheriff was showing beneath Daniel's weekend cowboy clothes.

She moved closer to him and patted his knee. "So, you like me? Maybe I should tell Mikey to stay around to chaperone."

He showed no sign of realizing she was kidding. "I do like you, Avery. Course, I don't know why. You're taller than most men, thin as a pole and you've already

told me you're flat chested, so no hope left there."
When he stopped at the stoplight he added, "When's he
leaving? I don't want him tagging along if we ever get
a chance to go out."

"I'm not sure. He had a friend who was driving
through town and dropped him off. The friend said
when he made the trip back from Lubbock to Austin,
he'd pick him up. Mikey showed up with a sleeping
bag but no extra clothes, so I don't think he'll be staying long." She smiled. The sheriff was complaining
about not being alone with her. She found it downright
adorable.

"Why do you call a grown man Mikey?"

"Just to irritate him. Same reason he calls me
'Stork' because of my long legs."

Dan leaned his hand across the space between them.
As he started the engine, he brushed her leg wrapped in
tight jeans just the way she'd touched him. "I kinda like
your long legs, lady. There's a grace about you that
danced through my dreams last night."

She thought of brushing his hand away, but in truth
she liked the warmth of his touch. She didn't know if
he was flirting or just being honest. He'd left no doubt
that he was attracted to her. And, as unlikely as it
seemed, she felt the same way about him.

When they pulled into the rodeo parking lot, she
was shocked by the crowd. Everything from local
honey to furniture was on sale.

"I don't think I brought enough money."

"Don't worry. Just tell them to stop by your place
Monday to pick up what you owe them. We can load all

we can in my truck. Anything too big for my truck they'll deliver later today. Trust me, no one wants to take their junk back home."

Two hours later the truck was loaded. A dozen chairs for twenty dollars each, a huge mirror for ten, an old, green half-moon desk for fifty, and an iron headboard that felt like it weighed a ton.

He watched her with gray eyes that missed nothing. She'd slept with a couple of guys while on tour. Once when she'd had too much to drink to care, and once when she thought one of the promoters really liked her. Turned out, he didn't remember her name the next morning. Both were disappointments. An awkward dance she didn't want to learn.

As they walked, passing in the shadows of the craft tents, Daniel put his arm lightly over her shoulder. "Cold?"

"A little," she answered, liking the nearness of this one man. They fit together easy and their steps were in sync. He didn't talk much, but they seemed to be communicating.

Avery spotted a lady with quilts. Beautiful quilts beyond anything she'd ever seen. Some standard designs, but others made to look almost like paintings. When the woman, whose name was Emily Ann, told her she used to teach quilting, Avery hired her on the spot.

"I want my shop to be more than showing notions and selling material. I want to teach the craft and the art of quilting."

Emily smiled with excitement in her eyes, as if she totally understood Avery's dream. "We'll start with a square-of-the-month class. You won't make much money from that, but you'll make quilters. Do you have room to put up a few frames? We could start a quilting bee. That's always fun and it would draw quilters in every week to see what you have new in the shop. There are those who love their machines that quilt, but there is something to be said for sitting around a square and talking as you work."

Avery wanted to hug Emily Ann. The lady knew quilting and was willing to help. "Can I hire you for twenty hours a week?"

"You can, dear, but I expect to get thirty percent off of anything I buy, and I do have an addiction."

Avery agreed. "I'll buy extra, and if you want to display any of these you're selling, I've got tons of wall space."

When Avery asked the woman to come by the shop next week, Dan leaned over and whispered, "You can't even think of being ready for a month."

Avery laughed. "Of course I can. I've got Mikey."

As they continued down the row, Avery couldn't stop smiling. For the first time she thought this might work. The only thing that worried her was this sudden urge she felt to hug people. She'd always been the one who stood back, holding herself away from touching, from getting involved. But Daniel's arm felt natural around her shoulder.

Suddenly she pulled him between a break in the tents. The urge was hitting her again and he'd have to run fast to get away. She'd never been a person who hesitated.

Daniel followed, then stood his ground as he raised one of his dark eyebrows in question, but she didn't give him time to speak. She pushed his hands away from his body and moved in for a full-body hug.

He remained a tree for a minute, then circled her in his arms and lifted her up in a bear hug.

Avery laughed, knowing he had no idea what was going on, but he was giving her just what she wanted . . . just what she needed. The pieces inside her were beginning to heal as he rocked her in his arms. For the first time in months she believed in herself. She didn't feel broken.

As he set her down she whispered, "Thank you," and he answered simply, "You're welcome." He lightly put his arm around her and they continued shopping as if nothing had happened.

When they made it back to the shop, her pretend-cousin was hard at work helping Ben Tucker paint. The shadow man did have more paint on himself than the wall, but he was trying.

Dan didn't say a word, he just joined the workers. He unloaded his truck and brought up the last of the boxes from the basement.

As soon as the paint was dry Avery planned to hang a dozen of Mattie's paintings of wildflowers on one wall and Emily Ann's quilts had to hang on the other side. The balcony space had newly polished floors and the bars were going up in the balcony. The area was starting to look like a classroom.

She was beginning to see the place in her mind. If she could see it, she could make it happen. A dance studio above a quilt shop.

The afternoon passed with Dan and her making the twenty-mile trip to Walmart for a bedframe, a mattress, a tiny refrigerator, a microwave, dishes, and all the other items needed to stock living quarters. Every time they unloaded she'd start her first sentence with "We forgot . . ."

Finally Dan shook his head. "This storage room is way too small to be a kitchen."

"Good. It's not a kitchen. It's a snack room. I can't cook. I'll eat one meal out and have cereal for breakfast and a health bar for supper."

"Squirrels eat better than that," Dan complained.

"It's how I've always eaten."

"Will you eat with me now and then?"

She laughed. "Anytime, cowboy, but don't drop by too often or I'll be fat."

He brushed her thin shoulder. "I wouldn't mind that at all."

"That will never happen."

An hour before dark, Ben Tucker headed home saying he'd be back Monday with Mattie. Dan brought back burgers on his last trip to pick up office supplies along with a pickup full of paper goods. Mikey said he'd eat his supper at the coffee shop since it didn't close until nine.

After he left, Dan and Avery settled on the steps to eat. There was just enough sunlight to see without turning on the lights. The sheriff leaned against the banister and watched her as if he hadn't been watching her all day.

They ate in silence for a while, then Daniel said, "You know Mikey doesn't have a chance with that girl across the street. She was hired a few weeks ago and I hear every single guy in the county has asked her out. She's turned them all down."

Avery smiled. "I wouldn't be so sure. Mike grows on everyone he meets. He told Ben he'd work as a day laborer on the farm if Ben would teach him how to drive a tractor. Ben said he'd teach him and give him as much practice as he wanted until they got a winter crop in."

"I guess you're right about Mikey. You should know, you've known him all his life. Tucker even seems to like him. I heard them talking about the navy."

Daniel spread his fries out on a napkin and frowned.

"What is it?" she asked.

"You think I should kiss you now before we finish supper?"

She smiled. "You worried I'll kick you out as soon as I eat?"

"No, I just don't want to wait any longer. What if Mikey comes back? Then I would have missed my chance after I've been waiting all day."

"All day? You poor man." She giggled and took a drink of her tea. "Then we better kiss. I've been told I need the practice."

He leaned over and kissed her softly, then pulled away like that was all the passion he wanted.

She pushed her dinner aside and dug her fingers in his hair, tugging him back to her. With her lips brushing his, she whispered, "Well, I've been wanting to do a whole lot more than a light peck, Sheriff. You started this and you're going to have to arrest me to stop me."

Nothing about her kiss was gentle. She was in a full-out attack.

When they finally came up for air, he laughed. Without a word he lifted her onto his lap and continued the kiss. Only now his hands were moving over her.

As she moved to his throat, he whispered, "I've been wanting to touch you all day. You have any objection?"

She popped a few snaps on his shirt. "I feel the same." Her hand moved over his chest as she kissed him deeper, then whispered against his mouth, "Touch me."

When his hand passed over her breast, he whispered, "You're perfection. You're also a demanding wild woman and I have no objections to that."

She pulled his mouth back to hers and realized this man was getting to her. No one had ever called her wild. She loved that for once in her life she could be demanding and this man didn't seem to mind at all.

When they were both out of breath, he pulled away and said, "Tomorrow is Sunday. Any chance you might come out to my place? I can cook outside, then we can watch the sunset over unbroken land."

She straightened. "You can cook?"

He laughed and Avery thought she might have just fallen in love. This might only be her first ever fling, or it might be something that would last forever, but for the first time in her life she was stepping toward love, not running away from it.

His kiss turned gentle as he held her like a treasure. This man was in no hurry to undress her; he seemed to want to enjoy every stage.

For a moment they were too involved in each other and barely heard the pop of gunfire.

When the second round came, Dan reacted. He set her down and ordered her to stay out of sight of the windows as he ran for the door.

She just stared. What kind man runs toward fire? A fool? A hero?

Another pop.

Glass shattered across the street and Avery disappeared beneath the stairs. Another shot rattled the still night air.

She could barely make out Dan standing beside his truck as he jerked his gun belt from behind his seat and pulled his weapon. Dan's white shirt seemed to glow in the streetlights like a target as more fire came from out of nowhere.

Avery heard screams and people running. More windows across the street being shot out.

Suddenly a car gunned its engine half a block away and seemed to hit fifty by the time it swung around the first corner, drove past and stopped. Dan fired as the car raced away.

Avery had to move closer. She had to see what was happening.

For a moment, the noise of the car and the pings of the glass still hitting the sidewalk were all she could hear, then Mikey's voice sounded from across the street. "All clear, Sheriff?"

Daniel fanned his weapon and yelled back. "All clear, here."

Mikey stepped out of the coffeehouse with a gun held straight out in front of him. Her pretend-cousin seemed to be searching the street looking for any sign of danger as he walked toward the sheriff.

Daniel's words broke the silence as he called for backup and an ambulance on his cell. "Location clear. One officer down."

Mikey must have heard the call too because he broke into a full-out run, his weapon still held at the ready.

Avery darted to the front of her shop. For a moment silence hung heavy in the cold air, then lights from almost every building blinked on. All looked as calm as if nothing had happened. A silent town square on a cold Saturday night. Christmas wreaths now hung from every streetlight.

Then, she turned to Daniel and saw a red stain spreading across his white shirt.

A scream shattered the silence. Her scream.

Dan was still standing at alert, his weapon drawn, but crimson moved over his shoulder.

Avery flipped on every light in her shop and the glow reached out to Daniel. People emerged from the stores still open and the apartments over the shops. All seemed to be running then circling the sheriff.

Mikey reached him first. "Lower your weapon, Dan. I've got your six." All easygoing talk was gone. It was an order. "Stand down, Solis."

Daniel slowly lowered his weapon into Mikey's waiting hand, then Daniel crumbled as the whole town watched.

Avery moved close enough to try to catch him, but she only slowed his fall as they both tumbled.

For one moment the smell of blood and the warmth of it covering her hand as she held his arm was all Avery was aware of.

"No," she whispered. "No!"

The only man who had ever held her as if she were a treasure closed his eyes. No longer seeing her. Silent.

Chapter 8
Silent Saturday Night

Daniel Solis had heard of county sheriffs who never discharged their firearm in the line of duty during their entire career. The stories of gunfights were always in big cities. County sheriffs might have to shoot a rabid animal, or a rattler, but they weren't in gunfights.

"Until now," kept playing through his head like a headline in a B-movie trailer.

The pain felt like his shoulder was on fire and a dozen people around him seemed to be screaming, but Dan was calm. The hurt didn't let up but he was floating, as if fighting sleep. He circled his still working arm around Avery in comfort. She was crying softly and shaking as if half frozen. He knew he was the one hurt, but he wanted to protect her.

Strange, he'd felt that way from the first night when he'd seen her dancing in the shadows of an empty room. She'd probably be mad as hell if he told her.

Avery was a woman who fought her own battles, and if she let him hang around, most of her battles would probably be with him.

There was passion in her too. Passion for life and maybe for him. Thinking back, every time they'd kissed she'd been the one to want more.

Dan's words came out in Spanish as he told her not to cry, then closed his eyes as the pain took control. All the things he'd thought about telling her seemed to fade into the night. They'd barely met, but there was something that drew him to her. He wasn't a man who knew what to say to a woman when it came to feelings, but with her it might be time to try.

His emotional clock had stopped ticking years ago. Maybe he should plug back into life. Avery danced through his dreams.

Someday he'd make love to her, he decided. He'd do it right. Let her know how he felt about her without words.

Not now while he was leaking from the shoulder. They needed to get to a doctor and then he'd try talking to her. Kissing the top of her head, he tried to think of the words he should say, but they wouldn't come. He had the oddest feeling of falling asleep in the middle of a crowd.

When he finally fought his way back, Avery was sitting up holding his head between her legs and the barista named Sunny from the coffee house was applying pressure on his shoulder. Her hands pushing against the wound hurt more than the bullet hole did. He wanted to talk, tell Avery he was all right. Tell the barista to stop. But he couldn't form words.

And somehow, in this nightmare, Dan had fallen into a reality where Mikey had taken charge. Avery's dumb cousin was shouting orders, talking on his phone and using terms only law enforcement used.

Dan decided his only chance of staying alive was to close his eyes.

Chapter 9
Midnight Black Saturday

The ambulance from Abilene was twenty-seven miles away, but Avery could have sworn it got there in ten minutes flat. She was crying, holding onto Daniel when they arrived. Before she could object, one of the EMTs gently pulled her away and two others surrounded her sheriff. The girl from the coffee shop let the emergency worker put some kind of pack over the wound as she slowly pulled away.

Her hands were red with blood but she looked more angry than afraid.

Avery felt the strong arm of the shadow man go around her. The guy she'd named Mikey was answering questions in rapid fire, but his grip stayed solid around her shoulder.

"Yes, the sheriff was shot."

"Only one shooter, but another man in the getaway

car. Most of the gunfire was aimed at the coffee shop." Mikey started pacing as he yelled into the phone.

"No customers except me and an old couple at the back table. All windows on the shop were out and both windows above in an apartment were damaged."

"No one was in the apartment at the time." Mikey's voice finally slowed.

"Total of six or eight shots fired, I think. Everything happened so fast. No, I did not get the license plate. Car was a black, late model, built like a Toyota, maybe a Lexus."

The blonde from the coffee shop, Sunny, stood beside Mikey and added, "I counted eight shots. The car had Oklahoma tags. First four letters were BTTB and I think the first number was nine. The old couple moved to the kitchen when the shooting started." She looked at Mikey when she finished her statement. "They seemed to have disappeared."

Mikey's nod was so slight Avery thought no one saw it but her.

Avery watched highway patrol cars pull up. An Abilene police car had followed the ambulance in. Two deputy sheriffs were questioning the crowd. The highway patrolmen were pushing the crowd back, leaving only law enforcement around Mikey, Sunny, and Avery as the emergency medics did what they were trained to do.

"I think I winged the shooter," Mikey whispered to Sunny and suddenly lawmen moved closer, firing off questions faster than Mikey could answer. With one hand raised, as if testifying, Mikey started talking. "I'm Agent Shawn Knight, supervisory special agent with the FBI assigned to the marshal's office to watch over a witness in protective custody." He locked his arm with the blonde's. "And this is Janet Edwards. She's my partner. We were planning to move our witness to a safer location later tonight. Sunny noticed a black car circling yesterday."

"Where exactly is your informant?" a deputy asked.

"I'm not at liberty to say, sir, but I'm sure the witness is safe. Not hurt. Not on scene." Avery's short-term cousin looked at her, but his words were for all to hear. "I can't go with the sheriff to the hospital. My witness is still my priority. If any of you have more questions, I'll be in the coffee shop trying to lower my adrenalin overload, then I plan to continue my assignment. My partner will work this scene with you men and talk to any eye witnesses."

The waitress-turned-partner seemed to think she was the traveling nurse on duty. "I'll walk you inside, Shawn. We'll tape up those cuts and bandage that hand. If you'd gone out the door, Agent Knight, and not the broken window, you wouldn't have gotten cut."

Shawn ignored her belated advice as he looked back at Avery. "Go with Dan, Avery. Once this is settled, I'll drive over and pick you up." His eyes met hers as he whispered, "Don't leave the hospital with anyone else but me, cousin. No one, understand? You'll be safe there with Doctor Henry Solis. Dan will have round-the-clock guards. Don't leave his room."

Avery's whole body felt his words. He was telling her she might be in danger, but why? "I'm not your worry."

"No, but you need to trust me and Doc. Anyone else is a suspect."

She barely knew this man but he was right. She did trust him. He was a chameleon but he'd run to Dan as soon as he knew the sheriff was hit. If he'd wanted her dead, he could have done the job the first night. Plus, he fed the cat every night and he bought the old man coffee who always wandered into the coffee shop without money. Avery wasn't sure that made him a saint, but it probably got him off the naughty list.

"Agent Shawn Knight. Somehow that fits you better than Mikey," Avery whispered.

As they lifted Dan on the stretcher, Avery heard Shawn ask Sunny how she remembered the car's plate.

"BTTB, who could forget that?" She was pulling her partner's hand toward the coffee shop and his body followed.

"Me, for one," he said.

She didn't slow but Avery heard her say, "Bad to the bone, Shawn. Where have you been all your life?"

"Under a rock, obviously."

Avery grabbed Daniel's jacket from his pickup and ran for the ambulance.

Daniel looked surprised when she pushed her way in and took his hand. "I'm not leaving you, Sheriff. I wasn't finished with our conversation on the steps."

"Me either." He grinned even though she saw pain in his gray eyes. "Don't you think you should stop calling me Sheriff, Avery?"

"I'll think about it if I ever wake up in your bed."

The man trying to get an IV in the sheriff's hand barked a laugh, then apologized. "Sorry a gunfight interrupted you two."

Dan closed his eyes without answering, but he didn't let go of her hand as the EMTs prepped him for transport.

"You're going to be all right, Sheriff, hang on. Your heart is pounding strong and you got a pretty girl propositioning you. Considering everything, even with that one gunshot, it's still a good day."

As they cut off his shirt, Avery watched. She'd never been afraid of the sight of blood, but there seemed to be so much. For a second she saw the bullet hole high on his shoulder and worried that there might have been more.

One of the men called in vitals and ended by saying, "Tell the doctor the sheriff's coming in stable."

Thirty minutes later when Avery ran into the emergency entrance behind the gurney, she almost wished she hadn't come. The ER was packed. This place was not where anyone would want to be on a Saturday night. Drunks sleeping on the floor, people crying, two cowboys in the corner still yelling insults and swinging at each other, and one lady strapped to a gurney was yelling that she'd been abducted and brought here against her will.

Avery zipped up Dan's coat and tried to be invisible. She almost looked official with the jacket's logo. Her hands curled around a ring of keys in one pocket and his phone in the other.

She heard one of the EMTs say to the nurse on duty, "We got a sheriff shot in the line of duty. We need to get him out of this crowd."

The nurse motioned with her head and they followed her down the hall. Nurses took over getting him settled while Avery stood in the corner trying to make sense of all that had happened. It wasn't long before the crowd was gone and they were alone. Avery moved close to Dan. He seemed to be studying her, almost as if he wasn't sure she was real.

She leaned over and kissed the top of his head, making no effort to stop a tear from falling. ·

"I'm going to be all right," he whispered. "You wouldn't want to climb up on this bed with me, honey? I've got enough painkillers in me that I don't even feel my shoulder, but I wouldn't mind feeling you close."

Avery laughed. "You're shot. We are not going to continue our make-out session in the emergency room."

"Considering what I'm thinking about you right now, I'm ready to leave and go back to your new bed and talk you into trying it out. You're kissing me on the head like you think I've got one foot in the grave. I might as well play that angle and prove to you I'm not."

She pushed his hair back, thinking a drunk might be easier to handle than a shot sheriff on painkillers. Leaning in again, she kissed him on the lips. As the kiss deepened, she thought this man would be so easy to love.

A few moments later the curtain rattled open and a low voice said, "That better be mouth-to-mouth you're giving him."

Avery pulled away and stared at a white-haired doctor who looked like he could double as Santa.

Dan spoke first. "Dig this bullet out, Uncle Henry, I got a date."

The doc smiled. "I never heard of taking a lady to

the ER for foreplay, but damn if it doesn't seem to be working for you, Dan. And by the way, we don't dig bullets out, we call it surgery, which is what you'll have as soon as we take a few X-rays."

Dan growled. "Avery, this is my meanest uncle, and that's saying something since I have eight. Don't believe a word he says. He got his medical license from the internet."

Two men dressed in green scrubs rushed in and strapped Dan back down to the bed. They both looked bored, like they'd been loading patients all evening.

Uncle Henry smiled. "I'm tempted to give you a brain scan. Something's wrong with you, boy. Didn't I tell you to stay out of the way of bullets and wild women?"

As the men started rolling him out, Dan shouted, "She may be wild but she's my date. First one I've had in a year so don't lose her while I'm gone."

"Great," Uncle Henry yelled back. "I'll try to talk her out of dating you and if you ask me, she's probably more woman than you can handle. If I hadn't gotten here fast, you would have talked her into bed with you and we don't allow that kind of thing at the hospital."

Half of the hospital could hear Dan yell back, "Hell, I've been thinking of just that all day."

Dan's transportation turned the corner but she could still hear him yelling.

The doctor laughed. "I love that kid."

She smiled. "He's a grown man, Doctor."

"I know, but that doesn't keep me from worrying about him. I'll send him straight to surgery from X-ray. You can head on home. He'll be out most of the night."

"I'm not leaving him." She was surprised how determined her words were. "He's my first date in years and I'm not going anywhere."

"You're as crazy as he is." Henry raised one bushy white eyebrow. "I'd better keep you safe; he'd want that. You can wait in my office if you like. I'll let you know as soon as he moves to a room." The doc looked her over. "I've got a private bathroom if you want to clean up. I'll send an aide in to patch up that knee. You are dripping on my floor, miss."

Avery looked down and saw a circle of blood staining her jeans. She hadn't even noticed. "Thanks."

She followed Dan's uncle down the hall to an elevator. On the third floor he opened his office and said, "I'll call my sister-in-law once he's in recovery. Dan's mother is a strong woman who should have had a dozen kids. But she only had Dan, so she pours all that mothering, worrying, and smothering out on him. If I were you, I'd start preparing for the storm that's going to hit come morning. Most of the family thinks Dan took this job half a state away from her just so she wouldn't ride in his cruiser with him on patrol. She'll be heading this way as soon as I tell her."

Avery smiled, but from the expression on Henry's face, he didn't look like he was kidding.

When the doc closed the door, she sat on the leather couch without turning the lights on. The windows let in a parking lot glow. She was up for dealing with Dan, maybe even sleeping with him, but she didn't know about an overprotective mother and apparently a huge family.

Avery didn't even know where Dan lived. A few kisses didn't mean she was his girlfriend.

She felt the weight of a huge key ring in one of his pockets and Dan's cell phone in the other. She'd hang on to them for him.

Then, without hesitating she curled up on the couch. For once she didn't have any trouble falling asleep. She simply pretended to be wrapped up in Dan's arms and drifted off. She might be just a bystander in all this, but deep down she knew there was something between them. They'd been together all day and she wondered if he felt what she had. Knowing he was near created a balance in her world and a need to be closer.

An hour later when an aide woke her, Avery asked where Dan was.

"He's in recovery. All went well. I'll take you to his hospital room. You can wait there with the deputy sheriff assigned guard duty."

Avery felt like she was living in a fog. She wasn't surprised when Dan's room came with a deputy outside the door.

Once in the private room, the aide helped her out of her bloody jeans and pushed a recliner close to his bed. "It won't be long. Doc said there was far less damage than he'd feared. Of course, I didn't tell you that, if anyone asks. I'll clean this bloody knee and wash out your pants. They'll only take an hour or two to dry if I hang them near the heater."

Avery nodded, but her thoughts were with Dan. Her knee didn't matter.

The nurse kept talking as she worked. "The front

desk also took a message for you. A Miss May called to say she was just fine and if you have time, let her know how you are doing. She even repeated her number twice to make sure the clerk got it right."

"That's nice." Avery grinned, then added, "If the front desk has her number could you ask them to call Miss May back and tell her I'm doing fine too?"

"Sure." The aide cleaned the scraped knee and asked, "Miss May important to you?"

"Yes," Avery answered. "I know her whole life story."

After washing the blood from her jeans, the aide left, already texting Avery's message to the front desk.

Avery paced for a while, feeling her skinned knee with every step but not stopping. When they finally brought him in, Dan was asleep. He murmured her name when they moved him to the bed and reached for her hand.

When he opened one eye, he managed a smile and mumbled, "Good, you're already half undressed for bed. Nice legs."

She grabbed an extra blanket and sat in the chair beside him. "I'm waiting for my jeans to . . ." He looked sound asleep. "Oh, never mind."

One of the nurses arranged his covers and then put another blanket over Avery as if her being there half undressed was totally normal.

Avery leaned back, remembering all the weeks she'd spent in the hospital the past year. No one had ever sat beside her. She'd been part of a world-famous company and with one fall no one remembered her.

She became a side dish in life, like Miss May had said she was. Only tonight Avery made up her mind that she was still someone and so was Miss May.

Avery did not let go of Daniel's hand even if he didn't know she was near. Moving his hand beneath her blanket, she curled around his uninjured arm and fell asleep.

Chapter 10
Bright Sunday Dawn

Dan opened his eyes and saw Avery's sunshine-kissed brown hair spread over his chest. Her head was pressed against his uninjured arm. "Morning," he whispered as he gripped her fingers tighter.

As she raised her head, she scrubbed her face like a kid pushing sleep away. "Morning," she echoed.

He smiled. "I guess we slept together. Have to say it wasn't as memorable as I thought it might be. I did have a great dream about seeing those long legs of yours."

She lifted her blankets, squealed, and darted for her jeans hanging over the plastic chair in front of the heater. As she jumped around tugging her tight jeans over beautiful legs, Dan could do nothing but enjoy the show.

Without asking she grabbed his bag of toiletries they'd dropped off and disappeared into his bathroom.

He thought of telling her to get her own room and supplies, but he wouldn't dare. She might do it. Except for a hole in his shoulder, this had to be the most exciting date he'd ever had. He couldn't stop smiling.

Uncle Henry bumped his way into Dan's room. "I wanted to check on you before I leave. My shift was over four hours ago, but I couldn't just leave you." The old doc looked around. "What happened to that wild woman? She finally ran off? Both of you were holding hands, sound asleep, every time I checked on you last night."

"She stole my toothbrush and disappeared into the bathroom."

"I'll get you another, kid. Course it'll cost you eighty bucks."

"Of course. Does it come with a little pitcher? Hospitals usually give a bag of stuff when you check out."

"I don't know. I'm the doctor, remember." He went to work on Dan as if to prove the point. "There's a few lawmen outside waiting to see you. I told them you've got to stay at least one more day. But I figure by nine your mother will be here informing me she is taking over."

"She flying in?"

"Of course. I haven't been able to keep her on the ground since my brother married her and gave her flying lessons." Henry pulled the bandage off Dan's shoulder. "Not bad. Already healing. I'm glad I read that book, *Bullet Wounds for Dummies,* years ago." As he taped the shoulder back up, he added, "Time you eat breakfast and talk to your cop friends. My sister-in-law should be here to smother her only chick."

"Order Avery a breakfast tray too," Ben said.

"Who is Avery?"

"My date, Uncle. Remember. The wild woman."

Before Dan could say more, Avery stepped out of the bathroom. Her face was still damp, her hair combed and pulled back. She'd tied her wrinkled shirt at her waist, showing off just enough bare skin. When she wasn't crying, she was a true beauty, Dan decided. And the way she moved would probably haunt his dreams the rest of his life.

Uncle Henry grinned and forgot about the patient. "Good morning, Avery. Thank you for watching over my nephew last night. There's no doubt you're an angel."

She smiled. "Can I take him home?"

"Soon, dear. I predict being near you will do him more good than any painkillers I could offer him."

"Stop flirting with my girlfriend, Uncle." Dan wouldn't have been surprised if Henry proposed to Avery any moment. He was in his sixties but he'd had five wives, so he knew the right things to say. His only flaw was he usually found the next wife before the last wife moved out.

Henry winked at her, then collected his charts, and sounding very professional, rattled off orders to the nurse who followed him out of the room.

Before Dan had time to say anything to Avery, the room filled with lawmen asking questions. Dan fired back with questions about the investigation. While-a-Way was in his county; therefore, the trouble was his problem.

The getaway car the shooter had left in had not been found yet, even with roadblocks. Which meant that it was probably hidden somewhere in his county. Dan wished he could get dressed, and started searching for something to put on.

Only he remembered his clothes had been cut off. He made a mental note to call one of his cousins to bring clothes, preferably a uniform.

No one knew what happened to Sunny from the coffee shop, or Mikey, Avery's cousin.

Correction: Shawn and Janet, the agents. They seemed to have disappeared. The coffee shop had been boarded up and no one knew where the guy who rented the upstairs apartment was.

The whole town square was a crime scene and half the people in town considered themselves self-appointed detectives.

Dan couldn't offer anything new to his testimony. He'd been worried about someone being hit by a stray bullet as he watched a tall man hidden in the night shooting at the coffee shop. When he'd finally pinpointed the shooter, all of his panicked worries had come true. Only he was the one hit.

"I took the hit and managed to remain standing for a few seconds. I kept my eyes on the shooter. He was a tall figure darting between the trees toward the getaway car. Well over six feet. Dark blue hoodie. White tennis shoes. As I hit the ground, I saw the car disappear."

Dan didn't add that a moment later he felt Avery against him as he dropped.

The lawmen asked the same questions over and over, but Dan couldn't remember more. He'd been on the ground. He hadn't seen the plates.

Another officer taking notes asked if Dan knew Agent Shawn Knight was on site. Dan said, "Yes, but he was undercover. He's done an excellent job. Almost had me fooled."

When two trays were brought in the lawmen left. Dan wanted to rest a bit, but Avery crawled up on the other side of the rolling tray and started opening everything like she was starving. One of her legs lay over his left leg and her bandaged right leg pushed against his side.

Dan grinned. "You got me penned in, Avery."

"You mind?"

"Not at all, but I'm really not very hungry," he said, thinking of pushing the button to lower his bed so he could sleep.

"Great. I'll eat both breakfasts. I'm starving."

He watched her eat, offering him a bite now and then. "I can feed myself."

"Then do it."

"I'd rather watch you. When we break out of here, I plan to fatten you up and call you Pumpkin."

"Never happen." She gave him a dirty look.

He winked at her as his hand brushed over her leg. "Did I fall on you last night? That why you've got a bandage on your right knee?"

"No. We fell together. You were falling and I tried to catch you." She stopped and looked at him. "I guess my legs were still too weak."

"Your legs are beautiful."

"You saw my scars?"

"No, I saw your legs."

To his surprise she looked away as if he'd seen the ugliest part of her.

Dan placed his hand on her jeans and slowly moved down from her hip to her knee bent over his leg. "This is probably a bit early to be talking about, but I'm looking forward to touching every part of you."

He studied her and lowered his voice. "Avery, would you go out with me on a real date? Not breakfast, not hamburgers, not wandering around a flea market. You know, I'll pick you up. We'll pick a nice place and I'll walk you to your door and kiss you good night."

She grinned. "Since you've already knocked me off my feet and I've slept with you, I might consider another date, but I'm hoping for more than a good-night kiss."

"How much more?"

"We'll negotiate over dinner on that date, but first you've got to tell me how you knew Mikey wasn't just my cousin."

"I don't really know. His accent wasn't right. He was too interested in Ben's job in the navy. And now and then Mikey moved like he was drawing his personal space in. You know, like he was used to being surrounded by people."

She squealed. "I noticed that too. Maybe I should have been a cop."

Dan was putting the pieces together. "Of course you

knew what he was. You knew he wasn't your cousin." He frowned. "Why didn't you tell me?" He hated that his questions came hard and almost angry.

She reacted. Wildfire in a bottle, he thought. Then she took a deep breath and answered his question.

"Mikey said it would keep you safe if you didn't know. But that obviously wasn't true. Why'd you run out in the middle of a gunfight? Only a man with a death wish would do that."

She pushed the trays away and he watched one long graceful leg swing over him, straddling his legs so close to him they were almost nose to nose.

He chewed on his anger for a moment before he answered. "I had to draw fire to find the shooter. I couldn't let anyone get hurt. I thought he was a drunk or someone mad at the coffee house. I didn't think he would actually shoot me."

"You are an idiot, Daniel Solis!"

Avery was so close he could feel her words. Anger built inside him, blocking out all except her furious eyes. She was right, of course, but that didn't cool him down.

Before he could form words, the door flew open and a woman, dressed in western clothes from her hat to her knee-high boots, rushed in.

"What is going on here?" The woman yelled even louder than Avery had. "Why are you attacking a man near death?"

Avery glanced at the intruder and said, "He's not near death. He'd better stay alive long enough to be my date."

The woman froze, her mouth open as she looked down at Avery straddling Dan.

Dan suddenly smiled, patted Avery on the leg and said calmly, "Morning, Madre. How was the flight? Glad you flew over to meet my girlfriend."

Chapter 11
Sunday Midday

Avery sat in the plastic chair in the corner watching Dan's mother fuss over her grown son. She'd straightened the covers after Avery climbed off, fluffed the pillows, and ordered a nurse to call Dr. Henry back to the room. She needed a full report on her son's condition, not just a text that said he was fine.

Avery watched as Dan tried calming her down, but she didn't listen. The woman was obviously taking charge. Within minutes the room began to fill with people she wanted to question. Her brother-in-law, the ambulance driver, and the night nurse if possible. The guard was pulled in from the hallway and asked to produce a list of all visitors.

Feeling like a rag doll that had been tossed aside, Avery looked down at her clothes. They were stained and wrinkled, while Mrs. Solis looked like one of the models in *Cowgirl Magazine*. The concho belt was made of solid silver and her boots were obviously hand tooled. She had to be in her late fifties, but her body was workout-an-hour-a-day shaped. Every time she glanced at Avery, she looked as if she'd just noticed the last patient had left something in the room.

Finally, Dr. Henry ordered everyone out of the room. Dan's *madre* frowned but followed orders. She had a list of people to interview in While-a-Way and first on her list was Shawn Knight. Avery had no doubt that she'd strangle one of the deputies to find out where he was.

Avery grinned. "Good luck with that," she whispered. Her shadow man wasn't easy to find.

As Dr. Henry passed her, he whispered, "Stay if you want to, Avery. I have a feeling you're all the medicine he needs from now on."

Suddenly the room was silent as morning sunshine warmed the air. Avery walked over beside the bed. "You look sleepy, Daniel. Did your mother wear you out?"

"She always does."

"How about you get some sleep? I'll watch over you if you like."

He frowned. "I don't want you watching over me. I want you sleeping beside me." He lifted his unharmed arm. "Climb in. Watch out for the IV."

"You can't sleep with me here."

"Why not? If people can have emotional-support pets on airplanes, I can have you beside me. This is a scary place. I need my support ballerina."

She slipped in beside him. "The scariest thing in this room was your mother. No wonder I couldn't scare you off."

"I would say her bark is worse than her bite, but that's not true." Daniel kissed the top of her head. "You've got about as much cuddle skills as I do. Maybe one of us should try relaxing."

"Should I leave?"

"No. We'll figure this out. Go to sleep." He laced his fingers in hers and closed his eyes. "Take a deep breath, Avery, and relax. We're only sleeping."

Avery lay close, her head resting on his bare shoulder. When his breathing slowed and she felt his body relax in sleep, she whispered, "I think I could love you, Sheriff, if you promise to stay alive."

A few hours later she was awakened by someone snoring. Moving her head slowly, she looked up at Daniel. Not a sound. Then she looked over at the recliner three feet away and saw Mikey, his head back, his arms folded over his chest, and sound asleep. Apparently, he'd joined the sleep-in.

Daniel's low words brushed against her cheek. "Should we wake up Agent Knight?"

"Should we?"

"Why not? He woke us up snoring." Daniel turned toward the undercover agent and said calmly, "Wake up, Mikey."

Shawn jerked wide-awake then looked around as if he'd forgotten where he was.

"How you doing, Sheriff?"

"I'm fine. Just sleeping with my lady until I realized someone joined us. You know, I really wasn't expecting you to drop in. Don't you have a witness to watch?"

"He's safe in a location unknown to everyone but me and Janet. She's watching them now."

"Them?" Daniel hadn't missed the hint. His brain cells were working at full throttle.

Shawn scratched his head. "Yeah, my top-secret witness, who had death threats from half a dozen directions, apparently wouldn't cooperate with us unless he could bring a date along on the relocation last night."

"That's not standard procedure," Dan said, adding the obvious.

"You're telling me. Nothing about this case is normal. I'm never stepping foot in Texas again. It all started with me feeding a fat cat everyone in town probably feeds, and ended up an hour ago with the sheriff's mother threatening to kill me. It sounded like she wasn't kidding, but damn, I don't even know where to file the complaint."

"Why would my mother want to kill you?" Dan smiled. "She doesn't know you yet."

"She claims I should be out looking for the man who shot you. I told her that was the county sheriff's job. Apparently, she didn't like that answer."

"Why are you here, Mikey? I gave up years ago accepting complaints about my mother."

"I brought you a uniform. If you're up for it, I thought you might break out of this place and help me find the shooter. Everyone around says you know every inch of this county."

Daniel pulled the help cord so hard the string came out of the wall and he heard bells going off three rooms down at the nurses' station. "I feel fine. Happy to get out of here. Avery, you stay here and tell everyone I had business to take care of."

"Stop telling me what to do, Sheriff!" Avery turned to Mikey. "And you are not pulling a gunshot patient out of bed to help you track down the shooter."

When she took a breath, Dan ordered the nurse hesitating to open the door to pull out the IV in his hand.

As he dressed, Avery listed every reason she could think of why he couldn't go. Finally, she added, "You've lost a lot of blood, Dan. You'll be light-headed."

"Good point," Dan said as Shawn helped him slide one arm into his shirt. "You drive, Mikey."

Avery was so angry she thought of slugging the patient. "If you're going, I'm going with you."

Both men yelled, "No."

She slipped on Dan's coat. "If your witness can take a date into hiding, the sheriff, who is not fit for duty, can take his emotional support date." When neither man moved, she added, "We'd better get out of here fast before your mother drops by. I have a feeling she'll want to tag along too."

Both men rushed toward the door as the deputy from Abilene blocked the entrance to the hallway. "If she goes, I'm going too. I'm your bodyguard, so where your body goes, Sheriff, I'm right beside you."

When no one objected, the deputy added, "Besides, I'm sick of hall duty. Everyone walks by and tells me I'd better do my job, like I might forget why I'm standing in a hospital hallway."

The sheriff mumbled a few curses and the agent said, "See what I mean, Sheriff? Everyone in Texas is crazy. I've had a dozen people complain to me because they missed the gunfight. Like I should have passed out invitations. One old guy told me the shooter wouldn't have got away if he'd been there."

As they all headed out, the panicked nurse asked, "What do I tell the doctor?"

"Tell my uncle I have a job to do." Dan put his good arm around Avery. "And tell my mother to stay here. I'll be back when the job is done."

Avery walked in step with Dan, linking her arm behind his back. He wasn't as steady as he sounded, but she matched her steps with his to make it less noticeable.

The guard ran ahead to pull his plain ten-year-old Land Rover around. As they came out the side door, the deputy popped the back. "It's not an official cruiser, but it's packed. Help yourself."

Shawn and Dan each took rifles. The deputy strapped on a gun belt and Avery pulled out the first aid kit. As they took a minute to check their weapons, she tried to breathe. This wasn't a game they were playing. Someone could get killed. Every cell in her body was voting to run, but she kept her eyes on Dan.

She barely knew him. A few almost-dates. A few kisses that warmed her all the way to her toes, and hugs when she'd been close enough to hear his heart. She felt him holding her, protecting her now. They might just be at the start of something, but the magic they had was something she didn't want to lose. He was the one man she couldn't just walk away from. The "what might be" was too great. More important than safety. More important than ballet had been.

For once she'd found a man worth fighting for, and as it turned out, that might be just what she had to do.

As he climbed in the front to navigate, she moved in behind him. Her hand closed around Dan's keys inside his coat. She had to hold on to something, even if it was just hope.

Chapter 12

Overcast Afternoon

As raindrops played on the windshield, Dan planned. With a storm coming in they didn't have many hours to search. The getaway car had headed west, not toward the interstate but toward rural roads. The ranches were big in that direction, measured in sections not acres. Not many roads.

If the getaway driver had any sense, he wouldn't turn around. He had a good head start, but the law would be racing toward him. If he turned north or south, he'd hit a major highway and someone would be watching.

Dan guessed the driver went west hoping to be safe, planning to hide the car the first chance he got.

Dan tapped the deputy's shoulder and pointed to a turnoff about five miles out of Abilene. With cop cars coming from every direction last night, their only chance of finding the shooter would be the back roads. Maybe he'd call someone to come pick him up, or maybe he'd wait a few days and try to drive out after midnight.

Dan's orders seemed to fill the Rover. "Look on your side for any building that would hold a car. Or a stand of trees thick enough to hide a car. Even stacks of hay might work. We've got an hour, maybe less, to find where he's hiding. Then the rain might cut off all roads that are dirt and not maintained."

The deputy added, "He likely wanted to get hidden as fast as possible last night, so my guess is he wouldn't have gone too far."

"I agree. But the way these roads cross, we've got a hundred miles to work through."

Shawn joined in. "I heard the highway patrol say they're covering every highway and interstate. Even the farm-to-market roads, so we can skip them. They were on guard within minutes of when you called in last night."

Silence settled in as all four watched mostly pastureland. Dan was mapping the roads out in his mind, making sure he didn't miss even a path wide enough to handle a car. If there was any chance a car could make it down a back road, they needed to investigate.

An hour passed and the sky darkened as if playing a game of hide-and-seek with them. Rain plopped on the windshield, seemingly wanting to slow them down.

Lightning flashed again and again, running across the land to chase them. No one talked. They simply drove and searched.

In one flash Dan spotted a hubcap ten yards into a field that looked like it hadn't been worked in decades.

"Turn around," he said calmly. As the deputy turned, he added, "Go back slowly."

"But there was no road turning off, Sheriff."

"I know, we're going off-road where the fence is down."

When they pulled onto the land, they all saw only a bit of the hubcap that was mostly covered in mud. It seemed to Dan that no one in the Rover was breathing as the deputy slowed and tossed his flashlight at where they had driven off-road. "Breadcrumbs," he said as the beam of the light shone toward the dirt road they'd just left.

Wheels spun as they headed straight for the metal building. Shawn slapped the window and yelled, "I think I see the roof of a barn hidden in the trees." On a clear day the barn might have been completely hidden, but now the winds were whipping the branches, allowing glimpses of a tin-roofed barn.

"Slow down a bit," Dan ordered, "but go straight in and cut your lights as we pass the trees."

As the deputy slowed and pulled up at the back of a rusty tin barn, Dan turned around. "Avery, stay in the car. Call 911. Tell them we're about twelve miles from While-a-Way, due west. My phone is . . ."

"I know," she answered as she pulled his phone out of the coat she was wearing.

A few minutes later the Rover rolled past the trees and came to a stop.

Slowly the men stepped out. Dan allowed himself one last look at Avery. Then he turned forward, mentally preparing to face the trouble he knew was coming.

Chapter 13
Bloody Twilight

As they walked toward the barn, Avery hit 911. The dispatcher picked up on the first ring. "Sheriff! Where . . ."

"No, but I'm with him." Avery said exactly what Dan had told her to say twice, then whispered, "Hurry," as if it were more a prayer than a demand. She was shaking so hard she feared she'd drop the phone.

For a moment she closed her eyes and wished her great-grandmother's wishing quilt was around her. If it was, she'd have only one thing to ask for. She'd wish Dan was safe.

"Got it, Avery," the dispatcher shouted. "Call is going out to all units now. They'll all be heading your way."

There was a moment of silence before the dispatcher asked, "Are you safe?"

"I am, but they may not be."

"Tell me the details. I'm patching it through to others, Avery. When both of you disappeared along with Deputy Collins, we knew something was up."

Avery related what was happening, then a man's voice broke in. "Avery, get down low in the car. Stay there. We have a dozen people heading toward you. You'll be hearing their sirens within less than ten."

She heard shouting and dropped the phone. There was no chance of her hiding, she had to see what was happening. She flipped on the blinkers, hoping if anyone did come they'd see the light.

Pulling the hood of Dan's coat over her head, she slipped through the dark night. Rain was so heavy nothing seemed solid.

As she rounded the corner of the barn, she saw a scene straight out of a black-and-white gangster movie. The light from one dull bulb over the barn door fought through the darkness, looking as flimsy as a watercolor painting being washed away.

She could barely see a huge van parked in the mud near the light and the bumper of a car peeking out of the dilapidated barn. BTTB reflected in the bulb's glow. They'd found the getaway car and the men. Only there were far more than two.

The men in front of the open barn doors were dressed in black and looked fully armed for battle. Two held their weapons shoulder high, ready to fire.

Avery counted four total on guard, a fifth was sitting in the driver's side of the black van. From the van's open back seat she saw two other men. One's long leg hung out of the open door. The shooter, she thought. The other man in the back was small and wide-eyed.

He may have driven the getaway car last night, but he didn't look old enough to legally drink.

She realized her posse had just interrupted the shooter's rescue. A few more minutes and all Dan and his team would have found was an abandoned car.

Dan, Shawn, and the deputy had their backs to her but she could see that their hands were up. Their rifles must be somewhere out of the barn light, probably at their feet. She wasn't sure how the bad guys had got the drop on three lawmen but they were in deep trouble.

In a blink she saw the circle of light as a stage. She'd danced on stages since she was five. Ballerinas don't watch the floor. They hold their heads high and sense where they are as they dance. None of the men were looking around, all were staring straight ahead.

Agent Shawn was arguing with the man in front of him, who must have been the leader. "If you let these two local cops go, boys, I'll give you what you want. I'm tired of watching the old guy anyway. I'll take you right to him."

Her almost-cousin's words were clearly Chicago-flavored, and the leader of the gang sounded the same when he called Shawn a dead man talking.

Shawn pushed. "Look, boys, we ain't got all night. Tie them up. The locals won't look near as hard for you if they find them alive. All we need is thirty minutes and you'll have that accountant, turned informant, in your hands. You can have him halfway back to Chicago before anyone knows."

The leader of the gang laughed. "You do know we'd take you with us for insurance. You screw us, you're dead. If you play along, we'll get you back to Chicago to be buried."

The biggest of the men in black laughed and mumbled, "He's walking dead right now, but it'd save us time if he takes us directly to the old man's hideout. We don't care about those two cops. I'm ready to be on the road heading north. The boss will be real happy to get old Howard back. We might get a bonus."

The leader shook his head. "I got an idea that won't have anyone following us. Since we're out here in the middle of nowhere, how about we stage a gunfight? I'm thinking these two lawmen stumbled on the nitwit local shooter you hired last night and his driver. With the rain there won't even be tire tracks showing we were here. It'll look like a real cowboy shootout, only in this case all four die. That way we get the accountant and don't have to put up with those two idiots in the van. I told the boss we didn't want to hire locals."

Shawn started arguing, but the leader was no longer listening. As the agent challenged their latest plan, he moved in closer to danger.

Avery heard one of the men in black say the idea made sense. The van was getting too full anyway. One even offered to pop both the shooter and the driver.

She wrapped her fingers around the keys in the pocket of Dan's coat. Heavy, thick keys like ones she'd seen that unlock gates. She should have picked up a gun from the back of the Rover. But she didn't know how it worked and she'd have no chance with four armed men.

Only she knew how this was going to end. Dan would be dead along with Shawn and the deputy. Suddenly all the drama of the theater looked calm compared to reality.

The men in black were arguing about who would kill whom. Shawn was yelling for someone to listen to him and the tall man hanging out of the van started choking the driver in the front seat. The tall shooter from last night must have realized, as the favored target to be shot first, he needed to get away fast.

Suddenly the wide-eyed kid jumped out of the far side of the van and slammed the door as he darted into the rain.

The four men in black swung into full alert as if they'd heard a cannon. All aimed their rifles toward the kid, but in a blink the rain seemed to swallow him.

Avery pulled the huge ring of keys from her pocket and tossed it as hard as she could toward the roof of the barn.

With the thunder and lightning and the panic, the keys clambered down the roof sounding like rapid gunfire.

All four men swung their rifles up as if a stampede was rushing toward them from behind.

That was all Shawn needed. He grabbed the closest man's rifle and slammed it so hard into the leader's face the crack sounded like a lightning pop.

Dan plowed into the second man, knocking him down with such force that the third man fell beneath the biggest man. Dan was on top of both, tossing rifles aside as he managed to get in a few blows on both.

The deputy hesitated for a second as if not believing he was part of the fight, then he leaned low and tackled the last man standing. Deputy Collins wrestled him in the mud until both were covered. The man was crying for help when the deputy sat on him as he cuffed him.

Screaming sirens sounded from every direction as chaos settled beneath the barn light's glow. Shawn shoved the unconscious man he'd hit toward the deputy. "Watch this one, while I go get the shooter."

The deputy pulled his service weapon and nodded.

A moment later Shawn came back with the tall shooter and a half-dead van driver.

The shooter was crying, saying he didn't mean to shoot anyone, only the windows. "I was just flushing out the guy in hiding. That's all. I ain't going to jail for some five-hundred-dollar job."

The van driver was cussing and swearing he wanted to press charges on the beanpole who tried to choke him.

Avery stood alone, yards away, letting the rain drip onto her face. Into her body. Into her mind. She couldn't move. She realized that seeing good men almost die mattered so much more than all her problems. She'd been feeling sorry for herself for a year.

She remained frozen, hidden in the shadows as other cars arrived. Troopers ran to help. Suddenly there were flashlights everywhere and headlights and men in uniform doing their jobs.

Chapter 14
Silent Night

One man, wide in the shoulders and slim in the hips, walked toward Avery. His movements were powerful, like he was storming the castle and he didn't stop until he stood directly in front of her.

Without a word he pulled her to him and crushed her against his heart.

For a while he just held her as she cried. She'd lived a hundred years in a few minutes. Her world had shifted and nothing in her life would be the same from this moment on.

Kissing his cheek she whispered, "Is it all right if I tell you I was afraid I might lose you?"

"Yeah, if I can call you Pumpkin just once."

"But I haven't gained a pound, Sheriff. You can't call me that until I stay around long enough to turn fluffy."

"I know, but I've decided I'm crazy about you just the way you are. You saved our lives tonight, you know."

Avery grinned. "I tend to throw things when I'm upset. And those guys threatening you made me mad."

He kissed her lightly. "I don't mind. Everybody has a few flaws."

As he kissed her again she wrapped her arms around his neck. If this man made love as great as he kissed she was definitely staying around.

Then he kissed her so deeply she forgot that she was standing in mud with rain pounding down.

Finally, a highway patrol officer tried to interrupt by clearing his throat.

Dan growled. "This better be important."

"Yes sir, Sheriff. We're loading up. Not much we can do in this rain. Agent Knight and Deputy Collins want to know if you two want to ride into the station with them. I'd take you in with me, but I got the kid who drove the shooter last night. He's throwing up in the back of my cruiser right now. We saw him standing in the middle of the road by where the fence was down. He was holding a flashlight and looking like he had no idea which way to go. He's only sixteen. Claims he didn't know what he was getting into."

Dan put his arm around Avery. "We'll ride with the guys who brought us to this dance."

The patrolman didn't smile as he stared at Dan. "Sheriff, your shoulder's bleeding."

Dan looked down. "Darn, I'm leaking again."

Avery tugged him toward the car where Agent Knight and Deputy Collins waited.

Shawn took one look at Dan's shoulder as he slipped into the back seat with Avery and yelled at the highway patrolman, "We'll be stopping at the hospital on our way in."

The patrolman saluted. "I'll call the doc and tell him to be waiting to patch you up again, Sheriff. He's not going to be happy to see you."

No one argued as they joined the line of vehicles heading out of the pasture.

Shawn and the deputy started talking about how mad Doc Henry would be even if the sheriff and his lady seemed to make a habit of ending their dates at the hospital.

Dan went back to kissing Avery. He obviously didn't want to think or talk. He just wanted to feel.

Avery seemed to be on the same page.

When Dan finally came up for air, he told the two in front to shut up; they were breaking his concentration.

"Oh," Shawn said in his Chicago accent. "You're bothered. That's real funny. We're in the front seat driving the make-out car. Seems to me, since you guys both have beds you could wait a few minutes, at least until you stop bleeding all over your partner in crime."

"Shut up, Mikey," both yelled from the back seat.

Neither man in the front seat said another word, so Dan went back to kissing, then suddenly pulled away. "Now, before we get to the hospital, I need to get a few things straight. No one calls my mother to tell her anything except me. Remember, I'm fine, if anyone asks. She's got spies everywhere. And second, I'm not spending another night in that hospital. You two are breaking me out if they start trying to strap me to anything but Avery."

Avery put her hand on his cheek and turned Dan's face toward her. "Shut up, Sheriff, and kiss me."

They both ignored the laughter coming from the front seat.

Chapter 15
Midnight

In the low lights of an abandoned office at the Abilene police station, Dan sat on an old couch beside Avery. She hadn't turned loose of his hand since they'd left the hospital an hour ago. Uncle Henry had given him a lecture as he'd added three more stitches to Dan's collection. He'd said he hadn't thought he needed to tell Dan not to get into a fight the day after he'd been shot, but from now on he'd add that to the discharge papers.

When they left, the doc hugged them both and said he didn't want to see them until Christmas.

Ten minutes later when they walked into the station with Shawn on one side and Deputy Collins on the other, every lawman in the front office cheered. By the time Shawn told what happened for the third time, they were legends.

Collins had been a rookie taking the hospital guarding assignment because no one else wanted it. Now he was part of the team and would never live down the fact that he must have learned his hand-to-hand skills of tackling bad guys on the football field.

As the hours seemed to drag by, all Dan wanted to do was take Avery home. She fussed over him and tried to tell him to take it easy. He didn't mind her trying to boss him around. He'd grown up with a dictator who poured all her love into her one child. Dan saw Avery's attempts as nothing more than proof that she was falling for him.

"Not much longer," he whispered as he kissed her hand. "As soon as Shawn finishes with the paperwork, I'll get him to take us home. Deputy Collins says he's going out at dawn to finish up the site. You do know that you saved us last night. If you hadn't tossed those keys, we might have never had a chance to get all four men at once."

"I wasn't a hero. I was scared to death."

"Most heroes are."

Dan tried to think of how to say what was on his mind. In a few minutes they could be surrounded again and all he wanted was to be alone with her.

"Avery, you know there are times when people live in double time. For a few days or maybe a few minutes you're totally alive. You breathe deeper, feel far more than ever before. Most of the time folks live their lives with their senses turned down to low. It's calmer that way, safer, more comfortable.

"Then there are those times we turn up the volume, run full out, feel every part of our bodies and minds alive."

She smiled. "I think that's the most words I've ever heard you say, Sheriff."

"Don't call . . ." Dan stopped and decided he'd fight that battle later. Right now he had to make her understand how he felt.

He looked directly at her. "Since the moment I met you, I've felt that way with you. I'm living in double time. I'm a hundred percent alive. I don't even want to sleep for fear of missing you. I've lived ten years thinking I'd do best if I remained alone, but the first time I saw you dancing in the night, I knew I was wrong." He took a long breath. "I needed you in my world."

She didn't move. Didn't even blink.

Great, he decided. She'd been through hell tonight and he'd finally frightened her to death by telling her how he felt. He should have just said something simple like "I think I'm falling in love with you." Then she could have told him to "Go do that crap somewhere else. I'm not interested in a bloody sheriff."

"In a few minutes we won't be able to talk alone, so I need to tell you that I don't want to go home without you. I don't want to sleep without you." Dan took a deep breath. "I don't want to live the rest of my life without you."

She was still staring at him with those huge blue eyes. The only hope she offered was her tight grip around his fingers.

"Avery, say something. Will you come home with me?" He wanted to say if he failed again at loving, he wasn't sure his heart would take the blow. If she said they hadn't known one another long enough. That was true. But she felt so right beside him and he didn't want to waste time trying to decide what to do, when he already knew whether she stayed or left she'd always be a part of him.

Dan leaned back and closed his eyes. He couldn't watch her go. "Say something."

He felt her pulling her hand away.

Dan couldn't move as she climbed up on him, her long legs folded on either side of him. She was above him as she placed her hands on his face and leaned down until her lips brushed his ear.

As he opened his eyes to face head-on whatever happened, she whispered, "I feel the same."

Then she kissed him as if waking him up to life all over again.

About the time they both were lost in passion, Dan heard his mother's voice.

"Daniel, I swear." Her words echoed down the hallway and came back, hitting him now from both directions. "Every time I see you two, you're stuck together. I'm not putting up with this. Do you hear me, Daniel? I don't care if you are in your thirties."

Avery's lips were still against his, but she was no longer kissing him. She was laughing. At that moment he realized she wasn't the least bit afraid of his mother. Avery was perfect for him.

His mother was yelling and Dan thought of arguing, then he picked up a few words in her rant.

He pushed Avery an inch away. "What did you say, Madre?"

"I said you might as well marry the girl. I'm tired of waiting around for grandkids."

He looked at Avery and smiled. "Marry me, Pumpkin, and make my mother happy."

"All right, Sheriff." Avery smiled at him with a hunger that had nothing to do with his mother.

He could feel future arguments building up. Nicknames. Where to sleep. Who was going to be on top, maybe. He decided he didn't care about that as he lifted her off him.

"Be careful of your shoulder," both women said at the same time.

Then, both of the women in his life nodded as if they'd just declared a truce.

Ten minutes later as Shawn drove them to Dan's ranch halfway between While-a-Way and Abilene, the agent said he'd be leaving in a few hours with his witness and his partner.

Shawn explained one last fact about this strange assignment. His state's witness had somehow found a woman he'd fallen in love with years ago and thought he'd lost. He claimed he met her in the third grade and never forgot her. That's why he suggested While-a-Way as a hiding place.

"Get this." Shawn laughed. "They were married this morning and apparently are planning their honeymoon in Chicago while he's testifying. Then they plan to settle in her hometown."

When Dan asked who the woman was, Shawn grinned. "Avery's friend. Miss May. The Baptist preacher married them for a dime, the same price they'd asked the preacher's grandfather to marry them for, when they were in the third grade.

"When the shooting started at the coffee shop, they ran out the back door and Miss May drove them to Ben and Mattie's place. She said it was the hardest farm to find in the county, so they'd be safe there."

Epilogue

Snowy Christmas Eve Morning

Dorothy Dawn's Quilt Shop had been open for three weeks thanks to the small army of townsfolk who helped. The quilting frames were up under the landing and shelves were packed with bolts of material. Racks scattered downstairs were slowly filling up with books and notions and squares.

The front counter was covered with Christmas quilts.

To Avery's surprise a few of the quilters who spent the day at the frames would stop and ring up customers while talking them into buying a few more supplies. Mattie, Ben's wife, came in to help with the books almost every morning. Emily Ann loved teaching a few nights a week and helping out with the ordering.

As Avery took the first step to the landing, where eight little girls waited for their dance lesson, one of the quilters stopped to complain about the noise. A few others joined in. "The girls' dancing makes too much noise and when they laugh it rattles down from above so loud we can't talk over them."

"Dancers and quilters don't blend together," another almost shouted.

Avery kept smiling and climbing. She loved teaching dance. She couldn't, she wouldn't stop.

As she started the class, she looked over at the gift Dorothy Dawn left her. Her wishing quilt. Miss May had showed Avery a tiny piece in the center of the quilt. A heart-shaped scrap that seemed to hold all the squares together, and embroidered in the center of the heart were Avery's initials.

The wishing quilt, pieced in many colors like Avery saw her life, was hers. Framed in blues the color of her eyes. And in one corner was a tiny ballerina dancing.

This one quilt belonged upstairs in the dance studio. Avery had no doubt it had been made with love, for her.

She smiled down at her students and said, "Let's warm up, then today we have a very special dance to do."

Thirty minutes later eight little ballerinas, some chubby, some awkward, one missing a shoe and most missing teeth, tiptoed down the stairs and began to dance around the displays to Christmas tunes playing.

The quilters huffed and mumbled for a moment, then stopped quilting as the girls circled them, smiling. Each dancer picked a lady and kissed her on the cheek as she whispered, "Merry Christmas," and danced back upstairs.

By the time Avery got back downstairs, the ladies were all lined up between the door and the checkout counter.

"Is something wrong?"

"Yes," one said. "You need to order more pink and yellow squares."

"And summer green," another shouted.

Another lady announced, "And you need to stay open longer or maybe on Sunday afternoons. We've got work to do."

"I could give one of you the extra key," Avery offered. "What's up, ladies?"

The lead complainer stepped forward. "We've got eight little quilts to make before Valentine's Day. I'm sure it's cold up there on that hardwood floor."

Avery smiled and began to ring up all their purchases.

She couldn't wait to drive home to the ranch and tell Daniel. She'd wake him up and tell him all about her two worlds coming together. Then they'd make love before he got out of bed, dressed, and had dinner with his wife. The next morning he'd wake her with breakfast and they'd make love before she got out of bed and went to work while he slept.

After all, they were living life in double time.

Wish Upon a Wedding

LORI WILDE

In memory of my grandmother, Glenna Osborn Reid, who didn't pass along her majestic quilting skills.

Chapter 1

Outside the metal double gate, Dr. Ellie Winter halted her extended cab pickup truck and stared at the overhead signage which read: Dusty Sagebrush Ranch.

Hauling in a deep, sustaining breath, she held it for several seconds and then released it in a soft, slow hiss. The sprawling thousand-acre spread had once served as a summer grief camp for children who'd lost parents or siblings. Now it was a dude ranch that served as a venue for western-themed weddings and other events.

So many memories here. Some good. Some bad. All of them emotional.

This extended weekend would be arduous, joyful, sad, blessed, and complicated. As kids, she and her younger sister Camille had attended the camp for three summers in a row after their father, a professional bull rider, had been killed in a rodeo arena when Camille was eleven and Ellie fourteen.

Ellie had packed plenty of tissue boxes along with

enough clothing for four days, her peach silk maid-of-honor dress, and an inventory of quilting supplies that included a rotary cutter, self-healing cutting mat, scissors, seam ripper, pins, rulers, and the twelve-inch block square she'd hand sewn in preparation for assembling the memory quilt planned for this wedding weekend.

For the past two months, she'd worked on her square whenever she had a spare moment in her job as a physician for the Professional Bull Riders organization. It was the first time she'd quilted since she'd started medical school eight years earlier, and her sewing skills were rusty.

Camille's bachelorette party, which started at ten a.m. today and would run until the rehearsal dinner tomorrow evening, would be unusual to say the least. Instead of whooping it up at a bar or strip club, her sister was throwing an old-fashioned quilting bee.

Although Camille wasn't above tucking dollar bills into sexy male strippers' G-strings or getting toasted on tequila shots. In fact, that was exactly what her sister had planned before they'd gotten the devastating news that Gram-Gram Winter had been diagnosed with Alzheimer's. Their grandmother was in the early stages and they were determined to make every moment count.

The wedding party would piece together the blocks each quilter had already sewn at home into a memory quilt top. Their father's mother, who'd taught Ellie and Camille to quilt, would be there for the quilting bee. While Camille was on her honeymoon in Fiji, Ellie would send the quilt out to be finished by an expert with a longarm machine.

A tear trickled down Ellie's cheek and she swiped it away with her knuckle. Yes, this weekend would be hard, but oh, the memories they would create! She would savor every second, both the bitter and the sweet.

Bittersweet.

Her perennial experience of the Dusty Sagebrush. Ellie pulled out her cell phone and took a snapshot of the sign. First photo in the memory books she would make for Gram-Gram and Camille.

Then she texted her sister: **Here.**

Camille texted back with a dancing woman emoji. **I'm N Cabin 6. Old times' sake. Text me once U check N.**

Ellie: **Will do.**

Camille: **Um, where R U exactly?**

Ellie: **Front gate.**

Camille: **Oh . . . BTW . . . There's something I 4got to warn you about.**

Forgot? Ellie frowned. Her younger sister was famous for "forgetting" to tell people uncomfortable things that she didn't want to deal with face-to-face and springing it on them in a text or email.

Ellie: **Oh?** Her response was mild. Nonaccusatory. She'd struck the right tone.

Camille: **Remember Dalton Branch?**

The love of her life? Ellie brought a palm to her chest. Um, yep. Dalton was unforgettable.

The suspicion she'd held in check slipped out and she couldn't control her own fingers. ***I* wasn't diagnosed with Alzheimer's.**

The second she sent the text, she regretted it. This

was Camille's wedding. She didn't want to be a fly in the ointment. Weddings were stressful enough. Immediately, she added: **Sorry, U know how I feel about Dalton.**

Camille: **Don't be mad . . .**

Ellie: **Please don't tell me U invited Dalton to the wedding.**

Camille: **Umm. Not exactly.**

Ellie: **What exactly?**

Camille: **Dalton bought the Dusty Sagebrush. U'll see him when U check in.**

Swearing under her breath, Ellie bit down on the inside of her cheek, an involuntary reaction to the montage of Dalton Branch memories suddenly running through her head.

Dalton on the first day of grief camp, a tall and lanky youth with an impossibly sexy grin, smiling at her as she and Camille stepped off the camp bus. He'd been wearing a white western shirt patterned with black silhouettes of bull riders, which stirred her grief. The hug he'd given her after Camille explained about their dad. How darn nice that hug had felt.

Dalton, as he waltzed her on the dance floor, his dark eyes lively, his arms loose around her waist, his gaze focused on her.

Dalton taking her fishing and laughing uproariously as she battled to reel in what turned out to be a large stick.

Dalton, as they grew older and their relationship deepened, kissing her for the first time underneath the midnight canopy of stars at Hope Lake the year they were counselors.

Ellie hadn't thought about Dalton in years, but the old memories were there, tucked down deep inside where she'd shoved them after he'd shattered her heart. Apparently, they'd just been waiting to tumble out. Being at the ranch stirred those memories like a long-handled spoon, scooping to the bottom to mix and blend the old emotions with the surging new ones—hurt, fear, betrayal, hope.

Part of her wanted to whip the truck around and blast out of here. But she was no longer that seventeen-year-old who'd gotten dumped on the same day she'd been accepted into Texas A&M with a full scholarship, hungry to pursue her dream of being a rodeo doctor, making the sport as safe as possible for bull riders and preventing other little girls from losing their daddy the way she and Camille had.

She could handle Dalton Branch. She was a doctor—accomplished, self-assured, in control.

Camille: **Ellie? U mad?**

Ellie: **Did U know Dalton owned the Dusty Sagebrush when U booked?**

Camille: **Not at first.**

Ellie: **Playing matchmaker?**

Camille: **No! I just wanted 2 get married here. It's where Cody and I met.**

Ellie believed her. **Thank heavens U aren't trying to play matchmaker. Dalton and I were never meant 2 B.**

Camille: **He's as hot as ever.**

Ellie: **Don't care.**

Camille: **Your heart belongs to your work.**

Ellie: **Who says I have a heart?**

Camille: **Haha . . .**

Pressure built at the back of Ellie's eyes. A sinus headache? Or tumbleweed grief?

Camille: **The gals and I will meet U in the dining hall at 8. Later.** The "gals" being her four bridesmaids.

Exhaling, Ellie shook off her discomfort. Her goal was simple. Make this wedding weekend unforgettable for her sister and grandmother.

Dalton Branch be damned.

Resolutely, she texted back: **See you soon, sissy.** She added a heart emoji.

Pasting on a bright, if somewhat shaky, smile, Ellie put the truck in gear and headed for the main lodge.

Dalton was antsy about Ellie's arrival. He'd been plagued by restless dreams of her for the past two weeks.

He shouldn't be nervous. He hadn't seen the woman in over a decade, but damn if the tiny hole in his heart hadn't cracked wide-open when the wedding venue request had shown up in his inbox from Camille Winter's wedding planner six months ago.

Had Camille told Ellie he'd bought the Dusty Sagebrush?

Bigger question. Why did he care?

For all he knew, Ellie was married with a passel of kids. All correspondence had been through the wedding planner, so he hadn't talked to Camille directly. He knew nothing of Ellie's life after they'd broken up, other than hearing through the grapevine she'd achieved her goal of becoming a doctor for the PBR.

He'd even resisted the temptation to look Ellie up on social media. The past was the past. Best let it lie. Except now, the past was the present and Ellie would be here any minute.

The wedding planner had told him the wedding party needed the conference room in the lodge for a bachelorette party/quilting bee and that Gram-Gram Winter had been diagnosed with Alzheimer's.

That sad news killed Dalton's soul. He'd watched the disease claim his favorite uncle and he ached for the Winter sisters. But the two women were tough. They'd gone through three years of grief camp, just as he had when his mom passed away from renal failure when he was a teen.

Dalton had set up extra tables in the twelve-hundred-square-foot conference room and brought in additional lighting. Hand-sewing a quilt was exacting work and the quilters would need plenty of lamps for their project. He understood because his stepmom, Carol, was an avid quilter and she'd recruited him more times than he could count to help her, and her friends, set up for quilting parties. His stepmother, whom he adored, had even conned him into learning to sew. The skill had come in handy when he'd bought the ranch. Instead of buying new curtains for the bungalows, Dalton had made his own and saved over a thousand dollars.

When Ellie had left for medical school, Dalton headed for the military, where he'd spent two tours of duty in the Middle East. The Army had been an eye-opener to a simple cowboy from the Trans-Pecos. Experiencing another culture had changed him in fundamental ways, and he'd come away with a renewed appreciation for American values. He was also much more cautious than he'd been before his military service. His heart was no longer available to anyone who wanted to just walk right in. When he was younger, he'd loved too fiercely, too quickly. He supposed that's what came of losing his mother at a young age.

"Need any help?"

He glanced up to see his ranch foreman, Kaddy Johnson, standing in the doorway. Kaddy had saved his hide in Afghanistan and he owed her his life. When he'd learned she'd been living on the streets of Houston after battling a severe case of PTSD, he'd offered her a job at the Dusty Sagebrush.

Kaddy was a proud woman, so he'd been a bit surprised when she'd accepted. She and her wife, Alma Gonzales, had moved into the small house at the back end of the property, and he wouldn't be able to run the ranch without them. Alma had become both the housekeeper and the ranch chef, specializing in Tex-Mex cuisine, which she catered for weddings. Because of these two amazing women, the Dusty Sagebrush ran like a well-oiled machine; they'd even gotten a small write-up in *Texas Monthly.* Business had boomed since the issue came out last summer.

"Perfect timing," he told her. "I've got four more lamps to bring in from storage."

Kaddy readjusted her Stetson. "I'll get it, boss."

"Thanks."

Kaddy paused, angled him a sidelong glance.

"What is it?" he asked.

She hitched her thumbs through her belt loops. "Are you okay?"

"Sure. Why wouldn't I be?"

"Your ex-girlfriend is arriving this morning."

"How do you know about Ellie?" He stared at her, perplexed. He hadn't shared his past.

Kaddy snorted. "How long have you lived in Fort Davis, boss? Just 'cause you don't gossip about other people doesn't mean other people aren't gossiping about you."

"The town is gossiping about me and Ellie?" Irritated, he jammed his fingers through his hair. *Dang it!*

"I've heard tell of your great love story." Kaddy shook her head. "I dunno. If I'd been that fired up over a girl from my past, I'd be a little stirred up right now."

"I'm not stirred up."

"You sure?"

"It was thirteen years ago."

"There's no love like the first love."

"What does Alma think about that?"

Kaddy gave him a sly grin. "Who says Alma's not my first love?"

Laughing, Dalton held up both palms. "You win."

"Seriously." Kaddy's boots echoed off the hardwood floor as she moved closer. "If the weekend gets a little rocky, you can always escape to our house. We can sit on the front porch and knock back shots of Limoncello."

She was teasing again.

When they'd finally gotten stateside, he and Kaddy had met up at a bar in San Antonio where the owner kept thanking them for their service and giving them free Limoncello shots until they could barely walk to the curb to catch an Uber. It had been a splendid night of blowing off steam, but after the three-day hangover that followed, Dalton had sworn off Limoncello for life.

"I think I can handle Ellie without an alcohol chaser."

"Suit yourself." Kaddy started out the door, paused and said, "Oh, hi there, Ellie, nice to meet you."

Ellie was here! *Oh damn, oh hell.*

Dalton moved left, then right, then left again as instant sweat ringed his collar.

Kaddy stuck her head back in the door, grinning like the Cheshire cat. The woman was yanking his chain. He should have known.

"Gotcha!" Kaddy hooted. "Look at you, running in circles over a woman. This Dr. Ellie must be hot stuff to get the likes of Cool Hand Luke riled up."

Cool Hand Luke was his Army nickname because he'd been so hard to ruffle, but right now, he felt as ruffled as ridged potato chips.

"Ellie's not outside the door?" His knees sagged with relief and his pulse slowed.

"Not yet." Kaddy chuckled.

"I should fire you."

"You won't."

"I might," he threatened without meaning it.

"Ha." She threw back her head and laughed. "Where

you gonna find someone else who'll work as hard as I do?"

"Point taken."

"Like I said, if you need someplace to hide out this weekend, I've got Limoncello with your name on it chilling in the fridge."

Chapter 2

You've got this, Ellie assured herself.

So what if Dalton owned the Dusty Sagebrush? That wasn't a bad thing. She was glad he was doing well. Although she did wonder why he'd turned the grief camp into a wedding venue. Probably more money in it. That made economic sense, and Dalton was nothing if not fiscally responsible. At least he had been thirteen years ago.

Who knew what he was like now?

He'd certainly put a lot of time, money, and effort into fixing the place up. He wouldn't have done that unless he expected a hefty return.

The ranch-style lodge was freshly painted a calming sage green, the long circular driveway had been refinished, a koi pond built and accentuated with gorgeous flower beds.

It took a lot of water and nurturing to maintain a pond and such plants in the arid desert climate.

Pulling into a parking area marked Guests, Ellie killed the engine and let out a long sigh she didn't even know she'd pent up. She was nervous, but she'd soon be quilting, and sewing calmed her.

She might as well carry in the quilting supplies now and start setting up as soon as she'd checked in. No point getting the key, heading to her bungalow, unloading, and driving back to the lodge. Although it was only seven thirty in the morning, she should scope out the conference room and get her bearings before Camille and her bridesmaids showed up.

Pocketing her key fob, Ellie slung the strap of her purse over her shoulder and got out of the truck to the familiar smell of livestock, sandy soil, and good quality hay.

Home.

That illogical, sentimental thought hit Ellie like a smack to the face. Truthfully, she didn't have a home. Yes, she rented a sparse one-bedroom apartment in Fort Worth, but her job was on the PBR circuit. The rodeo was her home.

Shaking off her melancholia, Ellie opened the back door of her pickup and took out the big cardboard box filled with quilting supplies and the quilt block she'd created from the purple flannel shirt she'd worn to her first rodeo to watch her dad compete when she was a preschooler.

She'd kept the shirt because Dad won that night, and he'd told her that seeing her in that purple shirt was his good-luck charm. She'd worn that shirt to every rodeo thereafter until she grew too big for it. Her mother had put it away in a keepsake box and Ellie had found it years later when going through her father's things.

Had making the quilt square from the flannel shirt been a big mistake? Would the memory of her son hurt Gram-Gram too much? Anxiety cut across Ellie's heart. *It's a memory quilt. Memories are the point.*

A light breeze rippled her long blond hair over her shoulders, and the supplies in the box rattled as she walked. She turned her face up, felt the early morning sun kiss her cheeks. She stopped walking, closed her eyes, and let the emotions wash over her—joy and sadness, anticipation and regret. She felt them fully and then let them go as she'd been trained to do in grief camp.

Yes.

She savored the release, but if she'd paid attention, she would have noticed that the red cotton fabric she'd brought to decorate the tables for the quilting bee had come loose from the bolt and was dangling over the edge of the box and flapping gaily in the wind behind her.

As it was, her rodeo doctor instinct grabbed hold of her the second she heard the *clop-clop-clop-clop* of hooves on concrete. Her first thought—*Why is a bull in the driveway?*

Her second thought?

Run!

Ellie flung her eyes open, spun on her heels and found herself face-to-face with a fat Angus bull. Fear flared through her body and froze her in place.

Head down, nostrils flaring, the bull pawed the ground, snorted, and before Ellie could react, charged.

Dalton took his Stetson from the hook by the back door and stepped outside just in time to see Danger Zone barreling toward Ellie.

Despite his ominous name, the elderly bull was normally a halter-trained cream puff, but right here, right now, he looked mighty provoked. Dalton didn't have time to ponder how the Angus had gotten out of his corral. The situation required immediate action.

Cowboy boots weren't made for running, but Dalton *ran*.

He sprinted around the old-fashioned hitching post used for pre- and post-wedding photographs, hurdling the flower bed filled with candy-cane petunias, leaping over the sandwich-board sign proclaiming: wedding this way→.

Dalton headed in the opposite direction, straight for the bull.

Time slowed and it felt as if as if he was barely moving. He heard Ellie give a tiny yelp. Her eyes went wide, and she stood immobilized.

Danger Zone was a freight train, snorting and pawing, his obsidian eyes locked on the red material fluttering from the cardboard box Ellie clutched in her arms.

"Put down the box! Put down the box!" he yelled.

Things happened so quickly, Dalton wasn't sure what came first. He saw Ellie drop the box. Listened as it smacked against the concrete. Felt his thigh muscles ache as he sprinted. Then he lost his mind as Ellie raised her hands to her face, looking terror-stricken.

Danger Zone was going to plow into her. No doubt in his mind. Not a second to spare. One thought throbbed through his brain. *Save Ellie.*

Chest heaving, pulse pounding, brain whirling, Dalton did what any honorable cowboy would do when he spied a lady in distress.

He dove between her and the bull.

Danger Zone didn't miss a beat. The charging, eighteen-hundred-pound bull lowered his head and smacked Dalton solidly in the belly.

Saving grace, Dalton thought, weirdly calm now that he'd taken the hit and spared Ellie. Danger Zone had no horns.

Horned or not, the bull wasn't through with him. He scooped Dalton up in a wild toss and slung him like a rag doll into the koi pond.

"Yee-haw! You ornery critter, get the hell out of here!"

From out of nowhere, a tough-looking woman wearing chaps, a cowboy hat, boots, and leather gloves appeared with a cattle prod. She headed straight for the bull, not the least bit intimidated.

What a shero!

Ellie had seen the same bold expression on the faces of the rodeo bullfighters in the arena. Gratitude flooded her body.

While the woman went after the bull, Ellie rushed to Dalton. She knew firsthand the damage a bull could do to a man's internal organs, and she heard herself praying, *Please let him be okay, please let him be okay.*

Just as she reached the pond, Dalton came up sputtering. Relief weakened her knees, and they were barely able to hold her up. *Okay. Good sign.*

She shot a glance toward the woman, encouraged to see the cowgirl had already turned the bull toward the pasture gate. The woman didn't have to use the prod. Just the sight of it changed the animal's aggression into compliance.

Quickly, she returned her attention to Dalton, who was standing zipper deep in the pond, soaked head to toe, his wet clothes clinging to every delineated muscle.

He was grinning like a possum.

In her head, she heard sexy, slo-mo music, recognized it as Marvin Gaye crooning, "Let's Get It On."

Yikes! Where did that come from?

Involuntarily, she slapped a palm across her mouth.

Dalton's gaze locked with hers and she melted like ice in the desert sun. Seeing him again brought it all back. Her first mad crush. Her deep, youthful devotion to true love.

God, she'd forgotten how handsome he was!

At six-one he was a match for her own five-foot-eight-inch height. Dampened, his hair looked pitch-black, although it was normally a delicious shade of dark chocolate. In high school, he'd wore it longish, letting it curl to his collar. Now, his hair was clipped short, barely two inches at its longest at the top of his head. The close-cropped style looked great on him. Although, once upon a time, she'd really enjoyed running her fingers through his silky locks.

He reached for his cowboy hat, which was floating on top of the water beside him, shook it off and then plunked it down on his head. Water droplets beaded off the brim, giving him a comical air that tickled her.

In the past, he'd been a cutup. Did that still hold true? Or had the years changed him?

"Howdy, Ellie," he drawled as if they hadn't been separated by thirteen years and a very bad breakup. "Long time, no see."

Ahh, he did still have a sense of humor, condensing time and distance into a lazy cliche. Good to know.

"I . . ." she said, then dropped her gaze to his flat belly, where the bull had head-butted him. "Are you hurt?"

"Me?" He turned his head in a laid-back swivel. "You know me. I can take a lickin' and keep on tickin'."

"You sure?" Her doctor brain was unconvinced. She'd seen him fly through the air and hit the water. A bovine assault was not something to take lightly.

Guilt. She was the cause of his getting catapulted. The bull had been coming for her because of the material fluttering from the quilting box, and Dalton had jumped in to save her.

If he was hurt, it was her fault.

Um, really, Ellie? Taking responsibility for something that was beyond your control again? Why wasn't the bull in a pen?

"I'm not one of your rodeo cowboys," he said. "You don't need to mend me."

She didn't know how to take that.

He was smiling, so she didn't think he'd been trying to insult her, but when they'd been together, he'd hated for her to baby him. Maybe he was playing macho man, trying to hide his injuries.

Narrowing her eyes, Ellie stepped closer, not trusting his assessment of his condition. She'd seen guys with multiple fractures jump to their feet and dust themselves off, declaring they were A-okay when they were anything but. Adrenaline and endorphin rushes could mask pain. Was that happening with Dalton?

She swept her gaze over his body. His breathing seemed a little fast and shallow but that wasn't surprising.

"Could you step out of the pond, please?" She kept her tone neutral and low-key instead of using the take-charge physician voice she wanted to adopt.

He held up both hands as if she'd pulled a gun on him. "Yes, officer."

Dalton didn't move.

"Could you do it now?"

"Sure." Still, he stayed in the water.

"Dalton?"

"Uh-huh."

"Do you need some help?"

"No." He nodded.

"Where does it hurt?" she asked, moving closer still. So close she caught a whiff of his pleasant cowboy scent—leather, sand, and soap.

He put his right palm over his heart.

"Your chest hurts?"

"No," he said. "I'd just forgotten how gorgeous you look in the sunlight."

She snorted, dismissing his flattery, but his words lit a warm fire in her stomach, a fire that had lain dormant for so long.

No. She wasn't doing this. She wouldn't romanticize him or what they'd once shared. Or rather, what she'd thought they'd shared.

Ellie extended her arm to him. The pond was only three feet deep, but there was a foot-tall brick wall surrounding the pond, which he needed to scale to get out. "Grab on. I'll hold you steady."

He winced. "See now, there's the sticky wicket."

"Oh?" She arched an eyebrow. "What's that?"

"When I raise my leg, it hurts likes blue blazes."

"Is the pain in your leg?" Could he have a hairline fracture? Oh heavens, she hoped not.

He moved his hand to his lower abdomen, at the waistband of his Wranglers. His long fingers fanned out over his zipper, indicating his groin.

Hernia? "What kind of pain? Aching, dull, stabbing, searing?"

He lifted a shoulder. "I dunno. Pain, pain."

She'd trained the young men she tended in the rodeo to describe their pain in distinct terms, and she shouldn't get irritated with Dalton for not knowing how to talk about his pain, but she was frustrated.

"Is the pain intermittent or sustained?"

"It only hurts when I raise my leg," he admitted.

"Scale of one to ten, how bad is the pain when you lift your leg?"

He cocked his head, considering her question. "Seven-ish, but the pain sort of freezes there, locks up and won't let go."

Whew! That sounded like a muscle spasm, but she wouldn't jump to a hasty diagnosis.

"How do you feel otherwise? Did you hit your head on the bricks? Are you dizzy?"

"Nope and nope."

"It sounds like your muscle is seizing up and that's why you can't step over the wall. Is that correct?"

"That's right. What do you think it is?"

"I won't know until I examine you, but from what you're describing, it sounds like a charley horse."

"Makes sense."

"I can't really examine and treat you while you're standing in the water. We need to get you out of there."

"Let's do it." He gritted his teeth.

She held out her arm to him again. "Hold on to me for balance."

He wrapped his hand around her forearm, his fingers warm and strong. His touch stirred old memories. They were together again. Not as boyfriend and girl-friend, obviously, but as *something*. . . .

Their gazes were welded to each other.

Something she had no name for.

Honestly, it felt as if they'd just seen each other yes-terday and no time had passed at all. It was a weird sen-sation, and it took her completely off guard.

To defend herself, she pulled up the mask of her doctor persona and spoke in a clipped, professional voice. "Bend your leg at the knee and then reach your leg backward from the hip."

"Huh?"

She demonstrated what she meant, bending her right knee and rotating her hip backward.

He looked skeptical. "I'm afraid I'll lose my balance if I do that."

"No, you won't." She locked her hand around his wrist and clung tight. "I've got you."

"Okay." He moistened his lips. "Here goes nothing."

He did as she asked, raising his leg with a narrow-eyed squint and bending it backward from his hip joint the way she'd shown him.

"Now," she said. "From that position grab hold of your ankle and pull your foot behind you toward your butt."

"Huh?"

She demonstrated again with her free hand, still holding her arm out for him while she bent in a dancer's pose. Her daily yoga practice kept her flexible while she was on the road.

"I can't do that. My body doesn't bend that way."

"Give it a shot. It'll help stretch out your abductor."

Wincing, Dalton held tightly to her and did his best to reach back to grab his ankle with his opposite hand. The motion was impossible in those skin-tight soaking-wet blue jeans. "Ow, ow."

He needed help.

"May I touch your body?"

"Ellie"—he drew out her name, enunciating both syllables equally, making it sound like L. E.—"I thought you'd *never* ask."

Chapter 3

Why on God's green earth had he said that?

Dalton could have bitten off his own tongue. He sounded like a total tool. Should he apologize? But wouldn't that just call attention to his gaffe?

Better let it slide.

Ellie did not seem put off. She grinned. "You're not in much of a position to flirt, Mr. Branch."

He wasn't in much of a position to do anything with Ellie Winter, the love of his life. Or rather, she had been the love of his life thirteen years ago, but that was water under the bridge. Hell, it was water that had evaporated over a decade ago. They were older and wiser, and the romantic melancholy of his teens was safely in his rearview mirror.

Except somehow it wasn't.

Not anymore.

Ellie stood in front of him, looking as pretty as the Davis Mountains in the distance behind her, her long blond beach-waves trailing over her shoulders, her crystal-blue eyes vibrant in the sunlight, her lithe figure sexy as hell.

Don't even go there.

Daydreams had no place in real life. She had her career doctoring busted-up cowboys on the rodeo circuit. He had his hands full running the Dusty Sagebrush. For all he knew she had a man in her life. Why wouldn't she? She was a gorgeous, accomplished doctor. He'd be foolish to think she wasn't involved with someone.

Why's that? You're not involved with anyone.

Yeah, well, he'd been busy converting the ranch from a grief camp to a wedding venue/dude ranch in the two years since he'd bought the place from the Farmingtons. Joe and Jill had retired and moved into Fort Davis and had given him their blessing to convert the ranch into this latest incarnation.

Dalton didn't have time for romance. He was happy just as he was, and he'd let Ellie walk away from him thirteen years ago for a good reason. A reason that still existed. She was so far out of his league. She was smart, beautiful, and accomplished. Dalton had never even gone to college.

He hadn't been wrong to let her go.

The past was the past. Best to leave history where it belonged. While he was turning all this over in his mind like burning flapjacks on a cast-iron griddle, Dr. Winter was leaning over, lifting the tail of his chambray shirt and running her firm palm along his lower abdomen just above the waistband of his jeans.

Holy Danger Zone, what was happening here?

Panic spurted through his bloodstream. Sweat instantly popped out on his forehead, mingling with the water as a blaze of wild tingles shot across his skin wherever her fingertips brushed.

His groin muscles bunched and jumped, sending a fresh twist of pain through his thigh. *Oh no, no. Not this*.

"Wh-what are you doing?" he croaked.

"Since your wet jeans won't allow you to fully stretch your abductor muscles, massage is the next best thing to ease the spasms." She put pressure against the muscle in question.

It pulsed and quivered at her touch.

"You are not about to put your hands down my pants, Ellie Winter!" He was losing it. If Ellie didn't stop what she was doing, muscle spasms or not, his body would react in an embarrassing way, and the last thing he needed was an erection.

"I'm a doctor," she said in a calm, professional tone. "I will keep my hand outside your underwear—"

"No!" He pushed her hand aside, tasting his own fear. The flavor was akin to cod liver oil mixed with sulfur. "I go commando."

"Oh." She raised both palms and stepped back, hands in the air. "I see."

"I swear it's no biggie. No intervention needed. I've got this. It's just a cramp."

"How are you going to get out of the pond?"

How? He'd crawl out when she left. "Let me work this out on my own . . . okay?"

To his relief, she nodded.

Thank God.

She straightened and stepped away.

Rather than try to get out, Dalton eased himself

back down into the water without bending his compromised leg. The spasming muscles hurt like the dickens, but the pain wouldn't kill him. Having Ellie see that he was getting hard over her? Well, that just might.

Good grief, why had she touched Dalton?

Ellie had seen his body's response to her touch, and it startled her. Was Dalton still attracted to her? Did Dalton still have sexual feelings for her? Or was it merely a natural male reaction to external stimuli? She hadn't intended to stir him. Absolutely not. But knowing she stirred him stirred her.

Well, that brought her up short. Ellie bit her bottom lip and fought off a blush.

"Shoo." Dalton waved her off. "I'll work this out on my own."

She hovered, wanting to flee to the safety of the lodge, but worried in case the injury was more than a muscle spasm. "I would like to examine you, in case it's not just a muscle spasm."

"Like what?"

"A nerve injury. That bull hit you pretty hard."

"Not *that* hard."

"I saw you fly through the air and land in the pond. Plus there's the whole *can't raise your leg high enough to get out of the water* thing."

He peered up at her from where he was stretched out in the water. He tried to grin, but she could see he was still in pain. "I'm fine."

"You're not."

"I will be." He gritted his teeth and his jaw muscle twitched. "Once my muscles stop seizing up."

"I shouldn't leave you alone."

"Not alone," he mumbled and nodded at the tough cowgirl, who came strolling back toward them, swinging the cattle prod like a baton. "Kaddy's here. Go on inside. Alma will get you checked in."

Ellie hesitated, uncertain. Most likely his pain was just a severe muscle spasm and he'd be okay once the muscle relaxed. That type of injury was extremely common in bull riding.

"I have muscles relaxers in my medical bag. If we get you inside, and out of those wet clothes, we can ice the area. That should do the trick."

"Seriously, Doc, I'll live. You've got a quilting bee to oversee. Camille is counting on you."

He knew her kryptonite . . . her younger sister. Truth? She wasn't his doctor. Dalton Branch wasn't her problem. Not anymore. Hadn't been in quite some time.

He leaned his head against the back of the brick wall, angled her a mind-your-own business glance. Damn, why did he have to look so gorgeous with those dreamy brown eyes and that cocksure grin? If he was smiling like that, he had to be okay.

"Don't let me ruin your day," he murmured. "Go."

"Dalton," she said in chiding tone.

"L. E." He bounced her tone right back at her. "Scoot."

The doctor in her wanted to stay; the former girlfriend in her wanted out of there STAT. It was the maid of honor in her that broke the tie. Camille was counting on her.

Nodding, she said, "I'll get my medical bag from the truck, and when you're able to get out, I'll give you a pill for the spasms and examine you. Fair enough?"

"Fair enough."

Relieved, Ellie turned and headed for the house, her heart thumping crazily and her mind spinning.

Behind her, she heard the cowgirl laugh and say to Dalton, "Well, boss, this is a fine kettle of fish."

Despite the spasms still rippling through his groin and upper thigh, Dalton couldn't help watching Ellie walk away. How he'd missed that wiggle!

What the hell? Ellie's not for you.

Right.

But he was a heterosexual man who hadn't had a girlfriend since he started transforming the rundown camp two years ago, and his urges were getting the better of him. No matter how hard he tried not to think about kissing Ellie, the image of her sweet pink lips was imbedded in his brain.

Leave the woman be. She's here for her sister's wedding.

Kaddy followed his gaze and let out a long, low whistle. "Your ex is *hot*."

"I can see that."

"How did you let that one get away?"

"Long story." Dalton sighed. "We were young, I was dumb."

"You're not so young anymore." Kaddy's blunt honesty could be a real pain sometimes. "Although I can't speak for the dumbness."

"Thanks for your input."

"You're welcome." She laughed.

"How's Danger Zone?"

"Better than you." Kaddy flicked her gaze to the mossy green water and the koi darting around his legs. He'd sunk down low enough that only his head and shoulders were showing.

"You get a boner? Is that why you're hiding in the water?"

"That question is inappropriate."

"I never claimed to be appropriate. I'll assume the answer is yes." She rested the cattle prod on a tree stump and reached out a hand to help him from the water.

Gritting his teeth against the fresh spasms gripping his leg, he grabbed Kaddy's hand and let her yank him from the pond. His foreman was a lot rougher than Ellie would have been, and that was good because, hey, he needed something to snap him out of the crazy sexual fantasies dancing in his head.

Memories blitzed him.

He and Ellie rowing a boat across Hope Lake fed from the spring runoff of the Davis Mountains. Teamed together in a relationship-building exercise as camp counselors their last summer. The summer they'd fully fallen in love. She'd worn denim cutoff shorts, a red halter top and flip-flops that showed off her cute feet and toenails polished a pearly peach.

He and Ellie hanging paper streamers for the end-of-summer dance. He'd held the ladder while she scaled it to staple decorations to the ceiling. He'd been naughty, staring at her sweet rump above him. She'd caught him staring, laughed sweetly, rolled her gorgeous blue eyes and muttered, "Boys."

He and Ellie hiking the mountain with a group of campers, exchanging private glances over the heads of their charges as they kept things lively singing soundtrack hits from Disney movies. Back then *WALL-E* had just come out. He recalled Ellie belting "Down to Earth" lyrics while he thought, *I want to stay right where I am. With you.* Ever after, he referred to the movie—in his head at least—as ELL-E.

He and Ellie watching the sunset from the pier on Hope Lake on their last happy day together, sharing a six-pack of beer he'd filched from the camp owners' refrigerator. She'd lain on her back, sighed dreamily and rested her head in his lap, her long blond hair trailing across his thighs. He still remembered the power of that moment. How he'd felt invincible. How being with her had him aching to conquer the world. Ellie and no one else. How his heart had been filled with so much love for her he could barely stand it.

Ahh, the romantic dreams of teenaged boys. If only he'd known that the next morning a letter from Texas A&M would arrive for her and ruin everything.

They'd been mad for each other, but they'd never made love. Oh, they'd gotten close to having sex, really close, but he'd had too much respect for her to consign Ellie to a summer fling. He'd wanted more. She was the one who'd wanted to take things to the bedroom, but he'd put on the brakes.

Over the years, whenever he thought about Ellie, that had been his one regret. That they hadn't gone all the way. Then again, maybe it was a good thing. He'd never really known what he'd missed.

Except now, he was acutely aware that he'd never had the pleasure of sinking into her warm, willing body and damn, if that wasn't a sudden craving. His mouth watered and his body tightened as he stood there dripping all over the concrete driveway.

Pure insanity, his lust.

Ellie was here for a long weekend that included a bachelorette party quilting bee, a rehearsal dinner and a wedding. She wouldn't have time for anything but events. Certainly no time to reconnect with him. It wasn't like he'd be lounging around either. He had plenty to do.

Romance was off the table. Why was he even thinking about it?

"Hang on." Kaddy disappeared into the barn and came back with a horse blanket. She held the blanket up around him, blocking him from view. "Shuck off those wet jeans. Alma will kill you if you get water all over her clean floors, and I'm in no mood for a funeral."

"It's my house," Dalton mumbled.

"Which Alma rules."

He couldn't argue with that. While Kaddy held up the blanket and kept her eyes averted, he stripped off his jeans and shirt, and then took the horse blanket from her and wrapped it around his body.

Dalton felt vulnerable as hell and eager to get dressed.

Kaddy picked up his soaking-wet clothes and draped

them over the fence. Dalton headed for the house, praying he could get to his bedroom before encountering anyone.

But alas, luck was not on his side.

Horse blanket clutched around him, Dalton shucked off his cowboy boots at the back door welcome mat, bolted through the mudroom . . .

. . . and ran smack dab into Ellie's breasts.

Chapter 4

Oof!

All the air left Ellie's body. Simultaneously, she and Dalton bounced off each other, staring with startled eyes.

"Whoa," she whispered.

"Sorry." His eyebrows shot up as his gaze fixed to her chest.

She brought her arms up to cover herself.

He glanced away, breathing heavily.

Glory! She was panting too. "How are the spasms?"

"Huh?" He blinked. "Oh, they stopped."

"You sure? I have medication for you."

"Don't need it. I'm good."

"Um, okay. I could take a look and help you ice it."

"No!" His eyes flared wider. "I'm fine."

"Let me know if that changes."

"I—"

"You—" She eyeballed him. Horse blanket extending from his chin to his knees, exposing black crew socks and nothing else. He was naked behind that blanket. She knew it as surely as she knew her own name.

Oh.

My.

Gosh.

Her skin heated, buzzed, and she felt slightly dizzy. How had she ended up back here, her hungry eyes and her insane heart filled with precarious notions about Dalton?

Longing. Dangerous thing. Desire. Not for this guy.

Please, no, not again.

And yet, and yet . . .

Hope.

Seriously? What's wrong with you? It's your sister's wedding. You have a quilting bee to throw. Snap out of it.

"Me?" He looked as hopeful as she felt.

Aww, dang it.

"You need to get dressed." She flapped a hand at his attire.

"Yes."

They stood there peering at each other. Somewhere in the distance a grandfather clock loudly ticked off the seconds. One, two, three . . .

"You're in my way," he said.

"Oh, yes." Stunned at her fuzzy-headedness, she hustled aside.

He rushed past her, carrying with him the scent of man, horses, and outdoors. Some of her very favorite scents in the entire world.

She inhaled, intoxicated.

He smelled like her girlhood. Blast from the past. Youthful optimism tangled up with adult reality.

Ellie turned to watch Dalton as he hotfooted it down the hallway. When he'd disappeared from sight, she sagged against the wall. With Dalton around, how in the world was she going to make it through this complicated weekend with her sanity intact?

An hour later the members of the bachelorette party were gathered in the conference room for their quilting bee. Ellie's spirits lifted as she watched her younger sister zipping around the room, high on prewedding excitement.

Camille had always been a social butterfly, the extrovert to Ellie's introvert. She couldn't help thinking her baby sis would be better served with someone more gregarious as her maid of honor, but Camille refused to consider anyone else.

"We're a team," Camille had said adamantly, when Ellie had brought up the matter six months ago, and she'd slipped her arm through Ellie's elbow. "The Winter sisters together forever. The ceremony wouldn't be the same without you standing beside me."

So Ellie channeled her professional persona and took charge of the morning's activities the way she took charge of a medical emergency, with confident calmness.

It had worked too, and everything was running smoothly until Gram-Gram Winter walked through the door, accompanied by their Aunt Olivia. Their late father's sister had recently taken early retirement from her job as a flight attendant for American Airlines so she could take care of her mother as the disease progressed.

Ellie and Camille's mother, Jennifer, didn't quilt. Besides, she and her former mother-in-law didn't see eye to eye, so she and her new husband, Fritz, wouldn't be arriving until tomorrow in time for the rehearsal dinner.

Watching her grandmother, knowing the reality of her tragic diagnosis, brought tears to Ellie's eyes. She swallowed back her salty grief, put on a bright smile and rushed across the room to greet her. She and Camille arrived at their grandmother's side at the same time.

Gram-Gram held up both palms and shook herself free of Aunt Olivia's grip. "I'm in the early stages. I'm not losing my marbles yet, so don't fawn, girls. I'm fine. Please, I want to enjoy every minute of this wedding. Don't treat me any differently than you ever would."

"Normally, I'd hug the stuffing out of you. Can I do that?" Camille asked.

Gram-Gram raised her arms over her head as if she were in a stick-up. "Hug away, Cammie."

Camille swaddled her in a bear hug.

Gram-Gram met Ellie's eyes over her sister's shoulder, gave her their "secret" look. The one Gram-Gram reserved for her oldest grandchild. Ellie smiled back, doing her best to keep the mist from her eyes.

Her sister released Gram-Gram and let Ellie go for

a hug. As Ellie did so, Gram-Gram whispered in her ear, "We need to speak in private later."

Ellie nodded and stepped back, letting other friends and relatives greet her grandmother, her mind whirling at Gram-Gram's request. Why did she want to see her privately? Was it about her diagnosis? Was the Alzheimer's more advanced than she was letting on? It was at times like these that the special closeness she shared with her grandmother felt burdensome. While she enjoyed their tight bond, she didn't like carrying secrets.

Everyone was chatting, visiting with each other.

Ellie moved to the corner of the room, letting the moment unfold naturally. She'd give them ten minutes, then call the quilting bee to order.

"How you doin'?" asked a sexy male voice.

Ellie looked over to see Dalton, fully dressed this time in clean Wranglers, western shirt and cowboy boots. He was carrying Gram-Gram's Singer Featherweight sewing machine.

When she and Cammie were growing up, their grandmother had been an avid hand-piecer, which was why Camille had asked everyone to hand-piece quilt blocks ahead of time, but in her later years, declining vision and arthritis had converted her to the sewing machine. The plan for the quilting bee was to help Gram-Gram sew her square on the machine and use it as the centerpiece of the memory quilt.

Seeing the sewing machine brought a lump to Ellie's throat. How long would Gram-Gram still be able to do the thing she loved most? She bit her bottom lip.

"Your grandmother looks good." Dalton nodded at

Gram-Gram, who was encircled by the quilters. "You'd never know."

"Camille told you about her diagnosis?"

"Yes." His somber expression touched her. "I am so sorry."

"Thanks," she mumbled, unable to hold his steady gaze.

"You okay?" Dalton set the sewing machine down on a nearby table.

She couldn't answer or she'd start crying. Simply, she bobbed her head.

"Els," he said, calling her by his pet nickname, and held out his arms.

She shouldn't have gone to him. The past was over and buried, but she couldn't seem to help herself. She rushed over and he enveloped her in a hug that was pure comfort. One person reaching out to another to ease grief.

Without even considering whether anyone was watching them, she dropped her head to his shoulder and just let him hold her for a moment.

He patted her back. "S'okay, s'okay. I'm here, I'm here."

Yes, he was, and with his tender hug, she was swept back in time. Her heart clutched now in the same way it had then, full of loss and longing.

Blinking, she pulled away from him. "Time to get this party started. Thanks for your help with the sewing machine."

Dalton dropped his arms and stepped back. "You need anything else?"

"No, we're good." Her gaze hung on his mouth. Dammit.

"You sure?"

"Yes." She put starch in her voice. "I've got this."

"Well, if you *do* need anything—"

"I know where to find you." She turned, anxious to distance herself. Ellie heard Dalton's footsteps behind her and the closing of the side door. She released a heavy sigh.

"Ladies, have you all brought your hand-pieced squares?" she asked.

The women present, eight in all, including herself, went for their totes, while Aunt Olivia led Gram-Gram to the Singer so she could start sewing her square.

The concept of a memory quilt was to celebrate the life of a loved one or an important life event like a wedding. Many memory quilts were constructed from the clothing of loved ones.

A quilt with many different influences and memories would by nature be a hodgepodge of color, design, and fabrics. The results would be scrappy, not professional and polished. A patchwork. But that was the point, wasn't it? To replicate the nature of memories and give Gram-Gram a touchstone when her memory stumbled. A way to bring her back to what was important when her mind got lost.

Ellie brought a palm to her mouth and turned her back on the group as she struggled to contain her sorrow.

Aunt Olivia lightly touched her back.

Ellie looked up to see her aunt extending a tissue. "Thank you."

"I've got plenty more," Olivia whispered. "It's going to be that kind of weekend."

Ellie dabbed at her eyes with the tissue. "How are you holding up?"

"I'm good," her aunt said, "I've taken up sound meditation. It's calming."

"If you ever need help with Gram-Gram—"

"I appreciate the offer, Ellie, but you've got your hands full. I will let you know when I need some self-care, but until then, focus on your career." Aunt Olivia's gaze went to where Camille was helping Gram-Gram get her scraps ready for quilting. "You know, she's deeply proud of you, and the last thing she'd want is for you to forgo your work to take care of her."

"You did it."

"One, I'm her daughter." Olivia chuckled softly. "And two, you've got a job patching up rodeo cowboys. Knowing you're helping to save young men like your dad means the world to her and . . ." Her aunt paused, and a clouded expression came into her eyes.

"What is it?"

"Sometimes she forgets your father is dead. The other night, she asked me if I would dial his number for her."

"Oh no!"

Aunt Olivia gave a small shrug. "The hard part is reminding her he's no longer with us. Sometimes I wonder if it would be kinder to let her believe he's still alive."

"I have no advice on that," Ellie said. "Do whatever you think is best."

"Thank you for your support." Aunt Olivia squeezed her arm. "It means a lot."

"Hey, you were there for us. You're the one who broke the news to me and Camille about Daddy. Mom was inconsolable."

"I remember. Those were dark days." Her aunt leaned over to kiss Ellie's forehead. "But we made it through. We'll make it through this too, but for now . . ." Aunt Olivia gleefully rubbed her palms together. "Let's have some fun!"

The quilters took a break at noon for the hearty spread of sandwich fixings that Dalton's housekeeper, Alma, set out for them. In two hours, they'd visited a lot but hadn't got much quilting done. They were still trying to hash out the final design, which would feature seven large blocks and the one which Gram-Gram had yet to sew on the Featherweight. They planned to lay out the squares inside a frame of fabric to tie everything together. Camille thought that design would unify the mishmash of styles, but when they'd drawn it out, Ellie wasn't convinced. Something was off.

Ellie would push the quilters to step up their game in order to finish hand-piecing the topper by tomorrow afternoon.

"There's a pitcher full of mimosas in the fridge, if anyone's in the mood," Alma invited, setting champagne flutes on the counter. "Please help yourselves."

"I'm game!" Camille said. "If you can't day drink at a bachelorette party, when can you?"

Oh great, Ellie thought, *drunken quilting*.

"Me too!" Gram-Gram sang out.

Aunt Olivia leaned in to whisper to Ellie, "Make sure Mom gets just orange juice. She doesn't need alcohol on top of everything else."

"On it," Ellie said and buzzed over to ask Alma for straight orange juice.

Once everyone at the lunch table had a mimosa in hand, Ellie moved to the head of the table and hoisted her glass. *If you can't beat 'em, join 'em, right?*

"A toast. To the woman who made this all possible. We wouldn't be here without Gram-Gram. We love you."

She met her grandmother's gaze. Gram-Gram blushed and smiled, looking for all the world like a little girl. Ellie felt a pang in her chest, fully aware that this might be the last time all of them were together like this. That awareness made the moment that much more precious.

"To Gram-Gram!" Everyone raised their glasses and downed their drinks.

Through a fuzzy orange glow of mimosas, they ate sandwiches, told stories of their times together, laughed and gossiped and had a grand old time for over an hour. Ellie kept glancing at the time on her phone, torn between getting the project started and letting everyone enjoy one another's company.

Just when she was about to make an announcement that they should all return to the sewing room, she spied Dalton standing in the doorway. He caught her eye and crooked his finger at her.

She put a hand on her chest. *Me?*

He nodded and moved out of the doorway as if he expected her to follow. Was something wrong? Was he having spasms again? Or more concerning symptoms?

Quietly excusing herself from the table, Ellie got up and went into the hallway. Dalton stood in front of a door, still gesturing for her to come with him.

To his bedroom?

Her pulse quickened. He must need her to look at his injury.

Ellie followed.

His room was neat as a pin, but she wasn't surprised. Dalton had always been tidy. There were pictures of horses on his walls and the décor was straight-up cowboy, but she didn't really notice any of that. Her gaze was fully fixed on the man in front of her.

The man she'd once loved with every bit of her heart.

He surprised her by his hesitancy. *Hesitant* was not a word that popped to mind in conjunction with Dalton. Looking awkward, he stood before a chest of drawers four feet away.

"Are you all right?" she asked, anxiety thrashing around in her stomach.

"Sure."

"Wh-what is it? What do you need?"

She could almost see the word *you* forming in his head. *C'mon. Get over yourself.*

"Can I show you something?" he asked.

"Um . . . I guess." She canted her head, feeling tongue-tied.

He opened the top dresser drawer, rummaged around

and pulled out a twelve-inch hand-pieced quilt square. "When Camille told me about your grandmother and the memory quilt, I felt inspired to quilt a square too."

"Oh, Dalton," she said, deeply touched by his kindness.

He looked sheepish. "Be honest, if it doesn't fit and you don't want to use it, no harm, no foul. I just wanted to be a part of your grandmother's memory quilt in some small way."

She crossed the room to take the quilt square from his hand. The stitching was competent, as good as her own. He'd labored over this for hours.

In her hand, the cotton was soft, and the print familiar. The pattern featured silhouetted bull-riders against a white background. The cowboys in the print had one hand in the air, the other looped around the holding rope as they struggled to stay on the twisting, bucking creature.

Her breath stalled in her lungs.

The material had been cut from the shirt Dalton had worn on her and Camille's first day at grief camp. The day Gram-Gram, their mom, and Aunt Olivia had driven them to the Dusty Sagebrush, only two months after her daddy was killed in the rodeo arena.

Looking at the pattern stirred up all the old pain, and she was back in the memory.

Dalton coming up to her, welcoming her and Camille to the camp. It was his second summer after losing his mother. Ellie had taken one look at that shirt, seen her father in the pattern and promptly burst into tears.

"May I give you a hug?" he'd asked, concern on his face.

She'd been aloof since her dad's passing, angry at him and unable to cry. Her lack of what Mom believed was appropriate reaction to losing her father was the reason she insisted Ellie and Camille go to grief camp.

Ellie had wanted to tell Dalton to back off. Had expected she'd tell him to stay clear of her because she wanted badly to punch someone, and he would do. Instead, she'd shocked herself by nodding, and he'd hugged her, truly hugged her to comfort her, and for the first time since Dad died, she'd burst into tears.

Now, looking into Dalton's eyes again, she saw the same kindness that she'd seen that long-ago day, and she wanted to cry in his arms all over again.

He'd remembered what he was wearing the day they met, and he'd kept the shirt all these years.

Grateful and honored, she clutched the fabric block to her heart.

"Oh, Dalton," she said. "What a beautiful gesture. Of course we'll use the square."

And immediately, Ellie knew the perfect design for Gram-Gram's memory quilt. Dalton's square, representing her father, would be at the center of it.

Chapter 5

At six o'clock, the quilters called it a day so everyone could get ready for the chuckwagon barbecue that Dalton, Kaddy, and Alma were hosting at the picnic pavilion. The event started at seven, and there would be line dancing with a local band.

Ellie was excited. She loved line dancing and live music, but she hadn't been boot scootin' in ages.

Pulse skipping, she spun in front of the full-length mirror mounted on the back of the door in her bungalow. She'd dressed in starched blue jeans, a blue gingham yoked shirt, and her dressiest cowboy boots. She pulled her hair back into a ponytail to keep it out of her face while dancing and applied fresh makeup. By the time she arrived at the barn, she felt ridiculously breathless and had no logical explanation for it.

Other guests included the minister, Fiona Harrington, and her husband, Dr. Karl Harrington. He was one of only two doctors in their small town. Fiona and Dr. Karl were making their way up the path from the bungalows to the barbecue. The fellas had arrived that afternoon—the groom, the ushers, family members, and Gram-Gram's boyfriend, a wizened, bow-legged cowboy with a loud belly-laugh and twinkling blue eyes. His name was Hank and he'd lost his wife about the same time Gram-Gram lost Papaw. They'd met at church and were adorable together. Hank had linked his arm through Gram-Gram's, and Aunt Olivia was hovering nearby with her husband, Justin. Ellie was so happy her grandmother had Hank in her life. It was a sweet connection for as long as it lasted.

Sadness swept through her, but she gently brushed it aside. This weekend was for celebrating. Tomorrow, while the women finished the memory quilt, the guys would visit the golf course down the road. Ellie counted twenty-five people in all, not including the three hosts, and Ellie was the only one without a partner. Except for Dalton.

"Ellie!" Dr. Harrington greeted her with his arm wrapped around his wife. "How in the world are you?"

Dr. Harrington had been their family doctor growing up, although she hadn't seen him since she'd gone off to college. He was in his early sixties with a trim goatee and an ebullient smile.

"Hi, Doc."

"Hey yourself, Doc." He eyed her up and down. "You look amazing."

"Thanks."

"It's been so long since we've seen you," Fiona said. "Since you went off to college."

"But you sent me a gift when I graduated from medical school." Five hundred dollars to be exact, and for a new graduate paying off school loans, it had been a godsend. "Thank you again. It meant so much."

"You're welcome," Dr. Harrington said. "We're so proud of you. Hometown girl makes good. How is the PBR treating you?"

"It's exciting," Ellie said. "An adrenaline rush."

"Rodeo junkie," he said, and then his eyes clouded as he added, "just like your dad."

"I wouldn't be doing this kind of medicine if it wasn't for him." She gave a wry smile, not missing the irony.

"Well, if the thrill of the road ever runs thin," Dr. Harrington said, "I could always use a partner. I'm getting older and I'd like to spend more time with Fiona."

"His practice has grown by leaps and bounds," Fiona said. "It's getting out of hand. Karl's been trying to find a partner for a couple years now and we've had some prospects, but most people don't want to live this far from civilization."

The Trans-Pecos was pretty isolated, but having grown up here, Ellie couldn't imagine living anywhere else if she ever decided to give up the rodeo and settle down.

They fell into step together as they headed toward the barbecue, talking about the upcoming ceremony and Fiona's role in it. Dalton was at the door greeting people as they arrived and handing out complimentary western-themed drinks.

The second their gazes met, a wide grin spread across his handsome face and Ellie's heart tripped right over itself.

"Virgin?" he asked.

Ellie startled. "Wh-what?"

His grin widened and he inclined his head toward the drinks lined up on the table beside him. "We have Roy Rogers for guests who prefer a nonalcohol choice, beer, wine, and two cocktails. The Salty Dog with a Leather Saddle and the Wild, Wild West."

Ellie peered at the array of beverages. She wasn't much of a drinker, but this was a party.

The Salty Dog was a drink of grapefruit juice, grapefruit vodka, and pink sea salt served in a martini glass and garnished with beef jerky fashioned to resemble a saddle. It looked so rustic and fun, but Ellie had gotten sick on Salty Dogs in college and she was no longer a fan.

"What's in the Wild, Wild West?" she asked, eyeing the drink, which was served in cowboy boot–shaped glasses.

"Basically, it's an Old Fashioned with tequila instead of bourbon, and garnished with a cream cheese–stuffed jalapeño pepper."

"Ooh," she said. "Spicy."

His eyebrow lifted. "You want one?"

"Nah," she said. "I'll take a beer."

"My choice too." He chuckled and reached into the galvanized bucket filled with ice that was sitting beside the drinks table, pulled out a longneck Lone Star, wiped the water off with a bar towel, and passed it to her.

"Thanks," she said, reaching for the beer.

Their fingertips touched in the handoff. A slight, bright tickle of flesh. Nothing more. Simple. Casual.

An accident, that touch? Or on purpose?

Ellie's crazy heart stumbled, making a big deal of it. Feeling out of step, she twisted the cap off the beer, tossed it into a nearby trash receptacle and took a long swallow, desperate to restore her equilibrium.

Dalton turned to the next guest in line, Camille's best friend, Breeanne, and her boyfriend, one of the groomsmen, Wesley Combs.

Glad to have Dalton's attention diverted, Ellie moved aside, stepping from the flow of traffic.

"Ellie." Camille's voice snagged her attention, and she turned to see her sister waving wildly.

Camille and her fiancé, Cody Coltrane, were sitting closest to where the band was setting up. Cody was a park ranger at Fort Davis, and that was where her sister and her new husband would make their home. For the first time since starting her new career on the road, Ellie felt a longing for home. It'd be nice to see her sister several times a week, instead of half-a-dozen times a year.

Ellie joined them at their table. They chatted about the day's activities and Ellie tried to get her sister to commit to the fast-paced sewing schedule needed to get the quilt finished before the rehearsal dinner the next evening. Camille shooed away her concerns.

"Chillax, Sis. It'll all work out."

Ellie forced a smile. She wished she was as laid-back as her younger sister, but she just wasn't made that way. "What if we don't get it finished?"

"Then you and Aunt Olivia can finish up. You're both staying until Monday."

"I thought I'd go ahead and leave Sunday morning. It's a seven-hour drive back to Fort Worth."

"Oh, hiss-boo." Camille made a pouty face. "Why?"

"You and Cody will be gone. No reason to stick around."

"Well, there is a reason if we don't finish the quilt . . ."

Ellie folded her hands in her lap. Camille was allowed to be as loosey-goosey as she wanted in her own life, but expecting Ellie and Olivia to finish the quilt just because she didn't want to commit to a rigorous work schedule crossed a boundary.

She opened her mouth to tell her sister that, but then Camille reached across the table to touch Ellie's arm.

"For another thing . . ." Camille murmured, nodding and glancing across the room.

Ellie followed her sister's gaze and saw Dalton had abandoned the drink station to Kaddy and gone to help Alma uncover the chafing dishes at the buffet. Almost as if he could feel Ellie's gaze on him, Dalton raised his head.

Their eyes met.

A long moment passed, just the two of them, staring at each other.

Sudden panic gripped her. That had been happening all dang day whenever they looked at each other. Ellie jerked her head around and gulped.

"*That's* reason enough to stay another day." Camille giggled.

"Tell the truth. Did you decide to have the wedding here because Dalton bought the Dusty Sagebrush?" Ellie asked.

"No," Camille said. "It was just a happy coincidence."

Ellie didn't know about *happy* . . .

The band was tuning up. The overhead lights dimmed, creating a cozy atmosphere. Camille's grin widened and she poked Cody in the ribs and nodded at something behind Ellie.

Before she could turn to see what or who her sister was eyeballing, she caught a whiff of Dalton's unique scent as he leaned over her shoulder to say, "We're ready—could you start the buffet line, Camille?"

Then Dalton briefly touched Ellie's upper arm at the same moment the band hit the opening notes to Patsy Cline's "I Fall to Pieces."

It was the first song she and Dalton had ever danced to. Her legs turned rubbery and her heart rate quickened. Darn it, there were just too many happy coincidences around here.

Confession time.

Dalton had asked the band to play Patsy Cline. He knew the singer was one of Ellie's favorites. She'd once told him that after their dad had died, she, Camille and her mom lived with her grandmother Winter for a time and Gram-Gram often played Cline's music on her old-fashioned record player. Ellie had fallen in love with Cline's smooth voice and mournful, heartfelt style.

Dalton was also fully aware it was the song that had been playing on the jukebox at the drugstore diner in downtown Fort Davis where he and Ellie had gone on their first date. The memory claimed a special place in his mind. He even recalled what they'd eaten. Grilled cheese sandwiches with bread-and-butter pickles washed down with a chocolate malt. When someone clicked the tune on the Wurlitzer, he'd reached out his hand and asked Ellie to dance.

In all honesty, he hadn't expected her to accept. She wasn't a fan of the spotlight, but she'd blown him away by letting him waltz her around the tables while the other diners clapped and cheered them on.

He wasn't sure what he was angling for with this trip down memory lane. The obstacles that had kept them apart as teenagers were still there. Although she was a doctor now, she was constantly on the road with the PBR, and the dude ranch he'd bought two years ago was finally turning a profit. Long-distance relationships didn't work. He knew that. It was why he'd lied to her thirteen years ago when he'd told her their romance was nothing but a summer fling.

Besides, she was smart as a whip and so out of his league. Always had been, always would be. He was a simple soldier turned ranch owner. That was as lofty as his goals got. The only way he'd been able to buy the Dusty Sagebrush was by watching his money like a mother bear getting ready for hibernation, sticking to a strict budget while he was in the military and saving every spare penny to purchase the place that had been his second home growing up.

No, Ellie wasn't for him.

So why in Sam Hill had he asked the band to play Patsy? He was opening himself up to pure heartache and he knew it.

But here was the deal. From the second he'd seen her again Dalton had been unable to think of anything but Ellie. Kissing her was never far from his mind. They had a chance for one sweet weekend. Why not seize it?

Ellie willing, of course.

He shot her a sideways glance, wondering if he'd overstepped by touching her arm, but when she smiled up at him, Dalton felt as if the sun had finally come out after torrential rains.

Camille and Cody got up and headed for the buffet. He didn't miss that Ellie's sister gave her a surreptitious thumbs-up.

"Do you mind if I join you?" Dalton asked.

"No, of course not." Ellie patted the spot beside her. "I'd love to catch up."

"Really?" He sat down on the bench seat next to her.

"You sound surprised."

"I just well . . . I didn't know if you'd want to have a conversation with me after the way I broke up with you."

She waved a dismissive hand and smiled, her ponytail bouncing jauntily. "That was thirteen years ago. If I got my heart broken, it was because I had unrealistic expectations. My youthful mistake. Nothing on you. You were just speaking your truth. You can't force feelings you don't have."

But he hadn't been speaking his truth. He'd lied his ass off when he told her he didn't have deep feelings for her.

Looking into her eyes at this moment, he knew he still did.

And that was problematic. If he were smart, he'd get up and go tend to his guests. Dalton, however, wasn't all that smart. He stayed where he was, locked his gaze solidly on Ellie. Doubled down.

A coy expression lit up her dazzling blue eyes. In that moment, she looked seventeen again, and all he wanted to do was hold her.

"I would like to spend some time with you this weekend, if you can spare it. I know you're slamming busy, so if you don't have a moment, I get it. No harm, no foul."

She rested her elbow on the table and her chin in her palm and leaned in, gifting him with her lovely lavender scent. "What are you doing after this?"

Whoa boy! She was game and giving off vibes that he'd only dreamed about. He was thrilled and, honestly, nervous as hell. They were getting a weird reboot. It felt as if the slate had been wiped clean and they had a chance for a fresh start.

Are you fooling yourself, Branch?

"Cleaning up," he said.

"What if I helped? Many hands make light work. We could go for a moonlight stroll afterward. Old times' sake?"

"Old times' sake," he echoed, his pulse galloping like a racehorse on the last furlong and he could hardly draw breath. He and Ellie together again.

Temporarily.

But that was fine. He was at the point in life where he'd learned to appreciate everything that came his way. Good, bad, indifferent. Life happened moment by moment and right now, he wanted to be with Ellie. Consequences be damned. He'd let the future and past sort themselves out.

"It's a date," she said, then leaned over, kissed his forehead, got up and sashayed to the buffet.

Dalton pressed two fingers to the spot on his skin she'd just kissed, in no hurry at all to wake up from this sweet reunion thirteen years in the making.

"Chicken or brisket?" Kaddy asked.

Ellie glanced up and met the ranch foreman's gaze. "What? No tofu?"

Kaddy's eyes widened and she looked momentarily disconcerted. "You're a vegetarian? No one mentioned you were a vegetarian. I'm sorry."

"Not a vegetarian." Ellie grinned. "Just pulling your leg. I'll have the chicken."

"Uh-uh." Kaddy shook the serving spoon at Ellie. "You're slyer than you look. No wonder Dalton's been hung up on you for years."

Ellie grunted. "Dalton's not hung up on me."

Kaddy rolled her eyes and snorted. "I thought you were savvier than that."

"Huh?"

"The man is gaga over you."

No. Ellie glanced around. Right now, she was the only guest at the carving station and there was no one in earshot. She searched for Dalton and found him on the opposite side of the room, talking to Gram-Gram, Hank, and Aunt Olivia.

"You kidding me? He's as nervous as a cat in a swimming pool." Kaddy chuckled. "I've known him for ten years, and I've never seen him so worked up over anyone."

"Me?" Ellie pressed a palm to her chest, still not quite believing her ears. Could it be true? Had Dalton been secretly carrying a torch for her?

"C'mon. Surely you know that. You were his first love."

The woman had it all wrong. "No, I wasn't."

Kaddy looked at Ellie as if someone had dropped her on her head. "You're pulling my leg again."

Ellie shook her head. "Sure, Dalton and I got close the three years we spent at grief camp together, but he was never in love with me."

Kaddy blinked, dangling a chunk of barbecued chicken breast over the plate Ellie extended toward her.

"What is it?" Ellie asked.

"Seriously? Are you that blind?"

Ellie shrugged off her galloping pulse. "You've misread things. Dalton wasn't that into me."

"I have a disturbing urge right now to whack you on the side of the head with this chicken."

"Please don't."

"I won't, but not because you don't deserve it." Kaddy grinned big.

"What are you talking about? Dalton broke up with *me*. He told me I was a summer fling and that I cramped his style."

With a tsk-tsk noise, Kaddy dropped the chicken breast onto Ellie's plate.

"You're saying that's not true?" She thought about that last night after the end-of-the-summer dance. The same day she'd gotten her acceptance letter and an academic scholarship to Texas A&M.

The night Dalton shattered her heart at Hope Lake.

"*Guuurl* . . ." Kaddy shook her head so hard, Ellie feared it might fly right off her neck. "That man loved you so much he lied to get you to take that scholarship. He knew you wouldn't go if you thought there was a future between the two of you. You were headed for great things, and he wasn't going to be the one to stand in your way."

"He told you that?"

"Not willingly. It took four shots of Limoncello."

Ellie placed a palm over her mouth, her other hand balancing the plate of chicken as a strange and wonderous sensation swept over her.

Dalton had been in love with her? He'd lied when he said she was just a fling? It was a possibility she'd never considered. Not once in the past thirteen years.

"That's ancient history," she said, desperate to collect herself and not drive her brain right over the cliff of logic.

"Doesn't have to be." Kaddy picked up her knife and went back to carving the prime rib roast she'd been working on when Ellie walked up.

"Meaning?" Ellie gulped, terrified of where her hopes were going.

"You're single. He's single. Perfect time for a brand-new start."

"I don't know him anymore."

"So go find out. Dalton is one of the most honorable men I've ever known and if you don't take advantage of this opportunity to reconnect, I'll never understand how someone as smart as you could be so dumb. That man's a keeper—if I wasn't married to Alma, I'd even consider switching teams for him."

Chapter 6

Dalton circled the room, making sure the guests were comfortable and their needs met, but there was one guest in particular never far from his thoughts.

Ellie.

He searched for her in the crowd and felt a blip of panic when he didn't spot her. Had she had second thoughts about staying until after the party was over? Had she gone back to her bungalow?

But no, there she was, helping Alma bus dishes.

His heart settled and a helpless smile crossed his face. She was getting a head start on the cleanup.

People were wandering back to the drink station for refills. Time to get the line dancing started. He hustled over to the band, waited until they finished the song they were playing and signaled that he was ready.

The band eased out of the song, and Dalton bounded up to the microphone. "Hey, y'all. Having a good time?"

The audience whooped.

"Ready for some boot scootin'?"

Cheers.

"Y'all know the Hoedown Throwdown?" As he suspected, most of the guests shook their heads. "Well, we're gonna fix that right now."

He picked up the cordless mike and hopped down off the stage. He locked gazes with Ellie, who was watching him from the back of the barn, her hands folded over her chest, her eyes amused.

"Ellie, could you come help me demonstrate the Hoedown Throwdown?" He hadn't planned to involve her; it just slipped out.

Whoa, Branch. You're springing this on her out of the blue. Uncool. Backpedal.

"No worries if you're rusty and you'd rather not," he said. "Kaddy's as wicked on the dance floor as she is with a carving knife."

From the carving station, Kaddy did a condensed version of the Hoedown Throwdown, butcher knife in hand.

"I'll do it," Ellie said, coming toward him, the *clip-clip* of her cowboy boots against the concrete doing strange things to his soul.

Dalton could identify her by the sound of her walk blindfolded. Brisk, determined, headed somewhere. And this time, that somewhere was toward him.

"Let's hear it for Dr. Ellie Winter." He started the applause, tucking the mike under his arm to smack his palms together.

Camille stood up and started chanting, "Ellie, Ellie, Ellie."

The rest of the guests joined in.

Ellie's cheeks were pink and her eyes bright when

she joined him at the stage. Everyone got to their feet and moved onto the dance floor. Even Ellie's grandmother and her boyfriend, Hank.

"I'll call the steps," Dalton said. "And Ellie will demonstrate." He looked over his shoulder at the band. "Hit it."

The band started into the song, keeping the sound low while Dalton explained the moves.

"First," he said. "You 'pop it.'"

Ellie exaggerated the "pop it" command for teaching purposes, extending her left arm as far out in front of her as it would go. She was standing a few feet from him, but he could feel her energy. She was into it. Her energy fed his, as past and present converged at the Dusty Sagebrush, where they'd first danced the Hoedown Throwdown together in 2009. Back then, the song had just come out in the *Hannah Montana* movie and everyone was doing it.

His mind flooded with pleasant memories and his heart bobbled like a boat on Hope Lake. "Then you 'lock it.'"

Ellie planted her right hip in a bold step that sent bolts of heat shooting through his body. Dalton couldn't take his eyes off her. For him, there was no one else in the room.

"Now, we 'polka dot it.'"

He watched Ellie shuffle her left foot forward with two definitive steps, straight toward Dalton.

Dazed, he almost forgot the next step. "Then you . . . um . . . 'countrify' it."

Ellie rooted her right heel at the same time she

lifted the ball of her right foot, then quickly duplicated the motion with her left foot and repeated the sequence.

It took every bit of concentration he had in him to go through the rest of the complicated steps. He wasn't even watching the audience. There was no one else in the room for him but Ellie.

"Jump to the left," he instructed.

She scooped her left foot, jumped to the right and spun to the left, getting closer and closer to him with each move. He should be moving too, demonstrating the dance as well, but he was too dazzled.

"Stick it and glide." Until now, he hadn't realized how dirty the instructions could sound.

Ellie brought both her feet together and glided back as if she'd been doing the dance steps every day of her life. How had she remembered the moves so flawlessly?

"Zig-zag touch."

She zigged. She zagged. She reached down at the same time she lifted her heel and touched her boot.

Dalton's heart somersaulted. He got a thrill out of calling and watching her play out his commands. The two of them working as a well-oiled team, he went through the rest of the complex lesson, demonstrating it beside her.

"One-eighty twist," he said into the microphone.

In unison, they spun, laughing. The drummer gave a hit to the skins, aiding them as they segued into the last part of the dance.

"Put it all together!" he sang out and turned back to

Ellie as they reviewed the complicated sequence again and the line dance began in earnest.

Maybe he should have picked a simpler dance, but the fun of this one was its complexity. It never failed to loosen people up as they stumbled, crashed into each other, laughed and shook off their self-consciousness.

And that's exactly what happened as the guests joined in.

He was so busy enjoying himself that he, too, goofed and went right when he should have gone left, smacking into Ellie's chest for the second time that day, but this time, instead of jumping away from her, he leaned in and the next thing he knew they were waltzing as the band quickly picked up on the change and shifted into Butch Walker's "I Love You."

Panting and breathless, Ellie spun from Dalton's arms as soon as the waltz ended and the band edged into "Cotton-Eyed Joe."

Almost everyone knew this dance and the guests automatically linked arms, leaving Ellie and Dalton to join in or not.

Dalton held out a hand to her, but Ellie was so dizzy and confused by what was churning between them, she shook her head, fanned herself and said, "I need some air."

She turned and rushed for the door, assuming he'd stay behind as host, but no, he came with her, matching her fleeing feet, step for step.

Gasping, she burst outside into the gathering darkness, thrilled and scared, her mind clogged with the things Kaddy had told her at the carving station. Dalton loved her so much that he'd lied about his feelings to get her to accept her scholarship and go off to medical school.

Cruel to be kind.

She couldn't blame him for it. She would have stayed and gone to school at Sul Ross just to be near him if he hadn't sent her on her way. She might have loved the idea of being a rodeo doctor to help men like her dad who got injured in the arena, but she had loved Dalton more than any ambition. Loved him the way only a seventeen-year-old in love for the first time could love.

But she wasn't seventeen anymore. Guilt for being so angry at him thirteen years ago dissolved into sadness at how things had played out. If only she could turn back time!

But she couldn't. What was the point in wishing to change the past? It was over and done with. What mattered was right now.

"You okay?" he asked outside the barn as the lively music echoed into the night.

"Sure. Fine. Why wouldn't I be? I'm just not used to that much dancing."

"You were amazing." He stepped closer. "I can't believe you remembered the Hoedown Throwdown. You didn't miss a step."

"Once upon a time that dance was important in my life." She met his gaze. Held it. Why wasn't her pulse slowing?

"It clearly made an imprint."

"*You* made an imprint. The dance came out when we were dating."

He stepped closer still.

She didn't move.

"How about that walk?" he invited, extending his arm.

"What about the guests? What about the cleanup?"

"Kaddy and Alma will handle it."

"Those two are a great pair. You're lucky to have found them."

"I am." He kept his arm extended. "Our walk?"

What did she have to lose?

Ellie slipped her arm through Dalton's and let him lead her through the shadows. Her heart—tight with old emotions and new anticipation—was pumping hot blood through her veins so swiftly, the only sound she heard was the frantic lub-dub.

There was a full moon out tonight, perfect for a stroll around the grounds, and Dalton was guiding her in the direction of Hope Lake. Somehow, she'd known all along that's where he would head.

The spot they'd shared their first kiss.

And their last.

They walked in silence, arm in arm, the moon lighting their path. It felt so good being here with him again. Once she got over her insecurities, being with Dalton was as easy as breathing. There was no need for conversation.

An owl hooted in the distance, calling to a mate who answered with a declarative, "Who-who."

"The barbecue was a success," she said. "Everyone was having fun."

"I saw your grandmother dancing with her boyfriend. They are so cute together."

"Thank you for showing her a good time. Each moment is precious."

"We should all strive to live life that way," Dalton murmured. "As if each day might be our last."

They passed by the corral where Danger Zone watched them with obsidian eyes. Dalton let go of her arm long enough to open the gate that went from the main grounds into the pasture that led to the lake. Once they were in the pasture and he'd closed the gate behind them, Dalton reached for her arm again.

Compelled by forces she could not explain or resist, Ellie rested her head on his shoulder, slipped her arm through his and thought about what he'd said. This moment *was* precious, and she was going to savor it to the marrow.

The darkness surrounded them like a soft hug, the shimmering moonlight reflecting off the water. The muted splash of a fish breaking the surface to catch a bug rippled through the air. The aroma of mesquite wood used to fire the barbecue smoker clung to Dalton's clothes and mingled with his own special scent.

Ellie licked her lips and wondered if he tasted as yummy as he smelled. She didn't have to wait long to find out.

At the end of the dock, Dalton drew Ellie into his arms, tugged her to his chest and peered deeply into her eyes. "Ellie."

Knees knocking, she whispered, "Yes?"

Cupping her chin in his palm, he tilted her face up, keeping his gaze trained on hers. "I'd like to kiss you now."

She sucked in a breath. "Oh."

"May I?"

"Yes, please," she croaked, knowing full well this wasn't a good idea, but aching for it anyway.

Dalton lowered his head.

As Ellie pursed her lips, anticipation tasted like honey in her mouth. She wrapped her arms around him. Clung to him.

Tenderly, he pressed his mouth to hers. Got a taste of her. Murmured a pleased sound and deepened the pressure. Her lips warmed beneath his, and she parted her teeth and closed her eyes.

"You're so beautiful," he whispered, his words vibrating against her mouth. "I'd forgotten how long your eyelashes are."

"Less talking, more kissing," she said, letting her eyelids flutter open and giving him a wry smile.

"Your wish is my command."

Ellie let out a soft sigh and he swallowed it. The pulse at her jaw spiked hot underneath his stroking fingertips. The smoky fragrance of his skin was an intoxicating contrast to her own lavender-scented bodywash.

Reaching up, she threaded her fingers through his hair, using him to hold herself steady as the kiss took on added dimensions.

Shocking how much she hungered for him.

She pressed harder against him, absorbing the feel

of his hard-muscled chest beneath the thin cotton of his western shirt, and she held on for dear life.

The kiss spun them into the timeless *now* and everything was part of their second-chance fantasy—the full moon, the taste of his lips, the familiar wooden dock. Transported to the past, she was seventeen years old again and filled with a bright-eyed hope that everything would work out for them.

Finally, they had to come up for air. When Dalton pulled back and gazed into her eyes, she felt a draw so compelling that she knew in her heart how this night would end, and there wasn't a thing she would do to stop it from happening.

She wanted him with wild urgency, and from the intensity of his kiss, he wanted her just as much. The wind ruffled her hair and, smiling, he reached out to smooth it.

"That was some mighty fine kissing, Mr. Branch," she murmured.

"Not too shabby yourself, Dr. Winter." He paused. "I'm so damn proud of you and all you've accomplished. You have no idea."

His words were a sweet and soothing balm. She'd worked so hard to get where she was, had made so many sacrifices. It had taken every bit of her concentration to get through medical school. Dalton had made sacrifices, too, for her dream; she just hadn't known it.

"Kaddy told me," she whispered.

"Told you what?" He smiled at her, soft and gentle.

"Why you broke up with me." She bit her bottom lip, paused. "I haven't had much time to process it, but despite the pain that decision caused us both, you were right to let me go. I wouldn't have become a doctor if you hadn't."

"I knew our relationship would distract you from your studies," he said. "And I just couldn't let that happen, Ellie. I'm sorry I lied about not loving you, but it was the only way to get you to leave for College Station."

She thought of what he'd given up for her, of how hurt she'd been when he'd sent her on her way, of how he'd been so brave and kind to do it.

"I was mad at you for so long."

He nodded. "I had to make you angry enough to forget me."

"It worked."

"I am sorry for the pain I caused." He stroked her cheek with his knuckle. "If it's any consolation, it killed my soul to send you away."

"Dumping me was a beautiful gift," she said. "I just didn't know it at the time."

"I'm glad it worked out."

This time, she was the one who kissed him, and he laughed aloud as she pressed her mouth against his.

"God," he said. "It's so good being with you again."

"A dream come true." It was her secret fantasy of one day reuniting with the love of her life—she'd just been too afraid to hang her hat on it.

She didn't know how long the spell would last, but here, under the moonlight, on the weekend of her sister's wedding, Ellie wanted nothing more than to spend the night with the one who got away.

"Walk me back to my cabin?" she whispered.

"Dr. Winter," he whispered back, "I think that's a brilliant idea."

Chapter 7

By the time they reached the cabin, Ellie's heart rate was out of control. This was it. Finally, she would have sex with her teenage crush and quench the desires, hot and dark and secret, that she'd tamped down for so long. Those simmering desires had turned into a full rolling boil.

How often she'd dreamed of this moment as a hungry seventeen-year-old, but now she was thirty and not so young anymore.

Slow down. Do you really want to do this?

One look in his eyes and she thought, *Yes, yes, I do.* She wasn't careless with her body. Had only had three lovers in her life, and she'd been in steady relationships with all three. She didn't do one-night stands, but this was Dalton. Sure, he'd changed in the last thirteen years, but he wasn't a stranger.

Still, she needed to set ground rules. Define what this night meant so that no one got hurt again.

"Dalton," she said with her head thrown back as he

burned kisses over her throat. "We need to talk about this."

He stopped and pulled back. "You've changed your mind."

"No, no," she rushed to reassure him. "I'm just . . . let's not . . ."

He raised an eyebrow. "Label it?"

"Yes. That."

"Okay." He went back to kissing her.

She squirmed away. "You don't have any expectations?"

"Beyond having a great time in bed with you? No, ma'am."

"You're sure?"

He dragged a hand through his hair. "Well, hell, Ellie, I can't promise how I'll feel in the morning, but right here, right now? All I want to do is make love with you."

Make love.

Not "have sex."

"You're absolutely sure?" She kept worrying her bottom lip with her top teeth.

"Let me spin this back on you, Els. What do *you* want out of this night?"

"To finish what we started thirteen years ago."

"And then?"

"I don't know." Honesty was the best policy, right?

"All right." He shrugged with such easy acquiescence it bugged her a little.

"Sex and nothing more?"

"If those are your rules, sure."

"No, no." She waggled a finger. "You don't get to

lay it all off on me. Ultimately, what do you hope to get from this encounter?"

"You in a bed," he said. "But I would be lying if I said the eighteen-year-old kid in me isn't hoping for more. That's the truth. If that scares you too much, then I should go."

"No! Don't go." Her sudden outburst surprised her. "I mean," she said, modulating her voice, "I want you to stay, but I can't make promises beyond that."

"Fair enough." He nodded. "Now, where were we?"

Okay, they'd sorted that obstacle. No reason to hold back.

What about tomorrow?

Ellie was a cautious person, but she'd let tomorrow sort itself out. Right now, Dalton was kissing the daylights out of her and she'd didn't want to miss a second of it.

"Would you like to come inside?"

"I would love that."

They peered deeply into each other's eyes, and then she turned to unlock the cabin door. Dalton put his arm around her waist and waltzed her inside.

They were both breathing hard, and their gazes were locked.

Cupping her face in both palms, he kissed her again, and then he bent and scooped her into his arms, literally sweeping her off her feet and carried her over to the bed.

The scent of honeysuckle blew in through the open window, bringing with it memories of summer on this ranch. Sweet, fond memories that stirred her heart and calmed her soul. With a girlish giggle, she wrapped her arms around his neck and nibbled his earlobe. Her pulsing blood filled her body with eager heat.

"I forgot how much you turn me on," she murmured.

"Me too." He kissed her forehead.

"It's been a long time since I've felt like this." She inhaled, added, "Maybe since I last kissed you."

"Ditto."

"Really?"

"Really."

Overcome, she turned her head, buried her face against his shoulder. He settled her onto the mattress on her back and then stretched out beside her. The full-sized bed was barely big enough for both of them.

Turning on his side to face her, Dalton propped himself up on one elbow and gazed at her with rapt attention.

She smiled at him, tentative to be sure, but so happy.

He traced the curve of her forehead with his finger, following the straight line of her nose to the tip, dropping off and pressing his finger into the little divot below her nose. The philtrum, in medical terms.

Leaning closer, he kissed the divot and got her hot and bothered all over again.

They kissed and kissed and kissed with the same passion as the teenagers they'd once been, but this time there was no restraint. His hands were everywhere, in her hair, underneath her shirt, at her bra. She wrapped her arms around his neck, pressed her chest against him as he freed her breasts and kissed them.

Ellie was spellbound. She could no more call this off than she could teleport. Dalton devoured her, groaning as she wriggled beneath him. She heard a soft moan slip from her throat, and they were at each other with an urge so blinding it stole her breath.

They undressed each other, wrestling out of their clothes and staring at each other. He grunted and narrowed his eyes as he took in her body and muttered, "Gorgeous." Her eyes widened and she gulped, thrilling at his nakedness.

His hands were gentle against her waist, his kisses hot and tender. He ran his calloused palms over her skin, sending sweet goose bumps along her flesh. He took his time, exploring her and she, intrepid doctor that she was, explored him right back.

He palmed her breasts and she cupped him between his legs, pulled a deep-throated groan from his throat. His fingers flew to the juncture between her thighs, gently parting her legs and finding her slick.

She was so wet for him. So eager.

His belly was bruised from where Danger Zone had smacked him yesterday. Tenderly, she traced her fingers over the darkened shape.

"Does it hurt? Maybe we should back off."

"It's nothing," he said. "I work a ranch. I get bruises, cuts, and dings every day. It's not going to stop me from enjoying this."

"You sure?"

"Shh," he said and kissed her again.

She shushed and let him do his thing. He lowered his head and this time his tongue did the exploring. She closed her eyes and absorbed the brilliant sensations, getting lost in the heat of his mouth.

"Oh, Ellie. You taste so good."

"Shh." She giggled. "I'm concentrating." How had she ever thought coming back to the Dusty Sagebrush and seeing Dalton again would be uncomfortable? It was explicitly and utterly sublime.

She'd feared he would upset her equilibrium and yes, he had, but in the most beautiful and special way.

They kissed and touch and explored. Foreplay was his specialty. He'd work her to the edge and just as she was about to tumble over, he'd pull her back, again and again. Then finally, a full hour into their blissful exploration, he said, "I can't hold off much longer."

"Me either."

"Hang on. I've got a condom in my wallet."

In the darkness, she heard him fumbling for his pants. Smiling, she closed her eyes as he took care of business, feeling the air conditioning cooling her heated skin, but not her ardor.

Dalton eased back onto the mattress beside her, his solid masculine presence tugging her eyelids up. He was gazing down at her, his face filled with rapt attention, his breathing shallow and rapid.

Their eyes locked.

He shifted, moved over her.

"If we do this," he whispered, "there's no going back."

"I know." She gulped.

"You still sure you want this?"

"You talk too much, Branch."

"I just want to make sure."

"Are *you* sure?"

Feeling troubled, she searched his face. Was she falling in love with him all over again? He'd hurt her once. Badly. But now she knew it had been for a good reason. She wanted to trust him, had trusted him up to this point. Her mind warred with her body. Her fears battled her desires.

But only briefly.

Desire won.

"C'mon, cowboy. Mount up."

Laughing, he cupped her head between his palms and eased his body into hers as he claimed her mouth for another spectacular kiss.

She gasped, filled with sensation, and raised her hips to greet him. *Welcome, welcome.*

He moved carefully, taking his time, sliding deeper into her body. Having him inside her wasn't strange, even though he'd never been there before. Their joining was as natural and comforting as a toasty fire on a cold snowy night as Ellie gave herself over to him completely.

He'd only had one beer at the barbecue so he couldn't be intoxicated and yet, Dalton was drunk with feelings.

Glorious feelings.

Complicated feelings.

Dangerous feelings.

Feelings for Ellie.

So many times he'd imagined being with her like this, and now his long-held dreams had come true. And reality was so much better than anything his mind could concoct.

He was stretched out over her, holding most of his weight on his elbows so he wouldn't squash her. Her eyes were closed, her mouth twitching as he moved inside her. Being with her like this felt like coming home after a long tour of duty.

Safe.

Sweet.

Surrender.

Ellie made a gritty sound of pleasure, a noise halfway between a groan and a moan. It charged him up and he picked up the pace, eager to take her up and over the edge of reason. They moved together as if dancing, their rhythm perfectly matched.

Finally, at long last, in sync.

The escalating pace demolished his control. At this rate he wouldn't last long.

"Please," she whispered. "Don't hold back."

Dalton let loose a groan of his own and buried himself inside her as far as he could go.

The final push to the summit was fast and frantic, in direct contrast to their leisurely foreplay. Tenderness gave way to hot, stroking power. The room echoed with the sounds of their jagged breathing.

It felt as if the walls were collapsing around them, the bed shaking and vibrating as Dalton spilled himself into her in an orgasm so powerful it rattled his teeth. Ellie was right there with him, gasping and writhing and calling his name.

It was the most beautiful sound on earth.

They shuddered together, sharing the release. Then he wrapped his arm around her waist and flipped them over as a unit. He tucked her into the crook of his elbow and pulled her up against his chest. Without hesitation, she rested her head on his shoulder and he could feel her heart beating against him.

"That was . . ." He panted. "You were . . ."

"Good?"

"Colossal."

"You're the colossal one," she murmured, turning her head and lightly biting down on his shoulder.

"Ellie," he said. "I've missed you."

She kissed his skin. "I might have missed you too," she said, then added, "a little."

He touched the end of her nose with his index finger. "No kidding?"

She shifted, flipping onto her belly and gazing into his face.

Reaching out, he ran the pad of his thumb over her full bottom lip, recalled her honeyed taste.

"Okay," she said, nibbling his thumb. "Maybe more than a little. Which leaves me feeling a bit . . ." She offered him a tiny, self-conscious smile. "Scared."

He reached for her, rearranged her, and kissed her gently, his hand brushing the tangled blond locks from her face. She made a quiet sound low in her throat, which tickled his lips.

And Dalton whispered, "I'm scared too."

He stared into her eyes, allowing her to see the truth of it. He wanted her. All of her. Not just her gorgeous body, but her sweet spirit and sharp mind as well. Dalton was falling in love with Ellie all over again, and he was utterly terrified.

*   *   *

The need in Dalton's eyes twisted Ellie up in countless ways, but what got to her most was that this rough, tough soldier cowboy *needed* her.

Here was the truly earth-shattering part. She needed him too. Her body burning, tingling, aching for more of him. So much more.

What had they started? What had she done?

She wouldn't let herself get giddy over him, never mind the sweet happiness pushing at the seams of her heart. She couldn't.

They'd shared a moment. A great moment to be sure. A moment that had been a long time coming, but that's all it was. She couldn't start spinning fantasies about happily-ever-after. Truth be told, what did she know about the man? He'd been an amazing boyfriend thirteen years ago, but since then he'd been to war and back. The experience had to have changed him.

But here in his arms, she felt safer than she'd ever felt in her life.

She was in too deep already and she knew it. The urge to hop out of bed and run away was so overwhelming it was all she could do to lie still. He'd hurt her once. Splintering her heart into glass shards, and it had taken her months to piece it back together.

He lowered his eyelids and suppressed a yawn, his sexy smile lazy and contented. Helplessly, she touched his jaw, running her fingers along the beard stubble.

"Hmm," he murmured sleepily. "That feels nice."

"Does it?"

"Uh-huh."

"How about this?" She stroked his throat with the back of her knuckles.

He shuddered. "Can you tell?"

She dropped her hand lower, trailing her hand down his chest. "And this?"

"Ellie," he said in a guttural tone. "What are you doing?"

She walked her fingers gently over his poor, bruised abdomen, heading south. She felt his body stir.

"Doctor Winter," he warned, "you're playing with fire."

"Am I?" she teased, threading her fingers through the curly hair down there. He was hot and hard again, as if they hadn't just spent the last hour having wild sex. She felt powerful. In control.

"You know you are." He grunted. "If you keep that up, I'll need a fresh condom."

"How about here?" She stroked the inside of his thigh and grinned into the darkness.

Dalton groaned.

The next thing Ellie knew, he grabbed a condom from his wallet, rolled it on and started touching her in the right places, showing her all over again just how much he needed her.

Ellie's chest tightened with a secret hope she was afraid to indulge for fear that if she did, she'd end up where she'd been thirteen years ago. Broken and inconsolable, yearning for the love of a man who did not love her back.

There it was. The scariest thing of all about this midnight tryst.

No matter how much she enjoyed his company, she simply didn't trust Dalton to take care with her heart.

Chapter 8

A noise outside the cabin woke Dalton.

Startled, he sat up and glanced at the clock on the bedside table. Four thirty. Still too early for Kaddy to be out and about. Had Danger Zone gotten out of the corral again? He needed to check on that gate. He couldn't have a bull loose with guests on the premises, no matter how aged the old boy was.

He turned to look at Ellie.

She was on her belly with her face buried in the pillow. Her breathing was deep and slow. Her long blond hair trailed down her back. She was sacked out.

God, she was so beautiful.

He felt his body stir all over again, anxious to be with her. The only thing he wanted was to shift her to her side and spoon her against him, but that urge would have to wait. There was trouble outside the door.

He canted his head, waiting for the sound to repeat. Heard the shuffling of feet and then a woman's voice calling, "Blue? Where are you?"

Immediately, he knew who it was.

Throwing back the covers, Dalton got to his feet. He pulled on his jeans as quietly and quickly as he could, letting Ellie get her rest. He searched for his shirt but couldn't find it in the dark.

"Blue?"

Forget the shirt. He had more important things to take care of. At the door, he looked back over his shoulder. Ellie hadn't moved.

"Sleep tight, princess," he murmured and stepped out onto the porch, softly closing the door behind him.

A few feet away, in a pool of light beneath the security lamp, stood Gram-Gram Winter in her nightgown. She took one look at Dalton and relief washed over her worried face.

"Blue!" she exclaimed. "There you are!"

His stomach nosedived. Blue was Ellie's late father, and Blue Winter had been dead for fifteen years.

"My son, my son!" The elderly woman raced toward him so quickly, Dalton feared for her safety. She could trip and fall. Break a hip in the dark.

He rushed to meet her.

She flung her arms around Dalton's waist and looked up at him, tears in her eyes. "I've missed you so much!"

Aww, damn. He didn't know what to do. Pretend to be Blue? Tell Mrs. Winter the truth? Wake Ellie and let her deal with her grandmother?

The elderly woman reached up to cup his cheek, but then her eyes clouded. "You're not Blue."

"No, ma'am."

She let out soft sob. "Who are you?"

"Dalton Branch," he said. "The owner of this ranch."

She dropped her hand, stepped back. "You're Ellie's young man."

"Yes, ma'am," he said, not wanting to complicate things by explaining his relationship with Ellie.

"Mother!" Ellie's Aunt Olivia appeared on the porch of the cabin next door. "What are you doing out here in the dark?"

"I went to find Blue," Mrs. Winter said, looking confused. "But he's gone, isn't he?"

Olivia moved down the steps, came over to her mother and slipped an arm around her shoulders. "Yes."

The elderly woman turned into her daughter's arms to whimper, "We lost him, we lost him."

Olivia met Dalton's gaze over the top of her mother's head. "Thank you for looking out for her."

"Of course."

"She's never done this." Olivia patted her mother's back. "They told me it would happen eventually, but I hoped we had more time."

"I've heard there are good days and bad."

"Oh goodness!" Olivia put a palm to her forehead. "In the hubbub of last night's party I forgot to give Mom her Alzheimer's meds. No wonder."

"There is a lot going on."

"Thank you for your understanding," Olivia said. "Ellie's lucky to have you in her corner."

That's when Dalton realized he was standing shirt-less on the porch of Ellie's cabin. Their tryst was no longer a secret. He'd apologize to her later for inadver-tently letting the cat out of the bag.

"Come along, Mom. Let's get you back to bed." With

a wave goodbye to Dalton, Olivia escorted her mother back to their cabin.

Dalton watched them go, his heart breaking for Ellie and her family. It occurred to him that Ellie was in a vulnerable place, and he wondered if that's why she'd let down her guard and invited him into her bed.

If that was the case, had he inadvertently taken advantage of her vulnerability? It was a sobering thought.

One thing was clear. He owed Ellie a big apology for his inability to keep his lust on a leash, and he'd tell her so the next time he got a chance. Wistfully, he looked over his shoulder and wished he could go back in time and not sleep with Ellie. Never mind that sex with her had been the best of his life.

He wouldn't wake her up and tell her what had happened. That would keep.

Although for him there was no going back to sleep. The best course of action? Get to work. They all had a busy weekend ahead of them and truthfully, he needed time to think.

When Ellie woke up, Dalton was gone.

Of course he was gone. He had a ranch to run. But he could have woken her up with a good morning kiss.

Oh damn, Winter, entitled much? You're getting clingy? That does not bode well.

They'd had a great time last night. Both of them. They'd enjoyed each other's bodies, released some long-pent-up sexual tension and gotten closure on their past.

That's all it was. The end of something, not the beginning.

Last night, in the throes of passion, she'd let her feelings run away with her. In the light of day, things looked clearer. Their reunion was temporary. Lovely, but it couldn't develop into anything more. Dalton was anchored to the guest ranch he was just getting started, and she was a doctor on the rodeo circuit. What chance did they have of creating anything solid and lasting?

None.

None at all.

She had no time to indulge herself. They had a quilt to finish and she was in charge. Pushing aside her worries and fears, Ellie hopped out of bed and got dressed.

By the time Camille and the rest of the quilters arrived at the lodge for breakfast, Ellie had her game face on. Shortly before the others arrived, she'd come into the communal dining room to find a hearty buffet of breakfast tacos, huevos rancheros, sausage casserole, fruit salad, and another pitcher of mimosas.

She looked around for Dalton, sticking her head into the kitchen to find Alma loading the dishwasher. She thought about asking for him but didn't want to look as if she cared, so she just said "good morning" and went back to the dining room. Just as she picked up a plate to serve herself, she heard the back door open and the sound of her sister's cheerful voice.

Camille was happy.

Ellie's sagging spirits lifted. That's all that mattered. This weekend was about her sister's wedding, not Ellie's wobbly new/old romance. She'd do her best to keep that in mind.

Chattering up a storm, Camille and her friends descended upon the dining room, greeting Ellie with hearty hellos as they dived into the food and talking about how much fun the barbecue had been.

"How'd it go with Dalton last night?" Camille sidled up to Ellie, a platter of tacos in her hand, and poked her playfully in the ribs.

"We had a nice moonlight stroll." Ellie spooned fruit salad onto her plate beside the helping of spicy huevos rancheros.

"And?"

"We talked."

"And?"

"No and."

"Oh, you Pinocchio," Camille said. "Cody saw Dalton coming out of your cabin at five a.m."

Did she admit it or try to come up with a story? Ellie wasn't comfortable with lying so she came clean. Lowering her voice so the others wouldn't overhear them, she said, "Okay, we spent the night together but don't go making a thing of it."

"Ooh!" Camille's eyes widened with delight. "I'm so excited! Let me set this plate down so I can give you a proper hug."

"No, no. You're making a thing of it. Stop making a thing."

"But it *is* a thing. You've rekindled your burning first love!"

"Shh!" Ellie darted a glance at the other women in the room, but their attention was on Gram-Gram and Aunt Olivia, who'd just joined them. Hopefully, no one had heard Camille. "Keep it under your hat."

"Aww, you're no fun."

"It's a one-time thing. Let it go."

"It doesn't have to be a one-time thing."

"I live seven hours away, Camille, and I'm on the road eighty percent of the time."

"So move to Fort Davis. It would be amazing to have you close. Gram-Gram would be thrilled to pieces. I heard Dr. Harrington is looking for a partner in his practice."

"Seriously, stop this." Ellie stepped away from her sister, but she couldn't step away from her wildly pounding heart.

For there in the doorway stood Dalton, looking at her with smoldering eyes and a smile so sultry it could blister paint.

Dalton crossed the dining room to whisper in her ear, his thoughts a mad jumble. "Could I speak to you a moment before y'all start quilting?"

Last night had been incredible.

So incredible that the remnants of the teen he'd once been started building fantasy sandcastles in his mind. Understandable, considering how much he'd once loved Ellie, but totally stupid in the daylight when she was giving him a blank stare as empty as if he were some random stranger on the street.

Still, he wanted to try and patch things between them. He yearned to be with her. To build a life with her. That longing scared him now just as it had thirteen years ago. Back then he'd been a kid, knowing they were too young, knowing he had nothing to offer her, knowing he was holding her back.

But things had changed. He wasn't eighteen anymore. He'd been in the military. Had seen and done things that honed and hardened him. Learned life was short and when you found something worth fighting for, you battled to hang on to it.

He studied her face.

She didn't smile.

Was she thinking of all the reasons why they couldn't be together? Had he totally misread what they'd shared at Hope Lake and in her cabin? Maybe she wasn't thinking of him at all. He'd gone to sleep with happiness in his heart. Determined to find a way to make this relationship work despite the obstacles.

But standing here, looking into her impassive eyes, shook his belief that last night had meant something.

"Sure," she said. "Is now okay?"

He waved at the plate she held. "Finish your breakfast."

She set the plate down on the table. "We can do this now."

That's when he realized everyone was staring at them. "No, no. It's no rush. Please, eat. Cold eggs are the worst."

"I'll eat your eggs," Camille volunteered. "You can get a fresh plate when you come back."

"Thanks," Ellie told her sister and without waiting, she headed for the door.

Dalton followed.

She went all the way outside, and hips swaying, walked to the koi pond. She turned, crossed her arms over her chest, and raised her eyebrows. "What is it?"

Her tone was clipped, and she didn't smile. Her shields were up.

Was she upset with him?

"You okay?" he asked.

"Fine, but I need to get this quilting show on the road, so if you can speed this up . . ." She spiraled a circular motion with her index finger.

Dalton had forgotten she made the gesture when she felt impatient or irritated. The familiarity of that moving finger stirred a mixture of feelings inside him—sadness, regret, the knowledge that somehow, he'd screwed this up.

"Ellie . . ."

"Please, Dalton, just cut to the chase. My time is precious."

Definitely irritated. She looked like what she was, a busy doctor who had no time for idle chitchat.

"I realize it must seem like I ran out on you this morning," he said.

The muscle in her jaw jumped. "Not at all. I understand. Life on a ranch starts early in the morning. You can't dawdle."

"I almost woke you up, but you were sleeping so soundly—"

She waved a dismissive hand. "It's fine. Don't think twice."

Ellie seemed completely unaffected by the night they'd shared. She looked so professional, so efficient, so damn out of his league, all the old doubts pushed away the shreds of his fading hope.

Clearly, they'd had a one-night stand. He'd been the only one thinking that maybe they could carve out a future together. Fighting for a cause you believed in was only worthwhile if you had a prayer of winning. The tightness screwing up her mouth said he didn't stand a chance

"I didn't want you to think I was using you."

"I didn't think that. If you were using me, I was using you too. Consider us even." She paused, tightened her arms around her chest. "Anything else?"

He should walk away. Leave it alone. But he took one last stab at changing her mind. "After the rehearsal dinner tonight would you like to—"

"As nice as that sounds," she said, her voice softening slightly, "I've got too much to do as Camille's maid of honor. I—"

He held up both palms. Took a step backward. "No need to explain. I get it. You're right. I'll be busier than a one-legged man in a butt-kicking contest. It was dumb of me to suggest it."

"Not dumb." Her voice softened. "Last night was fun."

"So much fun."

"It's a great memory." For the first time since they'd come outside, a small smile played lightly at the corners of her mouth. Memory. Yes. He'd already been relegated back to the past.

"Well," he said, "you have a good day quilting. Just text me if you need anything."

She pulled her phone from her pocket. "Will do. What's your number?"

He gave it to her.

"Thanks." She tapped his number into her phone, slipped her phone back into her pocket and walked away.

Even as his heart sank, his stupid hopes whispered, *At least she's got your number.* But she'd had his number thirteen years ago and she'd never once called.

Why would she? You were the one who sent her away.

Now here she was, turning the tables.

He deserved her dismissal, Dalton supposed, for having lied to her all those years ago, but that didn't make it hurt any less.

Ellie could not act on her growing feelings for Dalton. Could not let him unravel her heart again. Even if he'd told her he loved her and vowed to spend every remaining day of his life proving it to her, she simply didn't trust him.

She'd lost her father and her teenage love. She wasn't about to put her heart in harm's way again. Never mind that last night had been beyond fantastic—she'd allowed lust to lead her astray. Sex was one thing; a relationship was something else entirely and she had no place for a relationship in her life right now.

And most especially not with Dalton.

Why not? whimpered the seventeen-year-old lurking inside her. True love could reunite two people.

But it hadn't been true love, had it? If it had been, he wouldn't have sent her away, not even for her own good. Truth was, he hadn't fought for their love. Hadn't figured out a way to keep her. His reason for letting her go was just an excuse. There'd been more to it, even if he couldn't acknowledge the truth to himself.

She'd known better than to let him in again. She had

no use for her reckless disregard of the consequences of inviting him into her bed. She had no one to blame but herself. Love didn't last. How could it? People died. She was a doctor. She was more aware of that grim reality than most. She'd lost her dad, and Dalton had lost his mother. Both their remaining parents had lost their soul mates. Dalton of all people should get that. And now she was losing her beloved grandmother to Alzheimer's.

Honestly, it was too much loss to bear.

Love always died in the end, and there was nothing you could do to prevent it. Best course of action? Avoid love altogether and keep your heart safe from the mess.

She'd been right to discourage him.

Yeah? Then why do you feel so miserable?

The same darn thoughts had been circling her mind the whole morning as the group quilted and drank mimosas and chatted about past wedding celebrations. She kept a smile pasted on her face so no one would guess she was upset. This was Camille's special day. A once-in-a-lifetime event for her younger sister.

Alma appeared in the doorway of the conference room and announced lunch was ready. A taco bar. Everyone headed for the dining room except Ellie, who hung back to evaluate their progress on the quilt.

For the design, they'd placed Dalton's square in the center of the quilt and framed it with a heart-shaped outline. The rest of the squares were patchworked around it. Although they weren't finished yet, the results would look a lot better than she'd imagined it could with a piecemeal project.

"The quilt is gorgeous, Ellie." Camille paused at the

door. "Your design is a stroke of genius. You pulled it off, but I always knew you would."

A flush of pride heated her cheeks at her sister's kind words. "I'm so glad you decided to have a quilting bee instead of a bachelorette party. We'll remember this event for the rest of our lives."

"It was sweet of Dalton to make a quilt square. How many women can say they have a man who sews and who is sentimental enough to save the shirt he was wearing the day he met her?"

"Dalton's not my man."

"No?" Camille lifted an eyebrow.

"No."

"You admitted he spent the night with you."

"So what?" Irritation, and at the bottom of it fear, tightened her chest. "It doesn't mean he's my man."

"Then you're not as smart as I thought you were." Shaking her head, Camille turned and left the room.

Chapter 9

Inside the reception barn, Kaddy was setting up for the rehearsal dinner that evening. On the sound system, Willie Nelson sang "Blue Eyes Crying in the Rain." Dalton thought of Ellie's blue eyes and felt his heart move sluggishly in his chest.

Worst of all? He'd known that spending the night with her was risky business, and he'd done it anyway.

But last night had been so sweet, how could he regret it? *S'right, s'okay*, he told himself. He'd gotten over her once before; he'd do it again. But dang if that didn't feel like a monumental task he just wasn't up to handling.

"What's wrong?" Kaddy asked bluntly, looking up from the Japanese lanterns—in the shape of cowboy boots—that she was hanging from the ceiling.

"Nothing."

"Liar." Kaddy climbed down from her ladder.

"Okay, something, but I don't want to talk about it."

"Ahh," she said. "You've got the Kandahar blues."

"Well," he admitted. "It's not as bad as all that. No one died."

"Best keep that in mind while you're busy feeling sorry for yourself."

"Is that what I'm doing?"

"I dunno." Kaddy shrugged casually. "Is it?"

Dalton swept off his Stetson and jammed his fingers through his hair. "I caused my own damn problem, didn't I?"

Kaddy nodded sagely. "Now we're getting somewhere."

"You're supposed to be on my side."

"Cruel to be kind, buddy boy." Kaddy sauntered over to punch him companionably on the shoulder. "Just like you were when you sent Ellie packing the first time."

An irrational thought popped into his head. "Do you think Ellie slept with me just to get back at me for dumping her thirteen years ago?"

"Do you?"

"No." Vigorously, he shook his head. "Ellie's not like that. She isn't the sort to hold a grudge."

"Ellie put you in the one-night-stand zone," Kaddy guessed.

Dalton shrugged, felt a churn of pain deep inside his stomach. "Yeah, maybe."

"It hurts because you had fantasies of reuniting with her."

He'd told himself he didn't, but Kaddy was right. He had been spinning what-if fantasies of getting back together with Ellie, trying to figure out how to make a long-distance relationship work.

"Yeah."

"And she's pushing you away."

Dalton blew out his breath. "Looks that way."

"You gotta ask yourself if she's just not that into you, or if she's simply trying to shield her heart the way you are right now."

He shouldn't have slept with Ellie, but he had, and he'd mucked everything up. Now what?

"Here's the deal, boss. You can either cowboy up and smell the coffee and tell her how you really feel, or wallow in your misery, pining away for a woman whose real feelings you don't even know. Your choice."

"Can we have a private conversation?" Gram-Gram asked Ellie as the other quilters lined up for a dessert of Alma's homemade ice cream in the kitchen.

"Certainly. Would you like to go back to the quilting room?"

Gram-Gram nodded, a peaceful smile on her face.

Anxiety over her grandmother's health tightened Ellie's chest as she escorted Gram-Gram to the conference room. Once inside, Ellie guided her grandmother to the padded folding chair she'd been sitting in before they'd taken a break for lunch. Then she plopped down beside her.

"What's up?"

Still smiling, Gram-Gram leaned over and ran her palm over the quilt. "It's so beautiful and touches my heart that you girls wanted to spend your time making this memory quilt for me instead of whooping it up at a strip club."

"We love you, Gram-Gram," Ellie said, "so very much."

"The feeling is mutual." Gram-Gram patted Ellie's cheek. "My grandchildren are the light of my life and with this quilt, I hope never to forget you."

Oh, what a bittersweet moment. Ellie felt the melancholy agony to the bottom of her soul. She was so grateful to be here with her grandmother, to be making this memory quilt for her with her sister and aunt. She was acutely aware how special this time was for them all, simply because it wouldn't last.

Just as her time with Dalton had been precious but ephemeral. Unpleasant life lesson. You couldn't hold on to anything, so it was best not to try.

"I didn't want to say anything in front of the others," Gram-Gram began, "but I needed to let you know something important."

Fear was an icy hand at Ellie's throat, even as she felt honored that her grandmother was confiding in her. "What is it? What's wrong?"

Gram-Gram ducked her head and cut Ellie a sidelong glance. "Hank asked me to marry him last night and I said yes."

Ellie stared at her grandmother, trying to process her words. She'd been braced for a heartbreaking confession about her illness. "Y-you . . . what?"

"I'm getting married." Gram-Gram giggled and lifted a finger to her lips. "But shh, I don't want to take the spotlight off Camille."

Dumbfounded, Ellie stared at her grandmother. "I . . . I don't know what to say."

"Say you're happy for me."

Feelings rushed in on Ellie—fear, concern, disbe-lief—and for a moment, she couldn't speak. "Is that wise?"

"To you? Overly cautious Ellie? Probably not."

"What does that mean?" She tried not to feel hurt.

"You're a doctor." Gram-Gram gave a casual shrug. "You see life through a tight lens of health or disease. Nothing wrong with that, but please just realize it's a limited viewpoint."

"But you have Alzheimer's!" Ellie could hear the dismay in her tone and wished she hadn't sounded so strident. "How can you get married!"

"Are you saying I should stop living long before I die?" Gram-Gram's voice held a steely note. "The doc-tor says I'm in good health otherwise."

Ellie's mouth dropped and she didn't know what to say. Good health other than slowly losing her grip on sanity?

Gram-Gram gave her a wistful smile and patted Ellie's hand. "Sweetheart, we only have the present moment. God doesn't promise us anything more than that. You of all people should know that. I can't spend every day in fear. I want to live the time I have left to the fullest."

Ellie blinked at her grandmother, struggling to process what she was proposing. "You're getting mar-ried."

"It'll be simple. At Hank's house in Marfa. Only the family. We don't want to make a big thing of it. Just a small celebration."

"But Hank—"

"Knows my diagnosis. It's not one-sided. I'm taking a risk too. He's got heart disease and could keel over on the honeymoon."

"Gram-Gram!"

"Darling, you're young, so you haven't gotten to the point where you realize there's no time to waste. Please, it's my life. Let me live it as I see fit."

What could she say? All she wanted was for Gram-Gram to be happy. In fact, she admired her bravery.

"Hank and I have talked it through. We'll have a prenup and when my mind reaches a certain point, he'll put me into a nursing home."

Tears pushed at the back of Ellie's eyes, and she couldn't stop them from rolling down her cheeks. "Wh-what does Aunt Olivia say?"

"I haven't told her yet. I wanted you to be the first to know."

"Why?"

"Because I hope to be an inspiration."

"You already are."

"Then prove it to me."

Ellie wasn't sure what her grandmother was talking about. Frowning, she pushed back a lock of hair. "How?"

"Stop running from life. The thing you need is right there in front of you, yet you can't embrace it. Time is short, Ellie. I know when you're young it seems as if you have all the time in the world, but you don't. Stop throwing away the best thing that's ever happened to you."

"What are you talking about?"

Gram-Gram looked alarmed, clicked her tongue. "Oh, poor girl, are you really that blind?"

"I don't know what it is I'm supposed to be seeing."

"Look at the quilt." Gram-Gram angled her head at the hand-pieced quilt topper stretched out on the conference room table. "What do you see?"

A lump formed in Ellie's throat as she studied the stitches. Some were precise, some were more hesitant, all were sewn with love.

"How can you deny what's in the center of the quilt? It's your own design. Your subconscious is leading the way, but you've got your heels dug in, afraid to follow."

Ellie leaned over to trace the heart-shaped cloth frame around the center square. The square that Dalton had quilted. The square made from his shirt. The square that represented not only the day they'd met, but her father's career as well. The career that had taken Dad away. The career he'd loved with all his heart.

She moved her fingers to the print on the material of the center square, to the pattern of cowboy silhouettes riding a bucking bull. Fresh tears filled her eyes.

"Your father went at life full throttle," Gram-Gram said. "He lived until he died. I want to do the same."

"But he left us too soon!" Ellie exclaimed, startling herself by how raw and hard the words spilled from her. "He devastated us." Her mouth twisted up. "He was so busy living life at full throttle, he didn't even think about what his death would do to his family."

"Ahh," Gram-Gram said in the self-satisfied voice of a doctor who'd just nailed a mystery diagnosis. "You haven't forgiven him for dying."

"What? No," Ellie denied, but the little girl inside her ached with abandonment.

"That's why you're running away from Dalton. You're terrified that if you let yourself love him, he'll leave you too."

"He sent me away, Gram-Gram. I loved him so much before, and he told me I didn't mean that much to him."

"Dalton still loves you. Anyone with their eyes open can see it on his face every time he looks at you. He loves you, Ellie. No man would sew a quilt square for you if he didn't."

She shook her head. "I . . ."

"You don't love him too?"

"I do."

"Then why are you standing there staring at me? Stop being scared. Forgive your dad and Dalton and yourself. Go find that man and tell him exactly how you feel before it's too darn late."

Chapter 10

Possessed by the need to see Dalton, Ellie couldn't sit still.

While the rest of the quilters put the finishing touches on the quilt, she mumbled something about using the bathroom, jumped up from the table and headed for the door. Before she left the room, she glanced back and saw Gram-Gram's knowing eyes on her.

Smiling, her grandmother nodded and mouthed silently, "Go to him."

As if winged, her feet flew down the hallway, her pulse a hammer at her throat, beating out Gram-Gram's edict.

Go to him, go to him, go to him.

She had no idea what she would say, or how to start the conversation. She only knew her grandmother was right. A guy didn't sew you a quilt square unless he was still in love with you.

And she was still in love with him.

Had never stopped loving him in fact.

She'd tucked him out of her mind for thirteen years, but he'd never been far from her heart.

Last night had been beautiful, but the light of day had scared her, and she'd pushed him away.

A sense of urgency shoved her to the mudroom, just as Dalton burst through the back door. They halted just short of smacking into each other and on a singular breath, said, "We need to talk."

Dalton's hand was shaking as he placed it against the small of Ellie's back and guided her over the pasture path to Hope Lake. After his discussion with Kaddy, he realized he couldn't wait one second more before telling her how he felt. If she rejected him, so be it, but he had to let her know.

Without speaking, they walked out onto the dock. No one was around as they turned to each other.

"You go first," he said.

"No, no, you."

Then in unison they said, "I was an idiot."

They looked at each other and laughed.

"Okay," she said. "I'll go first."

He took her hands in his and drilled her with his gaze. "I'm all ears, Els."

"I made a mess of things."

Me too, he thought but didn't interrupt her.

"I've been walking around with a hole in my heart for the last thirteen years simply because I was too terrified to admit the truth."

I have a hole in my heart too! He tightened his grip

on her hands and deepened his smile, sent her a message with his eyes. *It's okay. Everything is going to be all right.*

She looked so beautiful in the sunlight, the wind gently blowing her hair back from her face, it was all he could do not to kiss her.

"I'm done running scared," she said. "I know it might be too late, that I've waited too long to see the light, but I have to take a chance. I have to tell you how I feel."

Hope on Hope Lake. Dalton wanted to ask a million questions, but he held his tongue. Let Ellie have her say before he began. He'd been waiting for her a long time. A few minutes more wouldn't make a difference.

"Before I do that, I have something else to take care of first." She withdrew her hands from him, and his heart sank.

"What's that?" he said, barely brave enough to ask.

She held up a finger. "I need to make two calls."

"Do you need privacy?"

"No. I want you to hear the conversations." She pulled her cell phone from her pocket, punched in a number and clicked the speaker feature.

Dalton heard the ringing phone vibrate the air.

"Dr. Harrington's office," a woman's voice said.

"Lisa, it's Ellie Winter. Does Dr. Harrington have a moment?"

"Hang on, I'll see if he can take your call."

Elevator music reached Dalton's ears as the receptionist put Ellie on hold.

"Why are you calling Doc Harrington?" Dalton asked.

"Shh." She put a finger to her mouth just as Dr. Harrington picked up the phone.

"Ellie! Hello. So good to hear from you. I was just about to pop into the exam room to see a patient, so I don't have long. What's up?"

"I've been giving your offer some thought," she said, her gaze locked on Dalton's.

His entire body went stock still, and he barely dared breathe.

"Yes?" Dr. Harrington sounded as hopeful as Dalton felt.

"I'd love to become a partner in your practice."

"For real?" Dr. Harrington asked.

"For real."

"What about the rodeo?"

Ellie locked eyes with Dalton. "I've found something that interests me far more right here in the Trans-Pecos."

Dalton fisted his hands, joy overtaking his heart. Ellie was moving back to Fort Davis?

"That's wonderful news. I'm thrilled."

"I'll let you go check on your patient now. Call me back when you have a chance, and we can schedule a time to discuss the details."

"Ellie, I can't tell you how happy this makes me," Dr. Harrington said. "Welcome home."

Welcome home.

Dumbfounded, Dalton couldn't speak. She was dead serious.

After she ended the call with Dr. Harrington, she phoned her boss at the PBR and told him she was moving back home and would need to leave her position as staff physician and would come in to make things official after Camille's wedding.

"I hate to see you go," her boss said. "We're all going to miss you, but I understand. Home is where the heart is."

She ended that call with her eyes firmly fixed to Dalton's face.

"Did you really just do that?" Dalton asked, overwhelmed by the grand gesture.

"I did."

"Why?"

"Can't you guess?"

"For me? You're moving back home for me?"

"For us," she said. "It's for *us*."

"I don't get it," he said, genuinely confused. "How can you give up the only thing you ever wanted?"

"Being a doctor on the rodeo circuit is not the only thing I ever wanted," she said. "From the second Danger Zone smacked you in the breadbasket and pitched you into the koi pond, I knew I was still in love with you. I was so terrified he'd hurt you, but even more terrified that I cared so much."

"But your dad. The rodeo. You worked your whole life for that. How can you just give it up?"

"Last night with you, and today with Gram-Gram when she told me she and Hank are getting married, I realized something important."

"What's that?" Dalton asked.

"I'd never forgiven my father for dying . . ." She paused, took in a deep breath. "Or you for sending me away. It seemed any man I loved left me."

"Ellie, I'm so sorry. I never meant to hurt you—"

"I understand," she said. "At least logically, but deep down inside, the hole in my heart never healed. Coming home, making love to you, cleared some things up."

"What things?" he whispered.

"I love you, Dalton Branch. I love the man who made a quilt square for my grandmother's patchwork quilt. So much that I'll rearrange my life to be with him." Tears misted her eyes.

"Ellie . . ."

"My knees are knocking here, please tell me you feel the same way."

"I can't tell you that," he said.

"Oh . . ." She stumbled backward, looked stricken. "Oh."

And then she turned and ran, blasting over the cattle guard and into the pasture beyond Hope Lake.

"Ellie!' Dalton shouted. "Stop!"

But she didn't stop. She just kept running, with Dalton's words ripping her apart. *I can't tell you that.*

What a fool she'd been! Assuming just because she was still in love with Dalton that he was still in love with her. She'd made a grand gesture, quit her job to prove to him how much she cared, and it had blown up in her face.

All she wanted to do was get away from everyone, curl up into a ball and lick her wounds.

She heard his footsteps pounding behind her and sped up.

"Ellie, please stop now! Danger Zone is in this pasture!"

Sudden terror froze Ellie to the spot and as her feet rooted into the dirt, she turned her head and saw the massive Angus bull standing there snorting, head down, pawing the ground.

Without missing a beat, Dalton ran at the bull, waving his arms with his Stetson clutched in his hand, stomping the ground and yelling, "Hee-yaw! Git!"

Danger Zone raised his head and shifted his attention to Dalton.

"Go on. Get out of here!" Dalton charged the bull.

Dear God! Ellie plastered her palm to her chest. Dalton was going to die!

To her utter surprise, Danger Zone swished his tail, turned and walked away.

Ellie's legs collapsed, but she never hit the ground. For Dalton was there, scooping her into his arms and carrying her to safety.

"Now," Dalton said, depositing Ellie in the rocking chair on the front porch of her cabin. "As I was saying before you ran away from me . . ." He dropped down on the floorboards beside the rocker and took her hands in his. "I can't tell you that I feel the same way about you—"

"I get it. It's okay." She swiped away tears with the back of her hand. "I'm glad to be moving home anyway even if you and I aren't a love match—"

"Woman," he growled. "Do I have to kiss you silly to make you listen?"

She shut up.

"I can't tell you that I feel the same way about you

because I love you more now than I ever imagined before. Seeing you again, realizing all that I'd given up, I knew I'd been a fool. I shouldn't have sent you away thirteen years ago. I should have moved to College Station with you, but I was terrified. You weren't the only one who had trouble moving on after losing a parent. I was so scared of losing you that I set you free before you could ditch me. I thought if I was in control, it would hurt less. It didn't. I went to war because I couldn't forget you. Not then, not now. I love you, Ellie Winter. I always have and I always will. You don't have to give up the rodeo for me. I'll sell the ranch and go on the road with you. Nothing means more to me than you."

"Dalton, are you serious?"

"I've never been more serious about anything in my life. But I don't want us to rush this. I want to date, as adults. I want us to savor our romance. And then, in a year when we've gotten to know each other all over again and we've made inroads toward forgiving our parents for dying on us, I'll ask you to marry me. What do you say to that?"

"I say, yes, Dalton Branch, yes to your wonderful plan that mirrors my own."

"Finally," he said. "We're on the same page."

She flung her arms around his neck and he kissed her for a good long time. Then they joined hands and walked back to the lodge, both knowing that at long last they could lay down their grief and walk wholehearted into love.

When You Wish Upon a Quilt

a Quilt

PATIENCE GRIFFIN

For all my quilting friends, near and far.
And for my readers. You make it all possible.
Thank you.

Chapter 1

"Pull it together, Paige," she whispered to herself.

Paige Holiday stood alone in the large sewing studio of the Sisters Three quilting retreat, packing her quilt samples back into her suitcase, knowing her fear and panic were irrational. Just the thought of returning to Houston today made her break into a cold sweat. The closer it came time to leave, the more anxious she felt. Good thing the Hanahan sisters, owners of the Sisters Three quilt retreat center, weren't in the room to see her fretting. They were in the office down the hall writing Paige a check for services rendered—a two-day workshop where she'd taught her Polka Dot and Plaid Mod quilt. This was one of many workshops she'd taught at retreats, quilt guilds, and quilt shops across the US, though her home was in Sweet Home, Alaska.

Paige's phone dinged and she looked down to see a meme from her best friend Lolly.

A bitter woman says "All men are the same."

A wise woman decides to stop choosing the same type of man.

Paige nodded and gave the screen a sad smile. "Easy for you to say." Paige had inherited her mother's and grandmother's penchant for picking charming, good-looking, good-for-nothings. Lolly, though, had great taste in men. She'd even gotten engaged, once or twice. Paige, on the other hand, had never made it that far. But if she had, more than likely, he—her imaginary husband—would've stolen everything from her and run off, leaving her pregnant and destitute with empty bank accounts. Just like what had happened to her mom and grandma. Paige came from a long line of women who had been taken in by con men.

Mom and Grandma Doris had undoubtedly passed along the legacy to Paige. The legacy was the reason Paige had grown up in Grandma Doris's cabin in Sweet Home with Mom constantly sniping at Grandma. Though their home had been filled with contention, living with her grandmother had been a blessing for Paige. Yes, her grandmother had been deceived by a man, but she wasn't angry and bitter like Mom. She used to say, "Oh, how your grandfather could make me laugh. But my parents were right about him. He was a ne'er-do-well." Grandma Doris taught Paige how to quilt and how to dream. She'd been the one to pass along a section of the Wishing Quilt to her, too, now made into the tote that went everywhere with Paige, as a large purse and part-talisman. Mom, on the other hand, was the opposite of Grandma. Mom was bitter about the life her husband had stolen from her. Paige spent her childhood trying to make her mother happy with straight A's, plus being the best daughter possible, giving Pollyanna a run for her money in the well-behaved department. When Grandma Doris died four years ago, Paige had taken to the road, accepting every quilt-teaching gig she could get, just to put space between herself and her negative mother.

Paige stowed another folded quilt in her luggage and took a deep breath, trying to let all the mistakes of the past go. Her mother was only human after all and Paige shouldn't judge. She had made some of the same mistakes as her mom and grandmother, especially when it came to men.

She slipped her scissors into the Wishing Quilt tote and ran a hand over the star motif crafted by her grandmother before putting her mind back on the task at hand. While she folded the last quilt, she searched for silver linings. She'd come a long way in getting over her disappointment from her trip to Houston two years ago, and was proud of herself for starting to be known in the quilting world. More importantly, she was making enough now to move to Fairbanks on her own. She loved Sweet Home, her hometown, but she needed to be closer to an airport to make it easier on herself as she spent so much time teaching in the Lower Forty-Eight. It was October now and she had plans to move in the spring.

As she carefully placed her last quilt in the large suitcase, the three Hanahan sisters—Lila Mae, Charise, and Betty—came bustling into the room. All three were characters, in their sixties, and husbandless. They had poured everything into the retreat center they'd started five years ago. For Paige, this was her fourth visit to the north Texas retreat center. After spending so much time with these ladies, she felt as comfortable with them as she did with the Sisterhood of the Quilt back in Sweet Home, her own quilting group.

"Why are you headed to Houston so soon?" said Lila Mae, the oldest of the Hanahan sisters, who was always in charge and a little bossy. "I know you want to see your quilt hanging in the International Quilt Festival, but the darned event doesn't start until next week."

Paige zipped up her suitcase. "I told you about Hope, who owns my local quilt shop. She tasked me with going to Quilt Market, which is right before the International Quilt Festival."

"I've never understood what Quilt Market is," Charise said, making a little pout. "Makes no sense to me why they have it if Quilt Festival is the next week."

Paige smiled and explained. "Quilt Market is the trade show for quilt shop owners and quilting professionals. Quilt Festival is open to the general public. I'm going to Market on Hope's behalf to meet with the fabric companies and order for our local quilt shop." Which was a daunting task. Paige wished a couple more quilters from the Sisterhood of the Quilt could have come with her so Sweet Home's quilt shop would end up with a wider variety of fabric. But Hope had armed her with a list of gadgets and fabrics she had seen online and wanted for the store. *Just use your best judgment*, Hope had said. Paige had laughed and warned her that she might only order polka dots and plaids, which were her favorite fabrics. Hope only smiled and said she trusted her. Funny, that trust came so easily to others but not to Paige.

Betty peered at her. "Your expression says there's something else going on."

There's a lot going on, Paige thought, but didn't know how much to share with them. Maybe only the good stuff. "Can you keep a secret?" She hadn't even told the Sisterhood of the Quilt. "I hope while I'm at Market I can make some connections. I've been thinking that I'd like to get into designing my own fabrics."

"Fabrics?" Charise asked.

"In my spare time, I've been drawing pictures that I hope will be printed on fabric one day."

Charise clapped her hands. "How wonderful!"

"Don't get too excited," Paige said. "This is an exploration mission. I need to find out how to get an introduction to a decision-maker." It was scary doing something so outside her comfort zone. But at one time, teaching others how to quilt had been scary, too.

"Can we see your drawings?" Betty reached for Paige's sketchbook, the one she kept close at all times.

"Sorry, no. I can't." Paige trusted these ladies but still felt burned from the last time she'd shared her designs, the last time she was in Houston.

"We understand," Lila Mae said. "You want to make them a surprise for us. We can respect that."

"I love surprises," Charise exclaimed.

"Thanks for understanding." As Paige set her suitcase on the ground, she received another text. "I better get going. The shuttle just pulled up outside."

Betty gave her a hug. "We'll see you in five days."

"I'm so glad the three of you are coming to Quilt Festival," Paige said honestly.

"Don't worry. While we're there, we'll watch out for you," Lila Mae said with a firm nod.

The older woman had no idea how much that meant to Paige. The Houston quilt show had been a disaster the last time. In truth, it had been Paige's fault as she'd been too gullible and trusting. She reminded herself that she was too smart now to repeat the mistakes of the past. At the same time, she wasn't completely sure. Trusting the wrong men was obviously in her genetics.

Charise and Lila Mae gave her their hugs, too, before Paige made it out the door. The ladies didn't say goodbye but followed her out, watching as she loaded the suitcase into the back of the shuttle. They waved to her—Charise even blew kisses—as Paige went to catch her flight.

Flying always gave her a chance to get a lot of design work done, which was baffling. The seating in coach was cramped and shouldn't make for optimal working conditions, but somehow, she always made headway on a project or conceived new ideas while flying. This trip was no different. Using her arm to block her sketch, Paige added more detail to the design of her Highland cattle drawing, inspired by the herd outside Sweet Home. She thought the Highland cattle would look great in a fabric panel sometime in the future.

When the pilot said to prepare for landing, a new case of nerves hit Paige. As the plane stopped and she pulled down her carry-on and settled her Wishing Quilt tote, her nervousness ratcheted up another notch. Memories of her last visit felt real and fresh, just as real as the heat and humidity that hit her as she stepped off the plane.

She had been so excited for her first visit to Quilt Festival, and had met Malcolm Landis at this very gate. Malcolm had been charming, chatting with her as they'd walked through the terminal together to get to baggage claim. He, too, was on his way to the quilt show and had swept Paige off her feet with his smile, his attentiveness, and, well, he was as handsome as all get-out. It seemed liked the perfect *How did you two meet?* story to tell their future children. She was so intoxicated with her crush on him that she didn't think to check him out on the internet. If she had, she would've seen that Malcolm was one of the up-and-coming men in quilting. She also would've seen that he was married. But that was only the first of many mistakes that Paige had made in Houston.

By the time the first day was over, she and Malcolm were inseparable. After a couple of romantic dinners, a nice kiss, and a leisurely walk through the quilts hanging at the show, Malcolm had asked to look at her quilt designs in her sketchbook. What he didn't know was that they weren't just her quilt designs. When her grandmother died, Grandma Doris had gifted her the sketchbook of creative star quilts she'd made over the years. Paige had added her own ideas to Grandma Doris's and had come up with something very unique. But foolishly thinking herself in love, and because she didn't see the harm, Paige had handed over the notebook when Malcolm insisted. She also believed with all her heart that the relationship was going somewhere. He was so complimentary that she didn't stop him from taking pictures of every quilt and jotting down notes as she spewed her inspiration and thoughts about the quilts on the page. He even copied the templates that she had planned to make out of acrylic to sell right along with her patterns.

When he didn't call her the next day or the day after that, Paige was extremely hurt and puzzled. She only found out the answer to what happened to Malcolm Landis eleven months later when Piney, the grocery store owner in Sweet Home, pointed out the cover of *Quilting World* magazine and said, *Isn't that yours and Doris's quilt design?* Paige was shocked. Malcolm's upcoming book, it turned out, was a compilation of the twelve quilt designs that he'd stolen from her!

She hadn't worked on a new star quilt design since. For a while, she hadn't sewn at all. But when she did start designing again, she'd gone in a completely different direction, really focusing on fabric as part of the design, instead of just the quilt image. And she was proud of herself that she was wiser now. She hadn't fallen for a sweet-talker from that time on, which meant she hadn't dated in the last two years. She told herself that she was too busy to date, that she was busy building her business. And it was true. But also, she was more than a little gun shy.

She grabbed her luggage from the carousel and ordered her Uber to get to the hotel. But forty minutes later, when the chatty female Uber driver pulled up to the Orchid Hotel, Paige was mystified.

"Um, this isn't the Orchid. I stayed at the Orchid two years ago."

"Yes, it is."

"But we should've driven by the convention center." Paige looked out the window, then behind her but didn't see it.

"Oh, right. You're talking about the old Orchid Hotel. That burned down a while back. They turned it into a parking garage. Apparently, the old hotel had flooded a couple of times and they decided for insurance purposes to move the location. This one is brand-new. Opened up just in time for the quilters coming to town." She seemed pleased about the move, but Paige wasn't.

"So how far is it to the convention center now?"

"I'd say at least five miles," Ms. Uber chirped.

Paige's heart sank and she felt a headache coming on. No wonder she'd gotten a much better rate than last time. No wonder there were so many rooms to choose from, too. From past experience, trying to get a hotel room for Quilt Festival was like trying to thread a needle during a hurricane.

Five miles away might as well be a thousand. One of the advantages of being close to the convention center was the ability to drop things off at the hotel, or change clothes quickly before a swanky evening meal, or to have a place for a siesta, and then hurry back to the action. By being five miles away, Paige couldn't be as spontaneous. Before she left for the convention center each day, she'd have to make sure she had everything with her because it wouldn't be easy to make a trip back for something left behind.

The driver hopped out and was getting Paige's luggage from the back of the SUV. Paige had no choice but to get out, too. If only she'd paid attention to the address when she'd booked the hotel online. She wondered if this was an omen. Because so far, this trip to Houston wasn't starting off on the right foot.

As Holt Champion walked his horse into the main barn, he heard his sister Ruth Ann cry out in the direction of the house.

"Rodger!" Holt called out to his foreman. "Come take Thunder." He wrapped the reins over the railing and hightailed it up to their sprawling ranch-style home with the long front porch.

Ruth Ann was lying on the ground at the bottom of the steps, clutching her arm. Quilting supplies were strewn about her and two very large Rubbermaid containers lay empty next to her.

"Are you okay?" he hollered before he actually reached her.

"What do you think?" Ruth Ann ground out.

When he got to her side, he stooped over and saw that her shoulder sat at an odd angle.

"Dang it, Holt," she wailed. "Help me pick those things up so I can get the van loaded. I want to be on the road within the hour."

Holt ignored the quilting things and stopped her with a gentle touch to her good arm as she was trying to get up but couldn't. "Stop thrashing about. This wouldn't have happened if you'd listened to me, little sister. I told you that I'd load the van for you. You should've waited."

"I don't want to be coddled and that's all you've done since I've been back." She rolled to her side, trying again to sit up. "Ohhh, fudgesicles, it hurts." Tears were forming in her eyes and Ruth Ann never cried. "I've got to get to Houston." Her words sounded between a command and a plea.

Holt carefully helped his stubborn sister to her feet. "The only place you're going is to the hospital."

"Just get me an icepack and I'll be good to go," she said stoically, though pain had caused a deep furrow between her eyebrows.

He pulled out his phone and made a call. "Rodger, get up to the house and put Ruth Ann's things back into the containers that are scattered around the yard. I'm taking her to the hospital. She's dislocated her shoulder."

Ruth Ann glared at Holt as if he was lying. Then she shifted her head to look at the injury and her expression turned to shock, then disappointment. "I don't have time for this right now."

He guided her to his truck. "From my experience, injuries never come at a convenient time." He'd dislocated his shoulder, too, but on the football field in college. He opened the passenger's door and boosted her up into the seat. "Hold on and let me get your seat belt." He hurried to the other side of the truck and climbed in.

As he got into the cab, he saw Ruth Ann brush at a tear and turn away as if nothing had happened. He reached over and buckled her in. "How bad's the pain? Like getting kicked by a longhorn?"

"I'm more mad than anything. Hurry up and get me there so I can get on the road to Houston. This is the last thing I need."

"I know."

Ruth Ann had had a rough time of it. Ten months ago, she'd taken a leave of absence from the university and moved back to the ranch when she'd discovered that her useless husband—now ex-husband—had been cheating on her with an undergraduate student. Ruth Ann taught textiles and her ex taught poetry, and they had only been married two years. Holt had hoped the university would fire him, but they only gave him a slap on the wrist. Holt would've liked to be the one dishing out the punishment! When she'd arrived back at the ranch after she and her husband had separated, Ruth Ann had been heartbroken and unmoored. Holt should've warned her off from the beginning, when he'd first met Bob after they'd eloped. The man's handshake had been subpar—wimpy with a clammy hand—which pretty much nailed Bob's character. But Ruth Ann had seemed happy, so Holt had stayed out of it. He'd learned his lesson. He wouldn't let another man get near her without Holt giving him an old-fashioned come-to-Jesus-meeting talk first. In the future, his sister would be treated right, or he would have to answer to him!

Holt started the truck and pulled out. "You should've listened to me." Yes, he'd already said it, but it was better to pick a fight with her than to see her tears. Actually, the last time he'd seen her cry was at their dad's funeral. Ruth Ann had been a senior in high school at the time. By then, Holt had graduated from the university and was living his own life. But he'd dropped everything to come home to take care of his dad and the ranch, plus raise Ruth Ann and get her through college. Ranching hadn't been in his plans—he'd thought he wanted something different when he graduated—but apparently ranching was in his blood as he didn't want to be anywhere else now.

Ruth Ann glared at him. "I didn't need your help. Besides, I knew you were busy today, checking on the sheep in the north pasture. And dang it, I just want to handle things on my own," she said, looking out the window again.

"You should've come to me first thing when you suspected Bob was cheating." Holt had said this before, too, and couldn't help but say it again. "I would've straightened him out, you know."

"I don't want to talk about it."

"Understood." He hated that he'd turned into a nag, but someone had to watch out for her.

Before Holt even got to the hospital, he knew what had to be done . . . because, well, Ruth Ann was as stubborn as Old Bess, their mule in the last stall in the barn. Also, because his sister hadn't been completely herself since her marriage broke up. However, this last month he'd seen a glimmer of hope. Ruth Ann seemed to be righting herself as she looked forward to Quilt Market and the International Quilt Festival in Houston. Those two events brought her out of her funk a little. She seemed excited about teaching a few classes there as well. So there was no way Holt was going to let her miss the quilting events.

At the hospital, while Holt paced in the waiting

room—with Ruth Ann getting her shoulder back in place in an exam room—he made a call to Rodger.

"I'll need you to take care of things for the next ten days. I think that's how long Ruth Ann plans to be gone."

"Yes," Rodger said, "that's what she's been saying—ten days. First, Quilt Market, then Quilt Festival."

"Good grief, Rodger, why would you be knowing the details?"

There was a pause, then Rodger answered. "I've been listening to her."

Either Rodger was implying that Holt hadn't been listening or something else was up with his foreman.

"Is Ruth Ann going to be all right?" Rodger asked, sounding anxious.

"You seem very concerned over a little fall," Holt commented. Rodger was as calloused as they came, the kind of man that could brand cattle while issuing orders to his men, without batting an eye over the bawling calves.

"Your sister ain't a regular gal." Rodger was riled up, which didn't happen very often. "She's both tough and fragile."

"What's going on with you?"

"Nothing. Sorry, boss."

"She'll be fine," Holt answered.

"Good. Now what do you need me to do?"

They discussed how the east pasture's fence needed mending, how the vet was to come on Monday to give vaccinations, and another hundred things that would need to be overseen while Holt was gone.

"You can count on me," Rodger said.

"I know I can." To Holt, though, or to any rancher, ten days was a long time to be away. *But that's what you do for family.*

"Boss?" Rodger asked. "Tell Ruth Ann I asked after her." He hung up.

Holt stared at his cell for a long minute, wondering if Rodger had a *crush.* But it seemed absurd. Rodger had ten years on Ruth Ann and was a hardened cowhand. Had the man gone soft now? Rodger was as faithful as they come, but Holt wasn't sure how he felt about his foreman hankering after his sister.

Holt put the thought out of his head and made the rest of his calls. Ruth Ann's hotel in Houston was fully booked, but he found one out of the center of things but still close enough that he could help her with all she needed. Next he called CeeCee, Ruth Ann's friend and owner of the Circle J Quilt Shop, to let her know what had happened.

"That poor thing," CeeCee said. "You tell her to not worry about working in the booth. She can just teach her classes at Market and Festival and spend the rest of the time healing in the hotel room. I'll find someone else to fill in for her."

Holt shook his head, though the woman couldn't see him. "That's the thing. I know Ruth Ann will still want to help you. Will that be all right?"

"Sure. I'll put her in a chair at the cash register. You said it was her left shoulder that she dislocated?"

"Yes, and she's right-handed."

"When she gets to Houston, text me, and I'll run out and unload the van for her."

"No worries on that count. I'm driving her so I can

take care of anything that needs hauling." He'd heard Ruth Ann talking to CeeCee about what had to be done in the booth. "Of course, I'm happy to lend a hand setting up the booth as well."

"Oh, that would be great. You don't mind climbing a ladder, now do you, Holt, and hanging Ruth Ann's quilts? I have a bum knee and I'm doing my best not to climb anything."

"No, ma'am. I'm happy to climb ladders for you. Whatever you need."

She gave him the particulars of where to park and what to do when he arrived. Holt finished his calls and waited until Ruth Ann was wheeled out.

On the drive home, Ruth Ann was in no pain.

Holt glanced over. "They drugged you up pretty good to put it back in place." *According to the doctor.* "Once you went to sleep, though, they had a hard time waking you up, little sister."

She gave him a goofy grin. "I was tired, is all." She squinched up her face. "Did the doctor really say I couldn't drive?"

Holt laughed. "Yes, he said you can't drive."

"Then how am I going to get to Houston?"

"I'm taking you."

"You can't. You have the ranch to run."

"Rodger will handle things. We've got it all worked out." Holt was torn. He prided himself that he'd trained his men well and his foreman was just as capable of running the ranch as himself. Holt just hated to be gone. But this was in service to Ruth Ann. Since she'd moved home, he missed her constant laughter, mischief, and even her jabs at him. Just this once, he was going to put his sister before the ranch. But if he confessed that to her, she'd argue with him.

She glanced over at his side of the truck. "You're a good brother."

"Yeah, that's not what you usually say. When I remind you of this later, you'll say it was the drugs talking."

"Nah. I wouldn't do that. I'm going to shut my eyes for just a minute now."

"Before you go to sleep, tell me if you're packed for the trip."

"All ready to go. The last thing to do was to load the van and head out."

"Good. You rest. I'll take care of everything."

And he did. By late afternoon, Holt had made it to Houston, gotten his sister checked into the hotel, and had her resting with the remote control in her hand. They'd had a huge argument about her lying about for the remainder of the day. Holt won.

He and CeeCee quickly put the booth together and got everything ready for Quilt Market, which was to start in the morning. He wasn't much on the big city but was glad dinner was readily available. He picked up Ruth Ann's food and walked across the street to deliver it to her.

She shot him a sour expression as he came through the door.

"What's that look for?" he asked.

"You don't have time to be here," she complained, acting more like herself.

"Well, I made time."

"What are you going to do while you're here? Look at the quilts? Go shopping in the booths?"

Holt had given it some thought while he'd driven to Houston. "I'll probably do what I did when I was taking Dad for his treatments and waiting for him to get done."

"Really? Going to taxi all the old ladies around the city?"

"Sure. Why not? I've dusted off my Uber sign and everything."

Chapter 2

Paige's first morning at the hotel didn't start out well. The blow dryer in her room was dead, which forced her downstairs to the front desk with wet hair, as the Orchid was short-staffed. The woman behind the reception desk was apologetic, so Paige smiled, took the replacement dryer, and hurried back to her room. Thirty minutes later, she was relatively presentable. She donned her lanyard with her credentialed nametag and headed downstairs for breakfast.

The dining room was only half full, compared to what it had been two years ago at the other location. Paige took her place in line for the buffet.

The short white-haired woman in front of her spoke with a shake of her head and a roll of her eyes. "I feel bamboozled. I thought this was the Orchid Hotel I stayed in last time. Now my Houston friend has to pick me up every day on her way in."

Paige gave her a sympathetic smile. "You're not

alone. I thought I was booking the same place, too, from two years ago."

The two of them exchanged pleasantries about where they were from and what quilt shop they were associated with. At the end of the buffet, they parted ways, as the older woman had friends to sit with. Two years ago, Paige was apprehensive about attending an event like this alone but in her travels since, she'd found that quilters at these events were a friendly lot and she wasn't worried as she took a seat by herself. Surely someone would claim the seat across from her or speak to her from another table.

She glanced around and chose her spot next to a table with other people wearing their name tags for Quilt Market. But as she sat, a tall, gorgeous man, sporting a Stetson, a black western shirt, nice jeans, and cowboy boots ambled into the dining room. All the women stared, some of them might have even drooled. Stetson was a big guy with big shoulders. He had dark blond hair with the perfect amount of beard that made him look like the all-American man, ready for the cover of this year's *Delectable Cowboys,* if there were such a thing.

"I do like a good-looking cowboy and I'm single," said the spunky senior at the table next to Paige's.

Paige smiled at her brazenness.

"Selma, he's young enough to be your grandson," the other senior chided.

"I don't mind. I like 'em young. What do you think, is he thirty-two?"

Stetson tipped his hat to the table. "Thirty-four, ma'am. Last April fifteenth. Tax Day." Stetson's dimples were captivating and his deep blue eyes weren't shabby either. Paige had the urge to stand up and push back that hat to get a better look at his face. But she came to her senses quickly. This kind of rash fantasizing was how she'd gotten herself into a mess before.

Paige's neighbor giggled. Selma put out her hand to Stetson. "I'm Selma. Nice to meet you."

Stetson shook it. "Are y'all here for Quilt Market?"

"What do you know about Quilt Market?" Selma's friend said skeptically. "You don't look like any quilter I've ever met."

"I'm just here to help my sister."

Selma pulled out a pen. "Now what booth would that be?"

Stetson looked like he was thinking. "Booth 1015, I believe. The Circle J Quilt Shop. The booth carries a lot of wool products. The right side has nothing but wool batting. You won't be able to miss it."

"Not if you're in it! We'll make it *number one* on our list today," Selma said.

Stetson beamed with mischief in his eyes. "She'll be mighty happy to see you. Her name's Ruth Ann. She'll be the one in a sling. Dislocated her shoulder while packing for Houston. You can tell her that I sent you."

Selma's smile faded. "You won't be there?"

"No, ma'am. I'm just the pack mule, helping her to move in and then to help move out again after the quilt show is over next weekend." Stetson didn't give them a chance to speak more. "It was lovely to meet you." He tipped his hat at them both and the ladies blushed.

Paige was quite amused by this exchange until Stetson's stunning blue eyes landed on her.

"'Morning." He tipped his hat to her as well before he sauntered away.

Paige thought she might slide out of her seat because she'd gone all soft and gooey on the inside. She immediately straightened and quit staring at him.

Selma leaned over to watch his backside. "Nice booty," she said, grinning.

"Leave the poor man alone and stop ogling," Selma's friend hissed.

Selma locked eyes with Paige. "What about you? How old are you? I bet you're just the right age to tame that cowboy."

Paige smiled but shook her head. "I'm thirty-three but I'm definitely not interested." He was the kind of man that could get Paige into all kinds of trouble.

Selma turned back to her friend. "Louise, take her pulse. We need to make sure that that girl ain't dead."

Paige laughed. "Not dead. Just taking a break from dating."

"It's time to get back in the saddle, missy," Selma said.

Surprisingly, Louise nodded. "You're too pretty to waste it." She patted her bob and Paige could tell she'd been a beauty back in her day. "You better use it now before you end up like us—"

"Old, decrepit, but can still appreciate a good-looking man," Selma finished.

Louise peered at her as if she had better than twenty-twenty vision, maybe X-ray vision. "You have a quilt hanging in the show." She'd said it as a statement and not a question.

Paige gasped. "How did you know?"

Selma laughed. "It's Louise's superpower."

Louise scoffed. "I recognize the name—*your name*. I helped hang the quilts this year."

"How do you know my name?" Paige was feeling a little exposed.

"It's on your name tag."

Paige usually kept it flipped over until she got to the show. Her broken hair dryer and feeling frazzled this morning must've made her forget. "Yes, of course," she said as she turned it over.

Selma pointed to the table where Paige had set her phone. "Do you have a picture of your quilt with you?"

Paige pulled up an image of her Sweater Sampler quilt, which had been inspired by the different designs on men's sweaters at their local hardware store in Sweet Home. She handed Selma her phone. "I like to play with plaids, dots, and stripes."

Selma laughed good-naturedly. "I can see that. I love how you put them all together—willy-nilly but still organized. Genius."

These ladies were a hoot, but Paige was feeling self-conscious and needed to redirect the conversation away from her. "So, where are you two from?"

For the rest of breakfast they got to know each other. She told them where she lived, that she designed quilts, and how she was a quilt instructor. The ladies riddled her with questions, especially her availability in the spring. Paige answered every query, feeling grateful that Stetson didn't take a seat in her line of sight, else she might've not been so clearheaded. Yes, a couple of times she leaned over to peek at him, to make sure that he stayed near the coffee station, but she had no interest in him at all.

She headed back to her room to brush her teeth and gather her rolling bag for the first day of Quilt Market. Before she returned downstairs, she ordered an Uber. She mused to herself on the elevator ride down to the lobby that this morning's breakfast had been very entertaining. But she had bigger things to think about, like whether she could get into the quilt side of the ballroom this early to see her Sweater Sampler quilt hanging in the show, definitely the pinnacle of her quilting career.

But her thoughts kept returning to the man wearing the Stetson, dimples that went on forever, and the smile that took her breath away. All ridiculous thoughts! She willed herself to see the weasel Malcolm Landis wearing that Stetson and stealing her designs all over again . . . and that did the trick. That would keep her from dreaming about Stetson for the rest of the day.

Holt sat behind the wheel of his truck and hung his Uber sign. He'd gotten a kick out of the ladies at breakfast this morning, which was the reason he didn't mind doing a little taxiing for people like them today. He turned on the app and a potential customer popped in right here at the hotel. He accepted and pulled around to the front.

Three minutes later, he was shocked when the filly

from breakfast, with dark hair and bright blue eyes, rolled her bag out of the hotel. She stopped short after looking at his truck, glanced at her phone in disbelief, and then frowned at him. What did he do to deserve that?

He hopped out and reached for her roller bag. "Howdy."

"Hi." She acted like she wasn't going to hand over her bag. But finally she did.

"Would you like to sit in the front or in the second-row seat?"

"The front is fine."

He carefully set her bag in the second row. "Your bag feels mighty light."

She was quiet for a long moment but then replied, "It won't be by the end of the day." She opened the door and climbed in.

As he got in the truck, he mused that he'd landed upon the rarest of females—a quiet one.

He started the truck and pulled out. "I'm Holt Champion," he said, though he normally didn't introduce himself.

She gave a perfunctory nod. "Nice to meet you." She didn't give him her name.

Smart lady. He admired that. At breakfast, he saw she was wearing a name tag, but from where he stood, he couldn't read it. Now her name tag was flipped over and he couldn't very well ask her to show it to him, now could he?

More small talk was in order so he said, "Those ladies this morning were something."

"Yes."

For a second he thought that was all she was going to say but then she added, "You made their day."

"Nah. They made mine. Nice ladies." The cab went quiet. But then he said, "Where are you from?"

While he was glancing at her, he caught her raised eyebrows and her it's-none-of-your-business look, the kind of look that said he might've crossed a line.

He filled in the empty silence with more information about himself. "If you're wondering, I'm not from Houston. I hail from a ranch a couple hours from here."

"I see."

But he didn't think that she did. "Normally, I'm a rancher. But since I have to hang around to help my injured sister"—for surely his passenger had heard the tale of Ruth Ann this morning—"I thought I'd turn on my Uber app."

"A rancher who's an Uber driver?" She sounded like she didn't believe him.

"Yeah. I started driving for them while waiting for my dad to get done with his chemo and radiation treatments." Which was more than he'd said to most people on the subject.

"How's—"

Holt cut her off. "My dad's passed. He's in a better place. Along with my mom." He didn't know why he was telling her all this and decided to clamp his lips shut for the rest of the short trip.

"Alaska," the filly said.

"Excuse me?"

"I live in Alaska. In an incredibly small town."

"It can't be smaller than Last Stop, the closest town to the ranch. Population 825."

"Population 573," she said as if she'd won the contest for smallest town.

Holt liked her smile. "I wonder if Last Stop would feel like a busy metropolis compared to where you come from. And you're certainly a long way from home. Do you own a quilt shop, then?"

"Oh, no. I'm just a quilt designer, here on behalf of our local shop to buy fabric and to check out what's new in quilting. I assume your sister owns a quilt shop?"

"Actually, she's a professor of textiles. She's on sabbatical"—though it wasn't exactly a sabbatical—"but she's here at Quilt Market to teach a couple of classes. She'll spend the majority of her time, though, working in the Circle J booth. Our friend CeeCee owns the local quilt shop. And as I said at breakfast, she specializes in wool products for quilts." He didn't tell the filly that CeeCee acquired a good amount of her wool from his sheep. "CeeCee also owns the Circle J ranch. Her quilt shop is small but she does well. She has a strong online business."

"I'm surprised how much you know about wool and the business of quilting. I would think the typical rancher would know very little."

"I was raised by a quilter and been around them my whole life," Holt said. "My mother was the president of the local quilt guild for many years. My grandmothers before her. And of course, Ruth Ann's life is all about the art of quilting."

"That's quite a legacy. Do you quilt?" she asked seriously.

"No. But I do appreciate the hard work that goes into making them."

"What's the focus of your ranch?"

"You know something about ranching?" he asked.

"We have a lot of homesteads near the town where I live. I have friends who have livestock, and of course, I keep a garden in the summer."

Holt realized they were almost to the convention center and he hadn't even gotten her name yet. The time had flown. He pulled in front, feeling disappointed that the drive was over. Maybe he'd see her at breakfast tomorrow morning. The odds of him being randomly picked again to be her driver were astronomical. It would surely unnerve her if he suggested that she reserve his Uber service while she was here. He would just have to be grateful for getting to talk to her for these few minutes.

He hopped out and retrieved her bag.

"It was nice to meet you, Holt," the mystery woman from Alaska said.

"Nice to meet you, too."

She looked at the ground and to the right of him and finally back to meet his eyes. "My name is Paige."

As soon as Holt's truck pulled away, Paige pulled out a folder and fanned herself. Probably because it was humid this morning and not because Holt was a one-hundred-percent manly hunk of testosterone with a high dose of charm, smiles, and that darn twinkle in his eyes. She'd never met anyone like him and doubted that she would ever again. She fought hard against figuring out a way to run into him—accidentally on purpose. She tried to stop her whimsical thoughts, but ideas kept popping into her head. She could be waiting when the breakfast area opened in the morning, hoping to see him then. She could call Uber and see if they would give her his digits. But she stopped her brain from spiraling out of control. *Pre–Malcolm Paige* would have spent many happy hours fantasizing about how to track down the cowboy, but *Post–Malcolm Paige* had learned her lesson. And that lesson was to flee as fast as she could in the opposite direction of men like Holt Champion. With all things being equal, and if the properties of mathematics held up in the realm of relationships—especially when it came to Paige picking guys—Holt had the potential to devastate her. Then why was she wasting one second thinking about him and how good he looked in that hat?

She wasn't!

She hoisted the Wishing Quilt tote securely on her shoulder, rolled her bag inside the convention center, made her way to the ballroom's entrance, showed her badge to the attendant, and then entered. She checked her phone and saw she had time to kill before her first fabric appointment, so she went to see her quilt hanging in the show. After ten minutes, she finally found it. She looked around to see if anyone was watching before she pulled out her phone and took a couple of selfies that would remind her, *My quilt was here!*

She still had a little time, so she headed back to the vendor section and started down the first aisle. She picked up flyers, listened to pitches, and made notes of several booths to come back to later. She almost stayed too long in the first aisle and then had to rush to make her appointment and place the quilt shop order for Hope. The whole time she was sitting at the desk, flipping through swatches, Paige was working up the nerve to ask if there was anyone she could speak with about her own fabric designs. But the truth was, she wasn't sure she was ready. Wasn't sure her sketches were good enough. And then too fearful to show them anyway. There was always the possibility that it could happen again, that someone could steal her designs.

In the afternoon, Paige met with the second fabric company, placed an order, and was still unable to work up the nerve to get her fabric ideas in front of the right person. Afterward, she visited several more aisles of vendors, being systematic, heading down one row after another, while taking notes for Hope about interesting new products.

She was embarrassed to admit that she was curious about Holt's sister in the Circle J booth. After one bathroom break, she found herself heading for aisle 1000. She didn't go directly to Circle J's booth but to the one across from it. She was ashamed of herself for being a stalker, watching Holt's sister as she talked to customers. Holt's sister seemed nice. After a while, Paige slipped away back to her place in aisle 600.

Before she knew it, Quilt Market was closing for the day. She was exhausted and exhilarated after taking in so many new techniques, new fabrics, and new gadgets.

Just like the last time she was in Houston, Paige watched as many groups of women left the convention center to have dinner together. A little pang of loneliness overcame her. But she was consoled, knowing that when the Hanahan sisters arrived next Wednesday that she, too, would have a group to hang out with in the evening.

Paige decided to order takeout from Pappadeaux before heading back to the hotel. As she rolled her much heavier bag to the end of the convention center, she wondered if Holt would somehow end up as her Uber driver again. Probably not.

She opened the restaurant door, near the pickup order counter . . . and couldn't believe her eyes! Holt was standing in line, chatting with three quilters who were waiting to get their meals. She couldn't decide whether to walk forward and take her place behind him, or to leave the restaurant before being seen.

From behind, someone tapped her shoulder. "Excuse me?" The woman was very tall with perfectly coiffed gray hair, and was very loud. "Are you waiting in line?"

Holt spun around as if his name had been called. His laser focus eyes landed on Paige and he broke into a smile. "Hello, Miss Paige."

She was between a rock and a hard place, worried for her good intentions that if she got any nearer to him, her resolve would disappear. But apparently, her growling stomach won out because she broke eye contact with Holt and turned back to the tall woman. "Yes, I'm in line." Paige scooted closer to him, trying not to stare at his dimples.

"Funny meeting you here," he said, before stepping to the side so the other quilters he'd been speaking to could see her. "Ladies, this is my new friend, Paige. She's a quilt designer and instructor from Alaska."

"Oh," they all said together.

He continued to tell Paige their names, but she felt too befuddled by the sound of his Texas drawl and the blue of his eyes to fully grasp the introductions properly.

As the quilters were telling Paige where they were from, they were interrupted by the cashier, who motioned them forward to pick up their food.

"Any plans for this evening?" Holt asked Paige pleasantly.

Too pleasantly for me. His smooth voice only got her heart to pounding faster.

And she wondered now why she'd let her guard down on the ride to the convention center this morning. If she'd had a bit of sense, she would've kept the wall up between them, as she'd planned to do when she'd seen him in his truck. He had looked all amiable and handsome and just the most perfect man to write home about.

"Well, uh," she started, trying to pull her thoughts away from the twinkle in his eyes. But she couldn't help but think that her and Holt's children would have blue eyes, too, since that was her only good feature and his eyes were, well, perfect. "Uh, yes, I have to go through all the literature I picked up today and call the quilt shop owner back home to tell her how much I spent." Paige gave an anxious laugh. "It's a little unnerving to spend someone else's money." She wouldn't admit that not all of her jitters were caused by the thousands she'd charged on Hope's account.

"I'm sure you did fine," Holt said encouragingly.

Paige pulled it together a bit and asked, "How is your sister doing? Feeling better?"

"She's plum tuckered. Ruth Ann left the booth early and got her meal to take back to the Hilton." He pointed out the window to the hotel. "She seemed in good spirits, though."

"That's good." Paige clutched her hands, not sure what to do with them. And also a little afraid she might reach up and run a hand along his jawline to feel his perfectly trimmed beard. "Quilt shows can certainly put quilters in good spirits but it's exhausting, too. Did you get a chance to look at the quilts today?"

But Holt was called forward to order his meal. When he was done, he didn't leave the ordering area but waited for her to order, too.

They conversed easily about the weather until his meal came. He continued to visit with her until her salad was ready, too.

But then she didn't know what to do as she'd been planning to order an Uber to go back to the hotel and chill out in her room. She looked down at her salad as if it could offer up any suggestions.

Holt must've sensed her uneasiness. "Listen, I'm headed back now. Would you like a ride, no charge?"

But this made her feel weird. At the very least, she should be paying him for that charming smile he was giving her. It kind of lit up her world. Made her think of flowers in spring. Love songs. And holding hands.

But wasn't it *charm* that had gotten her into trouble the last time she was in Houston?

Holt turned and put a hand on her back. "Come on. You look hungry. The truck is this way."

Oh, well, what could one more ride in his truck hurt, as long as she protected herself and didn't fall for him.

On the trip to the hotel, Holt chatted about his ranch. When he parked, he didn't immediately open his door but turned to her. "It's nice out tonight. I thought I might eat at one of the picnic tables in the courtyard. I wondered if you would like to join me? I would appreciate the company."

Why was he doing this to her? Could he see that she was an easy target? Was WILL FALL FOR ANY GOOD-LOOKING GUY stamped on her forehead? "Do you not like to eat alone?"

He laughed. "I guess not. I'm used to eating with my rowdy cowhands around our large kitchen table."

"I wouldn't be able to fill their shoes because I'm not feeling all that rowdy. Quilt Market has zapped some of my reserves," she confessed.

"But I am enjoying your company." He stared at her for a long moment. "Can I be honest with you about something?"

"That depends on whether I want to hear it or not," she said truthfully.

His eyebrows furrowed. "I feel as if we've met before. Like we're old friends. Is it just me, or do you feel it, too?"

Great line, she thought. But honestly, it didn't feel like he was delivering a line. And she was feeling it, too, that they'd known each other for years. But she couldn't trust herself to know what was real and what wasn't. Her DNA was programmed to leap before she looked.

She was right back to that spot between a rock and a hard place. If he'd opened his arms, she probably would've stepped right into them. She should say *good night* and head to her room. But she couldn't make herself do it. Finally she opened her mouth, but what came out was uncensored. "I would remember a man like you." If she was being romantic, she'd tell him that she did know him from another place, another time. Another lifetime. She'd say all kinds of ridiculous things but would only end up regretting them later. For now, she was regretting what she'd just said. "I'd remember you because you're . . . so *tall*," she said awkwardly. Then frantically tried to come up with something else to say. "Um, I don't know many men that are as tall as you." She sounded so lame! Someone needed to gag her! "You're so kind. I think you're the friendliest man I've ever met. Something about the way you engaged the older women today was quite endearing." The second it came out of her mouth, she thought she was going to die of embarrassment.

He gave a hearty laugh. "You are the funniest little thing." He smiled and shook his head. "This morning I could hardly get you to say a word. And now . . ."

She had to take control of this thing before she said or did something more idiotic. "Were you close to your grandmother?" Which was the natural progression from what she'd said before.

"Grandmothers," he corrected. "Grandma Aida and Grandma Margaret. How did you know we were close?"

"A lucky guess. You don't seem to mind the elderly women here."

"Not at all. As you guessed, they all remind me of

my grandmas. Both sides. Ruth Ann and I were lucky to have one set of grandparents living with us at the ranch when we were growing up, and the other set just down the lane." He got a twinkle in his eyes again. "Having them both right there was a real advantage for a growing boy."

"How's that?"

He laughed. "Always bound to be homemade cookies either at home or in walking distance."

She laughed right along with him this time as they both got out of the truck. She'd never answered him about sharing dinner together but followed him to the courtyard and sat at the covered picnic table across from him.

Tomorrow I'll be on my guard, she told herself. But right now, her meal tasted wonderful and they talked and talked. She told him how she'd loved growing up in a small community, her plan to move to Fairbanks to be closer to the airport, and even a little about her disgruntled mother. Paige was having a really good time and tried not to worry that the reason might have to do with the company she was keeping.

He glanced at the ground and then reached down. "Did you drop something? A notebook?" He held it up for her.

She plucked it out of his hand. "How did that happen?" She glanced at her Wishing Quilt tote bag and frowned. She must've forgotten to snap it shut after she replaced her wallet. She stowed her sketchbook safely away.

"What is that? A drawing pad?" he asked.

"Yes, just some sketches of quilts. And something

else." Because she was feeling all warm and cozy with him, she told him her secret. "I'm thinking about getting into fabric design." But she immediately regretted sharing that. Revealing secrets—whether her own or others'—was never a good idea.

"That's funny. At one time, Ruth Ann talked about getting into fabric design, too."

It wasn't funny at all. But there had to be tons of people here at Quilt Market that dreamed of creating their own fabric, just like her.

But then he continued. "Apparently, Ruth Ann has given up on the idea because she hasn't talked about it for ages. Not since she got married and now divorced." Holt smiled at Paige so congenially that she decided to forget the coincidence.

When they finished eating, they remained there, chatting, getting to know more about each other until well into the night.

Even though she wanted their time together to continue, she stood and was quite proud of herself for having the willpower to call it quits for the night. "I better get to my room. I need to check in with the shop owner."

"Hope Stone, right?"

"Yes." It pleased Paige that he'd remembered the details of their conversation.

Holt stood, too, and once again, she imagined herself stepping into his arms and being held. But that was fanciful thinking—harmful thinking—the kind of thinking that had gotten her into trouble before.

"I'll walk you in," he said, sounding protective, in that baritone of his.

When they reached the elevator, she was feeling self-conscious again.

"What floor?" he asked.

"Fourth." She was surprised when he gave her a look. "What is it?"

"That's my floor, too. Room 418."

Oh, the universe was having a heyday with her as Paige was pretty sure that Holt's room was directly across the hall from hers!

She kept her eyes trained on the doors as the elevator went up, feeling certain he was looking at her. She wasn't scared of him but she was scared of herself—how easily she'd been fooled before and how easily she could be fooled again, if her heart had any say in the matter over Holt Champion.

When they reached the fourth floor, Holt waited until she walked out first. They strode down the hallway together in silence. When she reached her door, she finally turned to face him. "Good night." She didn't know what else to say because what was coming to mind was ridiculous. *I had a really great time.* Or *I wish the evening didn't have to end.* Or even more pressing, *Do you want to have breakfast in the morning and then hang out with me all day at Quilt Market?*

But she kept all those sentiments and invitations to herself.

"If it's okay, I'd like to chauffeur you in the morning," he said, taking her off guard.

"Um, sure."

"See you at breakfast around the same time?" he asked.

She nodded, speechless.

From his door, across the hall, he tipped his hat. "Good night, Paige."

She wished he hadn't done that because it made her resolve melt a little . . . okay, melt a lot. Her resolve had been dwindling all evening. With every smile from him. With every kind word. With the way he looked at her as if he could see into her soul.

She shook the sentimental thought away, quickly slid her key card, and locked herself inside. She leaned against the door. "What's wrong with me?" But she knew, and couldn't blame *Houston* anymore. She should've lifted her moratorium on dating a while back. She should've been going out with every guy in Sweet Home and the surrounding areas. She should've been stockpiling jaded feelings toward men. Then maybe she wouldn't be wound so tight and having romantic notions about riding off into the sunset with that cowboy across the hall.

She pushed away from the door, knowing she should call Hope. Or call Lolly and hash through the day—talk about the cowboy she'd met and how she feared she was heading down the same path of heartache again.

But instead, Paige pulled out her sketchbook because something more pressing was on her mind. She was going to design a new plaid quilt, something different, something with a cowboy, a Stetson hat, cowboy boots, and a nice pickup truck. Just to get it all out of her system now. Then she'd be able to put her focus back on what she really wanted out of this trip to Houston: a fabric line of her own, but most of all . . . peace of mind. She wasn't going to let what happened before . . . happen again.

Chapter 3

As Holt sat in the chair by the window in his hotel room, he pulled out his phone and called his sister. When she picked up, he asked, "Hey. How are you feeling? Rested?"

"Where have you been?" Ruth Ann started in, her words dripping with irritation. "I've been trying to call you!"

"My phone was on silent."

"That doesn't answer my question."

Holt was at a crossroads. These days he seldom, if ever, talked to his sister about his personal relationships. At one time, they were on the same page as he'd pretty much been dating Allison since he was fifteen and she'd lived on the next ranch over from theirs. He, Allison, and Ruth Ann had all played together as kids. But things changed when he called it quits with Allison. Since then, whenever Ruth Ann tried to grill him about his breakup with Allison, he'd shut her down. Ruth Ann still hadn't forgiven him, as Ruth Ann had always viewed the two of them as sisters. In the last two years, Ruth Ann had been relentless, arguing that Allison was part of the family and Holt had no right to break up with her. What Ruth Ann couldn't comprehend, and what he'd learned the hard way, was that long-distance relationships didn't work. No ifs, ands, or buts about it. He'd moved on in his mind, though he hadn't had time to date, with taking care of the ranch and all.

But he wanted to talk to someone tonight and it might as well be his sister. "I had dinner with one of the quilters."

"Either you work fast or you're talking about one of the older ladies."

Definitely not one of the older quilters. "Her name is Paige. She's about my age. We ran into each other when I was getting my supper." He left out the part where he'd seen her at breakfast and thought she was the prettiest little thing he'd ever seen. Or the part where the breakfast ladies had caught up with him at the convention center and told him that Paige had a quilt in the show, a gorgeous plaid Sampler quilt that would look great hanging behind his desk in his home office. And he definitely didn't tell Ruth Ann about how he'd been Paige's Uber driver. It rang too much of a pickup.

"So was it a *date* date?" Ruth Ann asked. "Or just a friend thing?"

He didn't know. "Just a friend thing." But strangely, he wanted it to be more. How much more, he didn't know.

"Tell me about her. Where does she live?"

This was the tricky part. He could've made something up, but in the past, he mostly told his sister the truth. "Paige lives in Alaska."

"What?" Ruth Ann was outraged. "You broke up with Ally because you said long-distance relationships don't work. But now you're dating someone from Alaska?"

"I told you it was just a *friend thing*. No one's talking about getting married. It was just two friends sitting in the courtyard here at the hotel, eating the food that we each paid for separately." He was thinking that Ruth Ann was acting pretty high-and-mighty about who he should date, when she'd chosen horribly for herself and had a painful divorce to show for it. He started to tell her so but he held his tongue to keep from digging at that wound.

"This woman is staying at the same hotel as you?" Her pitch had risen and her words were an accusation.

He should've kept his mouth shut in the first place. "Yes, she's staying at this hotel. Can we just drop it? I called to find out how you're doing. Not to get the third degree." But it occurred to him that the shoe was on the other foot. He was usually the one giving the lectures. He tried again. "Are you feeling all right?"

"I'm fine. A little sore. But mostly I'm exhausted. I feel like I've been rounding up cattle all day. But there's no need to worry," she said.

"Okay. I trust you'll tell me if I need to circle the wagons."

"I will. Listen, I made some plans today. Between Market and Festival, CeeCee and I have scheduled a few days at Pinwheel Place Retreat Center near Lockhart. Apparently, there are cows right outside the window to watch while we're sewing. We should feel right at home."

"Are you sure you're up for it? Maybe you should stay at the hotel here in town instead."

"Stop being a mother hen. I said I'm fine. You know how much I love to go on retreat."

"On second thought, I think it would be better if you go home to the ranch for a few days to recoup." Holt wondered if Rodger was going to read him the riot act by not stopping Ruth Ann from going with CeeCee.

"I'm headed to bed now," Ruth Ann said, putting an end to it. "What about you? Are you headed to bed?" She had a tone which implied, *Or are you staying up for late-night drinks with this so-called friend?*

"I'm going to watch some TV before hitting the hay. See you tomorrow." He hung up.

He walked over to the bed and picked up the remote, but he didn't turn on the TV. He stared at the blank screen.

Maybe Ruth Ann was right. Maybe he shouldn't have befriended Paige. Not *befriended* exactly, more that he'd set his sights on her. What was wrong with him that he was interested in someone who lived on the absolute other end of the country, almost the other end of the world! Hadn't he learned his lesson with Allison? True, he and Allison had both grown up together in Texas, but once she experienced Chicago, she'd never come back for longer than a day or two to see her dad next door. It took a long time to realize that Allison had no interest in being a cowboy's wife and living out the rest of her days with Holt on the ranch.

But Paige wasn't the rancher's wife that he needed either, the person he saw himself with when he closed his eyes at night. He wanted someone to share his life with, not someone who was off galivanting to another quilt guild to teach like Paige was doing.

He wished he hadn't made plans for her to ride with him in the morning. Once again he thought, *what the heck had I been thinking?*

He dropped the remote on the bed and got to his feet, deciding he needed something to drink. He thought about going to the bar, but instead, he decided to grab a soda from the machine down the hall. He made sure he had his key and left the room. He couldn't help but glance over at Paige's door for signs of life. He didn't see any.

He trudged down the hall toward the vending machines. Before he turned the corner, he heard ice rumbling from the icemaker. He started to turn around and head back to his room; he really didn't want to see anyone right now. But he was already here. He stepped around the corner and stopped short.

Paige was standing in front of the ice machine in men's red striped pajamas with her dark hair pulled up in a ponytail and big horn-rimmed glasses on her face, making her bright blue eyes stand out even more. Which he didn't think was possible. She kind of took his breath away. A completely different side of Paige than he'd seen before. She was adorable and looking very clumsy, trying to juggle her ice bucket, a very large stainless-steel tumbler with a metal straw poking out of the top, and a paper cup with ice in it.

He reached out and successfully relieved her of the ice bucket. "Fancy meeting you here."

She looked stunned. "Oh. Hi." She glanced down at her men's pajamas as her cheeks turned to the same color as the stripes. "I, um, was thirsty. I like a lot of ice."

"I can see that." He couldn't help but grin at her. "That's one big cup you have there."

"Yes, well, when I travel, I try to stay hydrated." She made a motion as if to take back the ice bucket.

"How about if I help you back to your room?"

She paused, then said, "Yes. Okay. I would appreciate it."

They walked side by side, with her glancing up at him every so often. He couldn't help but stare back. *So much for keeping my distance.* But hadn't his father told him, when he was a boy, to always come to the aid of a lady who was in distress? It was the cowboy way.

At her door, Holt took the key from her and held the door wide for her to enter.

When she passed by, he got a whiff of something flowery, mixed with vanilla. Had she scrubbed her face with blossoms?

"Can you set the ice bucket by the TV?" she asked.

Her bed was covered with catalogs, pamphlets, and pieces of fabric. He didn't know where she was going to sleep tonight.

"I'm trying to get organized," she explained.

"You might need an extra suitcase to get all that home." He set down the ice bucket. Now was his chance to retract his invitation of breakfast and driving her to the convention center in the morning. But he couldn't. Instead, he headed for the door. "Sleep well."

He didn't wait for her to say anything but hightailed it across the hall to the sanctity of his own room. His heart was racing a little, as if he'd been chasing down a wild filly with a lasso in his hand.

But Paige wasn't a prize for him to win, because she would be nothing but trouble for him, if he kept wanting her the way he did. It was best if he went back to his original plan. After he gave her a ride in the morning, he would turn off his Uber app and put away his sign.

The next morning, Holt walked into the dining area, not looking for Paige, but in search of coffee. At least that's what he told himself. Of course, he couldn't stop his eyes from scanning the room, searching for her dark hair and stunning blue eyes. She sat near the coffee station. Selma and Louise were at her table, too. He wasn't exactly up to seeing them this morning either.

The second he walked by, Selma said, "Morning, cowboy. What did you think of Paige's quilt yesterday?"

He swung around and caught the shocked look on Paige's face.

"You didn't say anything last night about seeing my quilt," Paige said, frowning at him.

"Last night, you say?" Selma winked at her. "You didn't tell us that you and Cowboy had been moseying about together."

Holt rescued Paige. "Yes, I saw the quilt. I really

like it." *It was wonderful.* But he kept that sentiment to himself. Today, he was supposed to do a better job of keeping his distance, which would be easier to manage if he had a cup of joe. "Excuse me, ladies." He grabbed a mug and poured his coffee. He took a sip before setting his cup across from Paige.

But when he returned with a plate of food, Paige seemed to be in midsentence. "So just call or email me to fix a date. I'm looking forward to doing an event at your shop."

Selma patted her hand. "We are, too, sweetie." She nodded at Holt. "You can always bring him along, too, if you'd like."

Paige dropped her eyes to the table, looking embarrassed.

That's when Holt noticed that the older ladies had switched places so now he was to sit beside Paige.

"The sun was in my eyes," Selma said with mock innocence. "You don't mind, do you, cowboy?"

"No, ma'am." Actually, sitting next to Paige was better because he wouldn't have her directly in front of him, keeping him from getting lost while looking at her pretty little face. Except he could smell her shampoo from here. He took a swig of coffee to steady his nerves, also to bolster himself, to keep from leaning closer to the woman next to him. He put his focus on Louise. "What are you two up to today?"

"We plan to get through the rest of the booths. We're finishing up this afternoon and heading home," Louise said.

Selma chimed in, "Monday at Market is a snoozeville."

Because he wanted to prove that he was treating them all equally—prove it to them and to himself—he turned to Paige. "What about you?"

She glanced at him and then looked down at her plate. She seemed mighty uncomfortable. "Just more of the same. I have my marching orders from the quilt shop in Sweet Home."

He wondered what was wrong with her because she wasn't acting like herself. But come to think of it, he wasn't either. Their easy conversation of last night was gone . . . which was just as well.

Paige stood in her hotel room, perhaps even stalling, knowing Holt was waiting for her downstairs. It had been an awkward breakfast, not only because she was trying to keep an emotional—and physical—distance from the cowboy, but because Selma and Louise were looking on. Finally Paige grabbed her roller bag and her Wishing Quilt tote and headed for the elevator.

She found Holt sitting in his truck. Paige looked around to see if the older ladies were around. Not seeing them, she quickly opened the door and climbed into the cab, laying her roller bag across her lap.

"Can I put that in the back seat?"

"No. Let's get going," she said, watching the hotel's doors like a hawk.

He put the truck in gear and eased out of the parking lot. "Did you sleep well last night?"

"Not really," she said honestly. "You know how hotels can be." But it hadn't been the hotel's fault. "You?"

the hotel, the one that smelled of onions, burgers, and something hearty—maybe fried chicken. Country music and chatter poured from the door into the street. This kind of excitement was just what she needed to put her mind on more important things than Holt Champion. And hearing the music, made her think of using dots and plaid fabrics as treble clefs and music notes, a design she hadn't done before. Yes, she would get a table and immerse herself in the atmosphere, while she drew in her sketchbook.

But when she walked in the door, Holt and two women sat at a table near the entrance—his front and the women's backs. Paige didn't get the chance to sneak out before his eyes landed on her, as if he had a couple of homing devices installed in his retinas. She was disappointed with herself that his gaze could root her to the spot like it did.

Smiling, he shrugged, waved her over, and then leaned in, apparently to tell his women friends what he'd done. What choice did Paige have but to walk over to him, even if it was to decline his offer? Seriously, he was already juggling two women at the table, how could Casanova handle a third?

When the two women turned around, Paige saw that they were his sister in her sling, plus her booth mate. Hesitantly, Paige moved forward to their table as they scooted to make room for her.

Holt stood as the band started playing Garth Brooks's song *Unanswered Prayers*. He leaned over to speak into her ear. "Paige, this is Ruth Ann, my sister and her friend, CeeCee. I told you about them."

Paige smiled and shook hands with the two, though Ruth Ann seemed to be taking her measure and not smiling like CeeCee was.

"The band is pretty good, don't you think?" CeeCee hollered above the din.

"Yes. Very good," Paige answered. "The sound and the delicious smells drew me in."

Holt slid his menu over so Paige could share. She didn't miss Ruth Ann's eyebrows furrowing at the action.

Finally Ruth Ann spoke. "Holt tells me you're a quilt designer from Alaska."

"Yes. A town of less than six hundred people. We have a strong quilting group, though. Not much to do in the winter but sew," she said, hoping to raise a smile. But didn't get one from Ruth Ann.

"Well, it seems like all of us at the table grew up out in the boonies, then," CeeCee said good-naturedly.

"Except the weather in Texas is much nicer this time of year than it is at home." Paige couldn't figure out what she'd done to Ruth Ann. Did she think that Paige wasn't good enough for her brother?

The waitress made it to their table and took their orders. When she left, Paige decided to make Ruth Ann like her. "Holt tells me you're a professor, teaching textiles. Sounds fascinating."

"Yes," Ruth Ann replied flatly.

Paige tried again. "What is your area of expertise?"

Ruth Ann stared at her stonily and for a second Paige wondered if she wasn't going to answer. Finally she sighed and spoke. "Most textile degrees focus on the fashion industry. I'm lucky to explore textiles with my students through furniture, wall coverings, and of course, the quilting industry. I enjoy opening up their minds beyond what cute clothes they can make."

But Paige could tell Ruth Ann did care about what she was wearing. With Ruth Ann sitting next to her, Paige was able to glimpse Ruth Ann's stylishly wide-leg pants, a white knit blouse with black trim at the neckline, tucked in at the waist, plus a pair of stylish mules.

Ruth Ann looked down at what she was wearing. "Besides helping out in the booth, I'm teaching classes while I'm here."

"Trust me," Holt interjected, "she doesn't dress like that during lambing season."

Ruth Ann rolled her eyes at him.

CeeCee jumped in. "Did Holt tell you about their latest venture? We've been selling his wool products in my store and online. They're a big hit."

"Your booth is amazing. So much beautiful wool," Paige exclaimed before she realized what she was saying.

The looks on all their faces made her wish she could've put a sock in it . . . about ten seconds ago. She decided to come clean. "Okay, so, yeah, I was curious and surveyed your booth."

"I don't remember you stopping by," Ruth Ann said as if it were an allegation.

Paige shrugged. "I was feeling a little shy." She wasn't sure how Holt would feel about her scoping out his sister before he gave her a formal introduction. "Sorry. It's really a great booth. In fact, your aisle is on my list for tomorrow." She glanced at Ruth Ann's sling.

"Could you use my help in breaking down the booth at the end of Market? I plan to be here for Festival, so I'm not going anywhere."

CeeCee laughed. "The booth stays up. We're here for Festival, also. But we're going to Pinwheel Place Retreat Center between the two events. Would you like to join us?"

Paige didn't get to open her mouth before Holt answered for her. "She can't. She's busy."

Ruth Ann's eyebrows shot up. "Doing what?"

"Sightseeing," Holt said evenly. "She told me her plans last night."

Paige decided to throw him a life preserver by chiming in. "NASA and Galveston." It felt like she was stepping between the two siblings to stop an impending argument. Right there, Paige made a decision. Later tonight, she'd knock on Holt's door and cancel their outings. She didn't want to make more waves with Ruth Ann than she already had.

"Sounds lovely," CeeCee said.

The waitress brought their meals and for a time they were busy eating. Until Paige accidentally dropped her napkin. She and Holt went to get it at the same time and bumped heads.

"Sorry," he said. "Are you okay?" He reached under the table and squeezed her hand.

She felt like her eyes were going to bug out as she stared at him. But Ruth Ann and CeeCee didn't seem to notice, so Paige cleared her throat first before trying to speak. "I'm fine." And yes, it came out a little high-pitched.

He dropped her hand and returned to his burger.

When the check came, Holt insisted on paying for everyone's meal, which earned her another stern look from Ruth Ann.

After the bill was paid, they all walked out together but stopped just outside.

"I have to take these two back to their hotel," Holt said, directing his comment to Paige.

Which made her feel self-conscious with Ruth Ann frowning at the interaction. He didn't owe Paige an explanation. It was only happenstance anyway which brought them together tonight.

"Good night," Paige said to Ruth Ann and CeeCee. "I'll see you both at the booth tomorrow." She really had been eyeing the wool batting for herself, but now that she knew it came from Holt's ranch, Paige wanted it that much more. Silly, but true.

Ruth Ann and CeeCee said good night but only Holt looked back while they walked away. Paige went to her hotel room, thinking she would go through all the catalogs and brochures she picked up today. But once there, with the literature spread out on the bed and her hovering over all of it, she couldn't concentrate, not when Holt would be back any minute.

It didn't help that she kept popping up to run to the door to look through the peephole to see if the cowboy had returned. But she saw no Stetson, no broad shoulders. Over and over, she went back to the pamphlets and fabric on the bed and tried to work.

An hour passed and she decided that surely he must've returned by now. But when she went out in the hall and knocked on his door, he didn't answer. Her mind started racing at the implication. Was he out wooing another unsuspecting female? As she turned to go back to her room, the elevator dinged and he stepped out, stopped, and stared at her. She felt like she'd been caught.

"We have to talk," she said loud enough so he could hear.

"Fair enough." He sauntered toward her. "Your room or mine?"

"Very funny. How about down in the lobby? There's comfortable seating there." But *comfortable seating* had nothing to do with choosing that location; it was a public space. Immediately she wanted to change her answer because she remembered how romantic the sofa seemed an hour ago, how it sat in front of the crackling fire with an ambience meant for lovers. Someone should douse the fireplace with water before they got downstairs. Come to think of it, the flame growing inside her needed dousing, too. She started to suggest somewhere else but he interrupted her.

"Come on. Whatever has put that worried look on your face, I'm sure we can work it out." He put his hand to her back and ushered her toward the elevator before the doors closed.

She hurried in and took the far side because his touch, though innocent enough, had felt . . . *comforting*. Which was disconcerting. But wasn't *comforting* a nice way to feel when in the presence of a man? She shook the thought away because going down that track would only leave her feeling like she'd gotten run over by a train when the inevitable betrayal happened.

When they reached the lobby, she waited for him to sit first before taking her seat.

"What's this all about?" Holt reached over as if to touch her hand, but she pulled away.

"We can't go sightseeing together," she blurted. "Your sister wouldn't like it. She doesn't like me."

"Nonsense. She doesn't know you. Besides, we're just a couple of friends who are going to NASA and Galveston together." Holt made it sound oh-so innocent when Paige's whole being yearned for more.

She sat there in front of the cozy fire on the cozy couch, feeling all cozy toward Holt and believing him. No, just rationalizing, she reminded herself. But what could a little sightseeing hurt if she went into it with her eyes wide-open?

"Okay. You're right," she finally said.

He stood and held out his hand to her, as if to help her to her feet.

She waved him off. "I have to stop at the front desk before I go up."

"I'll wait for you," he offered.

"No. That's okay."

She watched him walk away in all his cowboy glory. She slumped back into the couch as the elevator doors closed, knowing the ugly truth.

"Man, I'm completely toast," she whispered to herself. And she was in too deep to really do anything about it.

Chapter 4

The room phone was ringing when Holt opened his door. He rushed to answer it.

"Hey," Ruth Ann said. "Have breakfast with Cee-Cee and me in the morning."

He didn't have to ask why. He already knew the answer: to keep him from having breakfast with Paige. He sighed. "What time and where?"

"Here at our hotel. Eight."

"See you then." In the next ten hours or so, he'd have to come up with a way to straighten out his sister.

First, though, he'd have to straighten out himself. But every time he looked at Paige or was near her, he forgot he was supposed to keep his distance. He kept telling both Paige and Ruth Ann that Paige was just a friend. But it sure didn't feel like it. He wanted nothing more than to pull Paige into his arms and kiss her. Just to see what it would feel like, what she would taste like. He kept imagining she was as sweet as the sugar cookies sold at church after Sunday service.

The next morning as he was leaving his hotel room, he considered knocking on Paige's door to let her know why he wouldn't see her at breakfast. But it was early and he didn't want to wake her. The first chance he got, though, he was going to get her number so he could leave her a message anytime he wanted.

But nothing she'd said or done gave him confidence that she liked him as much as he liked her. Actually, quite the opposite. He needed to find out what she was thinking. Just because he was curious, and not because he had any business starting up something with a woman who lived 4,200 miles away. Not that he was going to admit to looking up that factoid.

Fifteen minutes later he met up with Ruth Ann and CeeCee in their hotel's dining room. As soon as they sat with their plates in front of them, Ruth Ann started. "Work with us in the booth today. We need you."

CeeCee seemed surprised by the news but she remained quiet.

"Well?" Ruth Ann prompted.

By the look in her eyes, he could see she was worried that Paige was going to turn into *something* and she meant to nip it in the bud. Holt was at war with himself but he gave in to his little sister. "Sure. I'll help out. But I might take a few Uber requests if you start getting on my nerves, understood?"

Ruth Ann gave him her famous stink eye as if she was telepathically commanding him to keep Paige out of his truck.

CeeCee laughed. "I think that's fair. We'll both work real hard to stay on your good side. With you in the booth, maybe Ruth Ann and I can sneak away to check out some of the other vendors."

"Oh, don't leave me in the booth alone. I don't think your business could withstand my ignorance when it came to quilting doodads." Which wasn't completely true. But he certainly didn't want to be stuck by himself.

"Don't worry. Monday is dead in the booth," Ruth Ann said. "It really is just other vendors walking around scoping out the competition or catching up with old quilting friends that we only see at these events."

But that's not what happened. Not long after Holt took his place at the cash register, quilt shop owners started turning up in droves.

One remarked to CeeCee, "You have such a brain for marketing. Having a cowboy in your booth? Brilliant! Do you think I can hire him to make an appearance at my shop? I live in West Texas and we have a large selection of Texas fabrics."

Though the booth was crowded with women fawning over him and buying stuff, he felt invisible, like just another piece of meat in the butcher shop.

CeeCee laughed at the woman's remark and gave Holt a pitying glance. "Sorry. He's exclusive to Circle J. Isn't that right, Holt, darling?" Her drawl was poured on thick.

He played along and tipped his hat at the woman. "Sorry, ma'am. I'm loyal. A one-store cowboy. I only work for the Circle J."

The women crowding around him looked as if they were going to swoon. He couldn't wait to get back to the ranch. Heck, mucking out the stalls was more satisfying than this.

The morning and afternoon droned on with more of the same. The only reason he didn't hightail it to his truck was because CeeCee told him that she'd never had so many orders placed on the last day of Quilt Market.

CeeCee hollered to Ruth Ann across the booth, "R.A., we should've had your brother in the booth all along!"

"Next year," Ruth Ann promised, though there wasn't a chance in Hades that he'd do it.

When Holt had a minute with CeeCee alone, he said, "Thank you for asking Ruth Ann to help out. I'm grateful. Being here with you has really made a difference in her." He looked over at his sister. She seemed more like her rowdy self as her melancholy was gone.

A memory came back to him of his mother and grandmother sewing at the dining room table. The two of them were discussing how their quilting friends were priceless, *always making our lives better, especially during the tough times*. This was something that CeeCee had done for Ruth Ann.

When the day was almost over, Holt spotted Paige as she walked up to the booth, not looking at him but keeping her eyes on Ruth Ann and CeeCee.

"I need to place an order for wool batting and have it shipped home to Alaska for me," Paige said to Ruth Ann.

Ruth Ann glowered and tilted her head toward CeeCee, deferring to her. "She'll take your order." Holt wasn't happy with how his sister had spoken to Paige.

CeeCee pulled out a pad of paper. "Show me which ones you want." Paige followed her over to the rolls.

Ruth Ann frowned as the other two women discussed what Paige wanted. Holt eavesdropped and found out that Paige had a backlog of quilt tops that needed to be quilted for an upcoming trunk show. In the end, she handed over her credit card to Ruth Ann, who rang up her total and gave her a receipt.

At that moment, the announcer came over the intercom to say that Quilt Market had ended.

Holt hadn't heard what Ruth Ann just said to Paige, but Paige didn't seem happy about it.

While CeeCee chatted with Paige, Ruth Ann joined him, crossing her arms over her chest. "So, big brother, you're heading home for a few days?" She'd said it more as a statement than a question.

Holt gave her a hard stare. "Never you mind what I'm up to."

She dropped her arms and turned on him. "Well, Rodger texted earlier to say you weren't coming home during the interim."

Holt shook his head, disgusted with his sister and Rodger. He'd have to inform his foreman that in the future ranch business was none of Ruth Ann's concern, though she did hold a thirty-percent share.

CeeCee gave Paige a hug. "Thanks for the order. I might take you up on the offer during Festival."

"What offer?" Ruth Ann asked.

"Paige said she'd watch the booth for us, if we wanted to run off together to look at the other booths."

Begrudgingly Ruth Ann nodded, then turned back to Holt. "You should go home."

CeeCee and Ruth Ann closed up the booth, grabbed their bags, and left. When Holt looked around, Paige had gone, too. He had to two-step it to catch up with that filly. "Where are you going in such a hurry?"

"I've got things to do," she said.

"Yes," he agreed. "It's early. And there's been a change of plans. We're off to Galveston for dinner."

"Listen," Paige said, "I told you we can't go to dinner. And Ruth Ann said . . ."

"Yeah, what did Ruth Ann say?"

"Never mind."

"Tell me."

"Nothing really. Just that you'd been in a long-distance relationship before. I assured her that we're not in a relationship, that we're only friends." Paige frowned, then. "I'm not sure she believed me."

Holt wasn't going to respond to that. "Do you need to drop your things off at the hotel first or can we head to Galveston now? I found us a restaurant online that I think we'll both like." When she was silent for a long minute, he added, "You have to eat. Why not do it with me?"

She didn't look convinced.

He did the only thing he knew how to do: he'd have to corral the filly to get her to go where he wanted her to go. He put a hand on the small of her back and guided her toward the exit. He liked how it felt to have her by his side and he savored the moment.

"Stop at the hotel?" he asked again as they approached his truck.

"No. I guess I can just leave my bag in your vehicle." She seemed perplexed.

"Relax. We'll listen to a little country and western music and sing to the best ones, okay?"

That raised a smile from her. "What about some pop music instead?"

He chuckled and opened the door for her. "Sorry, Miss Paige. My ole truck here can only play country."

"Your truck looks brand-new."

"That's true but she's old at heart. A classic, really."

She laughed good-naturedly and he liked that about her. Once they got inside the vehicle, he felt the evening was going to turn out perfectly.

All the way to Galveston, they chatted easily about their day and he even got her to add her number to his phone. She seemed to enjoy his tales about how the quilters flooded into the Circle J booth, hounding him to speak so they could hear his Texas accent, and the countless selfies he'd been in today. He smiled over the number of miles she'd clocked on her pedometer from tramping all over the convention center. She seemed very animated when she talked about the new bookings she'd secured for her workshop in the new year. At the restaurant in Galveston they ate, with more lively conversation, while they watched the sunset from their table. Very romantic.

As they left the restaurant, he wasn't ready to head back to Houston. "Do you want to take a walk along the beach?" he asked.

"Sure," she said, grabbing her tote bag and following him outside.

On foot, they headed to the sand and surf with the night crowding in. He took her hand and was surprised

at how right it felt in his. In fact, her hand fit so perfectly that he was certain that they were meant to be together in this moment. Paige seemed content for them
to be linked, also, which made him even happier.

Earlier, they'd talked and talked but now they were
silent with only the sound of the crashing waves between them. No one else was around and he felt compelled to stop and pull her into his arms just to feel her
against him. She looked up into his face and he leaned
down to kiss her. She was sweet as cotton candy, so
much so that the kiss went on and on. So long that he
began hearing ringing in his ears.

She pulled away but not too far. "It's your phone."

"Oh." He didn't let go of her as he retrieved his cell
from his pocket. It was Rodger. "What's going on? Is
there a problem with the horses? The cattle? The
sheep?" Paige tried to step away but Holt pulled her
closer.

"No, no," Rodger said. "It's R.A. She's here. She
says she wants you to come home. She says she's not
feeling well."

"What's wrong?" Holt wanted specifics but decided
it didn't matter. "Never mind. I'm on my way." He
hung up.

"Is everything okay?" Paige asked.

"Problem at home. I have to get back. Now." He
took her hand and started walking. "I want you to
come with me." He wasn't ready to put distance between them yet. And to heck with what Ruth Ann felt
about it. But he was worried about his sister. It wasn't

like her to ask him to come home, even if she wasn't feeling well.

"You want me to come with you?" Paige seemed stunned.

"Yes. I want you to come to the ranch with me." He'd said it twice, mostly to make sure that he really meant it. This was an impulsive invitation but steeped with purpose, too. Since meeting Paige, he'd wondered how willing she would be to spend time at the ranch, see what a rancher's life was all about. He wouldn't let himself delve any deeper into the *why* of it.

"Okay," she said without hesitation.

He gave her a quick kiss and kept walking to the truck. "Don't worry about Festival. I'll get you back in time."

"My clothes?" she asked.

"We'll make a quick stop at the hotel on the way. And about seeing NASA, well, maybe you can play hooky one day from Festival. Even better, let's go early Wednesday morning before Preview Night starts?"

"I don't know." Paige frowned. "What about Ruth Ann?"

"She can find her own date for NASA," Holt deadpanned. But he would have to deal with his sister at some point, most certainly in the next several hours.

"You know what I mean. Ruth Ann won't like it, when she hears I went to the ranch with you."

He probably should've spoke up then and told her that Ruth Ann was already there. But if Paige knew, she would certainly say no to visiting the ranch.

Paige continued. "Let's make this clear. Going to NASA or the ranch, for that matter, is not a date."

Speak for yourself, Holt thought as he squeezed Paige's hand. He just hoped that Ruth Ann was okay. But maybe her not feeling one hundred percent might be just the thing to temper her response to the guest he was bringing home tonight.

Chapter 5

In her hotel room, Paige zipped up the small carry-on case she would use for the next two nights. She'd gone from being skeptical to excited at the prospect of seeing Holt's ranch. Not because she liked him, of course, but because she had a feeling that the ranch would give her more inspiration for the new line of quilts that she'd been designing—her Texas plaid and polka dot quilts. The ones that Holt inspired. An amazing idea came to her. What if she designed some Texas country fabric, too, to go with her quilt designs? She hadn't seen any fabric like the images that were popping into her head. As soon as she got into the truck, she would start sketching them.

But misgivings about going to the ranch with him floated alongside the amazing designs she was imagining. Well, she would ignore the misgivings and refuse to listen to the little voice in her head that told her that this could all go horribly wrong.

Holt texted. **I'm pulling the truck to the front now.**

"I better not keep the chariot waiting," she said as she grabbed her Wishing Quilt tote and wheeled her small bag out.

When she got to the lobby, she could see Holt's truck but didn't spot him at first. As she got close to the entrance, she saw him playing bellhop by transferring baggage from a taxi onto a luggage trolley. And that's when she saw who the women were that he was helping.

She ran outside. "What are you doing here?"

The Hanahan sisters turned to her with a surprised look on each of their faces but it was Lila Mae who spoke. "Betty and Charise were worried about you so we came a few days early. This was the only hotel in the area that currently had a room for us. I see now it was serendipitous."

"Yes." Suddenly Paige was back in the same quandary—*Should I stay or should I go?*—but for different reasons . . . *three* to be exact.

Charise pulled out a ten and held it out to Holt. "For your troubles."

Holt waved her off. "No, ma'am. No trouble at all." He looked at Paige. "Are you going to introduce me?"

The three sisters' mouths fell open, but it was Charise who squealed, "You know this handsome cowboy?"

"This is Holt Champion, *my friend*." Paige was trying to make that clear, but the ladies were peering at her as if they knew something more substantial was going on. "Holt, these wonderful ladies are my friends—Lila Mae, Charise, and Betty. The Hanahan sisters."

He tipped his hat at them. "Nice to make your acquaintances."

"How do you know our Paige?" Lila Mae asked protectively.

But Paige answered for him. "His sister dislocated her shoulder and he brought her to Houston and has been helping out in the booth."

"Booth 1015. The Circle J. Lots of wool products for quilting," Holt said, but he seemed pleased that Paige had spoken for him first. "I hope you can stop by the booth on Preview Night to say hi to my sister, Ruth Ann, and the owner of the shop, CeeCee."

"We'll do that," Lila Mae said, staring at Holt intently.

He turned back to Paige. "Do you need to stay here with your friends?" His mouth turned down more with each word as if he were disappointed that she might actually stay here instead of going with him.

Paige felt the need to explain to the sisters. "Holt asked me to go to his ranch with him until Wednesday. But if you ladies need me to, I'll stay here with you."

Once again Lila Mae took the measure of Holt before answering. "You go ahead. As long as there will be a proper chaperone when you get there."

Holt gave her an approving nod and a smile. "We have fifteen full-time ranch hands, a housekeeper who has a room in the main house, and Paige will have the guest room upstairs. My room is downstairs," Holt said, giving his last words the heaviest weight. "Does that fit the bill, ladies?"

"I guess," Lila Mae answered. "Paige, you will text if you need us?"

"Of course," she said. "But what will you do until Festival begins?"

Betty pulled out a notebook. "I've planned a two-day shop hop for us. Every quilt shop in the area. Doesn't it sound wonderful?"

"It does," Paige said.

"But going to the ranch with a cute cowboy sounds even better," Charise commented, which seemed to align with what Paige was thinking.

"All right, then." Lila Mae laid her hand on the trolley's bar. "Call when you get back to Houston."

Holt moved forward. "Ma'am, why don't you let me get your luggage up to your room for you?"

"Nope," Lila Mae said. "We're strong Texas gals. But thank you, anyway."

Paige hugged each sister and then smiled at Holt. "I'm ready."

The sisters watched while Holt opened the door for her and she climbed inside.

Paige waved. "I'll see you Wednesday."

They waved back, then went inside, each of them pushing a corner of the trolley.

Paige watched a second longer before pulling out her sketchbook and writing down and half sketching her new fabric ideas as they were coming to her fast. She didn't even care that she only had the dash lights to go by.

He glanced over. "What are you doing there?"

"New ideas that can't wait," she answered.

"I'm glad you're coming home with me," he said.

"Me, too," she replied. She had to admit that she liked to see him happy. But then she felt the need to backpedal. "The ranch should be a great place for me to get ideas for my quilts and future fabric." *Fingers crossed about having a line of fabric.*

"Oh." He sounded a bit disappointed.

She didn't mean to hurt him but she held her tongue instead of trying to fix things. More than anything, she wanted to reach over and squeeze his hand and make it better. "I can't wait to see your cattle, horses, and sheep."

"Good enough," he said.

They headed off to his ranch in the dark. "I noticed you carry your quilted tote everywhere with you," he said.

She hugged her tote bag. "It's made from a section of a quilt that my grandmother made a long time ago that she called the Wishing Quilt. It started out as lap-sized, but when I was in junior high, Grandma Doris subdivided it between us, giving me a piece, my mom a piece, and then keeping a piece for herself." Paige shrugged. "As you can see, I made mine into a tote. It's the last piece left of the heirloom." Somewhere along the way, Paige's mom had lost her piece. When Paige's grandma had died, her section of the quilt was accidentally thrown out by her mom; she hadn't realized how much Paige would've treasured having the old, tattered piece. She was still heartbroken over the loss. At least she still had her tote bag. "I'm worried about my Wishing Quilt tote, though. When I get back to Alaska, I plan to retire it by framing the motif for preservation's sake." She doubted she would ever have a daughter, but if by some miracle she did, she'd have a piece the Wishing Quilt to pass down to her.

"Why did your grandmother call it the Wishing Quilt?" Holt asked. "Does it grant wishes?"

Paige laughed. "I used to believe it did. But the truth is that the Wishing Quilt's only power was to make a little girl dream big. During naptime, I used to lie in Grandma Doris's bed and wish for the world. In a way, I guess, my wish did come true. I get to travel the world, or at least the United States, doing what I love." She wouldn't tell him how all three generations of women in her family, at one time or another, had wished upon the quilt, hoping Mr. Right was indeed just that. But in the end, they'd been disappointed. The Wishing Quilt didn't possess an ounce of magic when it came to bringing them the true love they'd wanted.

She glanced over at Holt's smiling face as he drove down the road and dared not to believe he could be the real thing, the one, but part of her wished he was.

Holt reached over the back of the seat and pulled out a quilt, presenting it to her. "This is my Truck quilt that Ruth Ann made for me. If you get sleepy, you can lay your head on it."

"Thanks." Paige stretched part of the quilt across her lap and used the rest to lean her head against the window. She felt very relaxed. Cozy. Warm.

She woke with a start as the truck stopped. "Are we there?"

"Yes."

Paige took it in. The house was a sprawling ranch-style home with a massive porch that stretched from one end of the house to the other and was lit up like it was noon on the Fourth of July. Nine rocking chairs were interspersed with four patio side tables, which were probably there to hold glasses of lemonade in the summer and hot apple cider for this time of year.

The front door opened and Ruth Ann came out, walking to the edge of the porch and stopping at the top step.

Paige's mouth dropped open. "I thought she was going on a retreat with CeeCee."

With the light behind Ruth Ann, her face was immediately plunged into darkness but her silhouette made her feelings clear as she'd slammed her hands on her hips. She must've seen Paige.

"What the . . ." Holt muttered as he opened his door and stepped out. "I thought she wasn't feeling well."

"Is that the reason you had to come home?" Paige asked. He should've told her!

He nodded and came around to Paige's side while she folded the quilt and stowed it behind the seat. Actually, she was stalling, trying to get a grasp of the situation, but mostly she felt like she'd stumbled into some kind of nightmarish drama.

Holt put his hand on Paige's back but dropped his hand when a second woman came out of the house and stepped on the porch. This one was tall, thin, and blond. Though it was dark, Paige could see that Blondie wasn't wearing blue jeans and a long-sleeved shirt like Ruth Ann. No, this one had on what looked like an expensive pantsuit that hung just the right way and swayed perfectly as she went to stand beside Holt's sister.

Blondie held up her hand. "Holt? Holt, honey, is that

you?" She had the sweetest Texan accent, which made Paige want to gag.

"What the heck is she doing here?" Holt growled.

With open arms, Blondie ran off the porch and threw herself at Holt, wrapping him up into a burrito hug. She kissed him! Kissed the same lips that Paige had kissed back at the beach!

Paige was disgusted with herself and mad at Holt. She'd been excited about coming to the ranch but clearly this had been a huge mistake. Just another tally to the mistake chart, the mental one she kept around for all those charming men that had swept her off her feet. *And my mother and grandmother off their feet, too.* Paige had been a fool to think Holt was different. And this was so much worse, because she was stuck. No Uber driver on duty to take her back to Houston so she could lick her wounds within the confines of her hotel room.

Holt set Blondie away from him. "What are you doing here, Allison?"

So Blondie has a name.

Allison reached out and pushed Holt's hair from his face. "I thought it was time for a visit."

Holt's eyes swung to Ruth Ann with deadly accuracy. "I want to talk to you."

Paige was glad he wasn't happy about Allison being here, but at the same time, she felt like the previously attentive cowboy had totally forgotten she existed.

But then he turned back and motioned to her. "Come on. Let me show you to your room."

Paige balked and stared at him. Clearly he'd lost his marbles. But she also felt helpless on what she could do while standing out here with the cool breeze chilling her while Ruth Ann's glare burned a whole through her. It would be easier to sequester herself in a room, call someone for help, anything to get away from these other women in Holt's life.

With as much dignity as she could muster, Paige followed Holt up onto the porch and into the house, while Ruth Ann shot daggers at her.

Once inside Paige couldn't exactly appreciate the Texan décor and how quilts were everywhere. Her stomach was roiling. If she could have, she would've found the heavy wood furniture, deep red, blue, and brown tones of the textiles very comforting. But nothing could soothe her broken spirit now.

Holt started up the stairs but spoke over his shoulder. "I'm really sorry, Paige. This was an ambush, meant for me, and here you got caught in the middle of it."

She reached out and touched his arm to stop him. "I know you can't take me back to Houston right now, but maybe you know of a shuttle service that I could call to come get me?"

He shook his head. "I don't want you to leave. I'm going to clear this up and then tomorrow, we'll have a whole day for me to show you around the ranch before we head to NASA the morning after."

Paige shook her head. "I can't stay here." *Not with Allison—beautiful Allison—of the long legs that go on forever.*

Holt ran a hand through his hair. "Why not?"

Paige rolled her eyes. "Because your girlfriend is here!"

Holt grabbed Paige's arms. "Allison is not my girl-friend."

"You kissing her just now sure told another story."

"I didn't kiss her. She kissed me."

"Potato, po-taw-toe."

"We broke up two years ago. I haven't heard from her or seen her since. Heaven only knows why she's here now."

Paige was pretty sure that Ruth Ann had had a hand in it.

"Give me a minute to find out what's going on, and to send Allison on her way."

"You can't kick her out into the night," Paige said.

"Don't worry about Allison. She grew up on the ranch next to ours. Her father still lives there. It's the reason we know her." Holt frowned at the window where he'd pointed. "I suspect it's the reason we were together for so long." The last bit he seemed to be saying to himself.

But that didn't make Paige feel better.

"Listen. In a nutshell, we grew apart, had separate dreams. Allison loves the big city and I don't want to be anywhere but here on this ranch."

That didn't make Paige feel much better either. Her life was in Alaska.

But realization hit like a bolt of fabric had whomped her in the stomach. Her life wasn't exactly in Alaska these days, but was on the road, doing quilting work-shops and presentations.

"Can you get unpacked? I'll be back in a few minutes to answer your questions. Okay?" Holt had a pained expression on his face.

"Sure." But she had no intention of unpacking or staying for that matter.

As soon as he left the room, she pulled out her cell phone, but that was a disappointment, too. She didn't have any bars to search for a ride back to Houston.

Holt stomped downstairs. He would get answers from his sister right now to find out what she told Allison to make her come.

But at the bottom of the steps, Allison waited with a cup of coffee in her hands, holding it out to him.

"I made it like you like it." Her voice was familiar, she was familiar, but he didn't reach for the coffee mug or for her.

"Tell me why you're here." Holt tried not to be angry with her as this surprise attack had to be all Ruth Ann's doing.

"I came to see you."

"But why now?"

She set his coffee on the side table that held a basket for keys and a larger basket for mail. "I've missed you." She stepped closer and laid a hand on his chest. "You're one of a kind, Holt Champion. I'm here to renegotiate the terms of our breakup."

He removed her hand from his chest. "This isn't the boardroom, Allison."

Her smile faded and the Chicagoan Allison returned—piercing gaze and demanding demeanor. "In a nutshell, I'm here to get you back."

A shuffling noise sounded from the top of the stairs. By the time Holt had turned around, he could only see Paige's back as she hurried away. *Dang it.* She'd heard Allison and once again he felt like a horse's backside for putting Paige in this situation.

"Go home, Allison." He started back up the steps but stopped as a strange thought hit him. Was his future really upstairs and his past behind him?

But then Allison spoke. "Yes. Good idea. I'll stay at Daddy's tonight"—she waved a dismissive hand to the upstairs—"while you take care of *that*. I'll be back in the morning for us to have a proper chat." She didn't wait for him to contradict her but walked out the door.

Before he could turn back, Ruth Ann appeared.

"Well?" she said, her tone expectant.

"Well, what?" He trudged back down the steps, glaring at his sister. "Never mind." He pointed to the door. "You and I are going to the porch for a talk." He didn't want Paige to overhear what Ruth Ann had to say.

Once they were outside, he realized he hadn't seen CeeCee. "Where's your cohort? Is CeeCee hiding out in one of the bedrooms while you stir the pot and meddle in other people's business?"

"She's not here. Why would you think that?" Ruth Ann asked.

Holt looked around. "How did you get home, then?"

"Rodger. He met us halfway."

"Rodger?" Holt was incensed.

"Yeah, Rodger. He does things, no questions asked," Ruth Ann said smugly.

"Listen. You shouldn't have used Rodger that way."

"What way?"

Holt really didn't want to say this but he had to wave off his sister. "I don't know this for sure, but Rodger"—the words got stuck in Holt's mouth, but then he pushed on anyway—"Rodger likes you." Holt felt like he was in fifth grade all over again, passing notes for a friend. *Mark an X here if you like Rodger.* "And I don't want you to take advantage of his feelings. He's my fore-man, not your lap dog."

Ruth Ann looked down. "I don't think of him as a lap dog. He's been a good friend to me since I've been back home. Actually he's always been a good friend to me. He's a good listener." She kicked at the railing. "And what do you care if he likes me? What would you say if I told you that I like him, too?"

That took Holt off guard. "Well, I guess that's be-tween you and Rodger then." Rodger was ten times the man that Bob could ever think of being.

"Just make sure it doesn't interfere with ranch busi-ness."

She looked up and smiled at him. "Okay."

But Holt wasn't ready to let her off the hook just yet. "Speaking of interfering, what the heck was Allison doing here tonight? Did you call her?"

Ruth Ann didn't answer right away but chose a rocker and sat, the same rocker she sat in as a kid when she was in trouble for taking her horse out when she'd been told not to. "Yeah, I called her."

"What were you thinking?"

"I was thinking that *you* weren't thinking clearly. Allison was supposed to be my sister and you ruined that by breaking up with her. Holt, you've invested so much of your life into her. I figured if she showed up, that you'd remember how much you loved her."

"You figured wrong."

"I worry about you," Ruth Ann said earnestly. "Someone in this family needs to have a happy ending. I want it to be you."

That knocked the wind out of him. Holt sat next to Ruth Ann and looked out into the dark, knowing that in the daytime their land stretched as far as the eye could see.

Ruth Ann glanced over at him. "I don't want you to be mad at Rodger. He was just as surprised to see Allison here as you were. I made the call this morning and told her to get down here or else she was going to lose you forever."

Holt shook his head. "Allison and I are too different now to ever make it work."

Ruth Ann hitched her thumb over her shoulder. "And you think that dark-haired female upstairs is the answer? She lives thousands of miles away."

Yes, that was bothering him, too.

Ruth Ann continued. "You're the one who said that long-distance relationships can't work. You tried for years to make it work with Ally, someone that you've known and loved your whole life. Is that what you want? Another long-distance relationship? Why not just make it work with Ally, here and now?"

Holt took off his hat and laid it on the side table. "I don't want Allison." He wasn't clear on what he did want beyond that. It's why he'd brought Paige here, to see if he could figure it out. He stretched out his legs and crossed them at the ankle. "I just know, Ruth Ann, it wasn't your place to interfere." He glanced over at his sister and all he could see was the eight-year-old that she'd been. "Also know that if you don't work at being nice to Paige, I'm going to put you over my knee and spank you like Dad used to do. Do you hear?"

"There won't be any spanking," came a soft voice from behind him.

He and Ruth Ann swung around at the same time to see Paige standing in the open doorway with her small suitcase and Wishing Quilt tote at her feet. She'd snuck up on them and he was kicking himself for oiling that squeaky door last week.

He stood as Paige spoke.

"I would appreciate it if one of your cowhands would give me a ride to the nearest town. I'll stay at a hotel and then make my way back to Houston tomorrow."

He opened his mouth, but it was Ruth Ann who jumped to her feet and took over. "You'll do no such thing." His sister glanced over at him. "Holt is right. I've been rude and I want the chance to make it up to you. So you have no choice. You have to stay."

Holt held his tongue, but raised an eyebrow at Paige as if Ruth Ann was the one in charge now.

"I don't think—" Paige started, but Ruth Ann hurried over and picked up her suitcase.

"Come to the kitchen. There's chocolate chip cookies and a fresh pot of herbal tea."

"Is there enough for me?" Holt asked.

Ruth Ann shook her head. "No. We're going to have some girl time. To get to know one another."

Holt ignored the plea in Paige's eyes, the one that was telling him to rescue her from having to follow his sister. "Okay. I'm sure I'm needed out at the barn anyway." He stepped off the porch without giving Paige a backward glance because he was afraid he might do something stupid . . . like give her a quick kiss before Ruth Ann whisked her off to make things right.

But as he got closer to the barn, he decided it wasn't his horse that he wanted to see, but Rodger. He checked the bunkhouse first but Rodger wasn't there. He found him in the stall with Thunder.

"We need to talk," Holt said.

"Sure, boss."

"About my sister," Holt clarified.

"I figured as much." Rodger left the bucket of oats with Thunder and stepped from the stall.

"You picked up Ruth Ann?" Holt knew the answer but wanted to see Rodger's face when he answered.

"Yes."

Holt liked that he didn't hedge.

"You didn't think to call and inform me that you were doing it?" Holt hadn't ever run the ranch as a dictatorship, but was thinking now that he should've.

"No. Everything was caught up and I was only gone a couple of hours."

"But she's my sister."

Rodger looked at him as if that had nothing to do with it. "Ruth Ann called and asked for help." He said it like there was no arguing with the common sense of it.

Holt looked over at the old mule, not wanting to

meet Rodger's eyes now. One man should not pry into another man's affairs, but he felt like he had no choice. "Do you have feelings for my sister?"

Rodger sighed heavily. "Listen, boss. For years I've cared for Ruth Ann, which I never intended. Honest. She's dumped that fella Bob—who is a liver-bellied so-and-so. He never treated her right and you know it. I just decided that she needed someone like me, someone that would treat her good. If she'll have me."

Holt had never heard Rodger string that many words together at one time. "Well, okay, then."

"So I have your blessing to court her?" Rodger asked.

"That's between you and Ruth Ann." Holt stared at him—a good, long, hard stare, making sure that Rodger knew he meant business. "You hurt her—"

"I never would. Ruth Ann is special. The kind of woman that only comes around once in a lifetime."

Holt couldn't argue with that because he'd been thinking the same thing about Paige Holiday . . . *once in a lifetime*.

Chapter 6

Ruth Ann set Paige's suitcase on the step. "The kitchen is this way."

Paige looked at her bag longingly, but reluctantly followed Holt's sister. She couldn't stop asking herself why and how she always got into these messes. But nothing had ever been this bad before.

Ruth Ann pointed to a barstool at the large island. "Would you like to take a seat?" It was the most polite thing that Ruth Ann had ever said to Paige.

She slipped onto one of the barstools as Ruth Ann poured a cup of tea from a teapot shaped like a cowboy boot. She slid the teacup over, along with the plate of cookies.

"Homemade," Ruth Ann said.

Paige took one to be polite but she wasn't hungry. One of the things she'd learned from the older women at the Sisterhood of the Quilt back home was to wait people out, even if it felt uncomfortable. Sooner or later, Ruth Ann would get around to saying what she wanted to say.

Ruth Ann took the barstool across from her and sat down. She blew on her tea, took a sip, but didn't take a cookie from the plate. "I know Holt told you that I'm a college professor?"

"Yes." They'd covered that territory at the restaurant near the hotel.

"Then he must've told you that I'm on leave from the university."

"No."

Ruth Ann frowned at that. "Well, that's not what I want to say anyway." She looked out the window but there was nothing to see but darkness. "I'm very protective of my students."

That statement came out of left field.

Ruth Ann continued. "I know other instructors that are very hands-off, neutral, not really invested, not caring if their students thrive or fail." She turned back to Paige and brought her eyes up to meet hers. "That's not how I'm made."

Paige still waited, though she wanted to tell her to get to the point.

As if she'd read her mind, Ruth Ann said, "The point is I will stop my students from cutting into an expensive piece of fabric if they are going against the grain, when they should be going with it. I guide them every chance I get. I figure I only have one shot to make a difference here on earth and I take it seriously, especially when it concerns people that I care about. Do you get my meaning?"

"No," Paige said evenly, though she had a clue.

"I stop my students from making mistakes."

Okay, now that made Paige angry. "So, what you're trying to say is that Holt is like one of your students and that him spending time with me is a big mistake."

Ruth Ann frowned. "Um, no. I'm just telling you how I usually operate. I'm a control freak. I hover. Okay, and yes, maybe I thought Holt was making a mistake. It wasn't like him to go trailing after you. It's usually women falling all over themselves to trail *after him.*"

Paige was trying to follow and wondered if Ruth Ann's words had an apology hidden in there somewhere.

Ruth Ann continued. "For so long, it was understood that Allison and Holt would be a couple, get married, and everything. I had just gotten married when Holt suddenly broke up with Allison. Frankly I didn't believe it. I wasn't around very much and really didn't understand until tonight that he meant it. He doesn't want Allison." Ruth Ann reached for a cookie and took a bite, as if to give Paige a moment to chew on that tidbit she'd just given her.

But what she said brought the obvious question to the forefront.

"Go ahead and ask it," Ruth Ann prompted. Apparently, Holt's sister was pretty good at reading people, at least reading Paige.

"Okay," she said bravely. "If Holt doesn't want Allison, then who does he want?"

Ruth Ann laughed. "You'll have to ask him."

Which wasn't fair.

"Listen," Ruth Ann said, "I've been awful to you

and I'm sorry. It's been easier to focus on Holt lately than to work on myself. I thought I could fix Holt and Allison's relationship, which now seems ludicrous. I'd scream to high heaven if he tried to pull the same stunt that I did here tonight." She sighed. "I told you I've always been a control freak but apparently I've taken it to a whole new level. I've been kind of screwed up since I found my husband cheating on me with an undergrad. What you saw here tonight was just me trying to control Holt's life since I've had no control of my own." Her face held the pain of betrayal, something Paige knew oh-so well. It made her think that at least on this one issue, she and Ruth Ann could connect.

"I could write a book on how men deceive women," Paige offered, commiserating. Her mom and grandmother could write a couple of chapters in that book from their expertise, too! "I have baggage from it. I have some serious trust issues, too."

"I bet it didn't help to find Allison here tonight either."

"It didn't," Paige said.

"Well, Holt had no hand in her returning. Promise. I'm really sorry for telling her to come." She paused for a long moment before going on. "But what I need to know now is am I forgiven?" Ruth Ann gave her a sheepish smile.

The lessons learned in Sunday school were always helpful in times like these. "Water under the bridge," Paige said. She knew forgiveness had a lot of *Fake it until you make it* built into it. Her grandmother had been a great role model for forgiveness, too. Besides teaching her how to quilt, her grandmother showed her that forgiving others opened up more room for happiness in one's life. Paige's grandfather, according to her mother, had been a horrible scoundrel, nearly as bad as Paige's dad had been. Mom was still bitter over Dad, which left no room for happiness in her mom.

Suddenly, Paige understood more of why she'd taken teaching jobs all over the country. When Grandma was still in the house, there was always positivity, even on the darkest days. But now there was only bitterness from her mom's broken heart. For not only had her dad stolen all the inheritance and escaped to a nonextradition country, but he'd taken her mother's spirit away as well.

Paige shared the wisdom of the revelation with Ruth Ann. "My friend Lolly sent me this text when I arrived in Houston." She read it out loud. "A bitter woman says 'All men are the same.' A wise woman decides to stop choosing the same type of man."

Ruth Ann smiled. "Rodger, Holt's foreman, said his mama used to say something similar. Rodger has been very sweet to me and has helped me to not be so bitter. He says everything happens for a reason." She stood suddenly, as if something had dawned on her. "Come to the sewing studio. I need your opinion on what I'm working on."

It took Paige off guard but she had to admit that she felt lighter. She wasn't sure if it was because Ruth Ann had buried the hatchet—and not into Paige's back, as she suspected she might—or if it was because it sounded like Holt liked her as much as she liked him. Maybe the kiss had been real. Maybe Holt wasn't like all the rest. Maybe Holt was a standup guy?

This time as Paige walked through the house, she let herself enjoy the quilts and even ask questions. "What about the Armadillo quilt hanging over the couch? Did you make that one?"

"Oh, heavens, no. My great aunt handstitched that for Daddy when he was just a boy. My grandmother made him take care of it, so that's why it's still with us today."

Paige thought about her tote bag made from the Wishing Quilt. Though her grandmother wasn't with them anymore, her grandmother lived on through the Wishing Quilt. Oh, how Paige missed her.

"Sometimes it makes me sad," Ruth Ann said, "that the quilts are here, but the people are gone. Most of the time, I take comfort in them, remembering the stories that go along with each quilt." She looked over at Paige. "That gives me an idea."

"And that is?"

"I'm going to catalog all the quilts in the house and all the quilts I've made, too. I'll write down the stories that go along with each quilt for future generations." Ruth Ann broke into a smile. "Maybe this is something I should add to the syllabus for my students, so they can get in the habit of documenting their projects with the stories that prompted them. The story is the important part, right? Thanks for the idea, Paige."

"I didn't do anything," she said.

"I think you did. Now, come see the Cowboy quilt I want to make for a special friend."

"For Rodger?"

Ruth Ann stopped and stared at her. "How would you know that?"

"Because you lit up when you spoke of him."

"Oh." Ruth Ann continued walking. Once in the sewing studio, she positioned her quilt blocks on the design wall and Paige helped.

"This room is an addition that Daddy built for my mom." Ruth Ann gazed around the room. "This room made me who I am."

"It's incredible in here."

"You should see it during the daytime. The sunlight hits it just right." She turned and gave her a serious look. "I need to make something clear. You know you have to stay, don't you? Or else I'll be in the doghouse with Holt forever."

Paige smiled at her. "I guess I can stay but only if you won't take offense if I want to rearrange some of your blocks."

"Of course not."

Paige switched up four blocks and stood back. "Have you considered adding a pieced border?"

Ruth Ann nodded at the quilt. "I hadn't, but now that you say it, I think that's what's been missing. Any suggestions?"

"You could play it safe and go with stars. But if I were you, I would add cowboy boots around the edge." Paige grabbed a blank sheet of paper from the center of the table and sketched a simple cowboy boot. "And of course, I'd fashion the cowboy boots out of different bandanna-type fabrics. But that's just me."

Ruth Ann smiled. "You have a good eye. That's something you can't teach. Believe me, I've tried." She laughed as if it were an inside joke. "You should see some of the design disasters and color combinations that my students have put together when they are trying too hard to be artistic. I hate to use the word *eyesore* but there's no other word for some of their combinations."

The two of them laughed together and it felt good to finally be able to breathe. But then there was a voice from the doorway, and once again, Paige was short of breath, for a different reason this time.

Holt leaned against the jamb, grinning. "I see you two are getting along now."

Ruth Ann took the boot template from Paige. "Quilting has a way of smoothing things over."

He smoldered Paige with his eyes. "Do you want to meet my horse?"

"Go on," Ruth Ann said. "We can work more on this later."

Paige felt ridiculously shy but walked to the door as calmly as she could. Holt pointed out the way. She stepped past him, breathed him in, and kept going as he followed her down the hallway to the front door. Once they were outside and walking toward the barn, he spoke. "Did she do it right or do I need to give her another good talking-to?"

"Do *what* right?" Paige suspected she knew. But who could really tell as she was giddy with her emotions all over the place tonight? Being near him was thrilling and scary. And for some weird reason, even after everything that had happened here, her gullible heart trusted him.

"Did my sister apologize? Just so you know, I don't think she's ever said *sorry* in her entire life."

"Yes, she apologized. And she asked for forgiveness, too."

"Maybe *the brat* is finally growing up after all." He said it with love, a smile, and a chuckle.

Knowing he could love his family like that made Paige feel safe, warm, and utterly happy. But before Paige fell for him completely, she had a few questions that needed to be answered.

"What about Allison? I heard her say that she'll be back in the morning." Paige also heard the disparaging way that his ex referred to her.

"I fixed it."

"What does that mean?"

"I called her at her dad's house and told her not to come back, that she'd be wasting her time."

That was all well and good, but it didn't exactly speak to where Paige stood with him.

He put his hand out and stopped her. "To be clear, I told her that I was interested in someone else."

Paige's heart skipped a beat, but she held back from letting her heart soar. Instead, she feigned innocence with an, "Oh?"

He slid his hand down her arm and intertwined his fingers with hers. "I'm very interested in you."

Paige couldn't believe this was happening. The cowboy with the Stetson hat cared for her, too. It was real.

Then he sealed the deal with a lingering kiss. If this were a movie, this would be where the curtain would come down, or the credits would roll, or the screen would fade to black as she and Holt rode off into the sunset together.

He gave her a hug and pointed to the barn. "We better get going. I promised Thunder that I'd introduce him to *my lady*."

Paige thought she would melt from happiness.

The next half hour was pretty perfect as she met Thunder and Rodger while holding Holt's hand. The evening ended inside the house at the bottom of the steps with a kiss good night before she went up to her room.

She had sweet dreams, knowing all was right with the world. The next morning, they started their day with coffee on the porch before he showed her the ranch by horseback. They visited his cattle and his sheep and she loved every second of it. By the time they were back at the house eating dinner with Ruth Ann, Rodger, and six other cowhands, Paige had fallen completely in love with Holt and was dreaming of spending the rest of her life with him. Or at least that was the assumption her heart had jumped to. But . . .

Not once all day together had he said a word about how their relationship was actually going to work. Did he want her to get an apartment in town so they could continue to date? *If that's what they were doing?*

When dessert was served, her concern had grown into doubt, and doubt was quickly transforming into fear. Was this just a short-term fling for him? Even though she was enjoying his company, she was making herself miserable about the future. If Lolly were here— or if Paige had cell reception to call her—she'd confess all her woes over her budding relationship with Holt.

Paige knew exactly what Lolly would say. She'd laugh and tell her to silence the voice that was trying to ruin a good time.

Paige groaned. She hoped she wasn't just a *good time* to Holt. She was going to try and chill out, just enjoy him, and push all her questions and worries aside.

Holt gazed at her. "Are you all right? You seem worried. Didn't you have fun today?"

She stuck a smile on her face, trying to trust once again that this was all real. Trying to trust him. "Best day ever." If only she could get past her reservations; her family's genes were prone to pick the wrong man instead of the right one. She glanced over at Holt and said a little prayer. *Please let him be the man that I think he is.*

The next morning, Holt carried Paige's suitcase downstairs. Her visit had been a success. "Let's get our stuff into the truck and head back. We should have just enough time to see a good portion of NASA today before I'm on booth duty for Preview Night at Quilt Festival tonight."

As he drove to Houston, Holt glanced over at Paige every now and then because she seemed to be talking to herself. He had to ask her again. "Is something wrong?"

She chewed on her lip. "No. I'm good."

"Okay." He was going to take her at her word. "When we get to town, we'll drop our things off at the hotel and then on to sightseeing. Sound like a plan?"

She nodded and smiled at him and he felt certain he

was falling in love with her. Not the kind of love that was familiar—old hat—like what he'd had with Allison when they were dating. This was new and exciting and made his chest feel strange. Like he wanted to hold Paige in his arms and protect her from all the craziness in the world. He reached over and took her hand, and out of the corner of his eye, he could see her relax . . . which made him happy.

Once they got to NASA, they rushed to see as much as they could before they were expected at Preview Night. Ruth Ann had guilted him into being the Circle J's mascot again. He'd laughed as Ruth Ann milked it by insisting her shoulder would heal quicker if Holt would spend at least half of his time with her and CeeCee during Quilt Festival. He agreed but planned to spend the rest of his time with Paige.

Coming back from NASA, they were running a little late. As he and Paige walked up to the booth, Lila Mae, Charise, and Betty were already there, speaking with CeeCee and Ruth Ann. They all stopped talking and stared at them, especially at how his hand and Paige's hand were joined together. Immediately Paige untwined her fingers from his and hurried over to the ladies.

But that's when the razzing began.

"Oooh, Paige has a boyfriend," Charise cooed.

"Grow up," Lila Mae censured.

Holt noticed that his sister had an easy expression on her face, no frown, which was a far cry from the last time he and Paige were in the booth.

"What's going on here?" he asked.

"We've been getting acquainted with the Hanahan sisters," Ruth Ann said.

"And making plans with the gals." Betty had a pencil and her calendar out.

"What kind of plans?" he asked.

"Dinner plans," Lila Mae answered, "for tomorrow night. Betty has already made the reservation. It was my idea."

He wondered if he and Paige were expected to attend.

Betty checked her calendar and then pointed at him with her sharpened pencil. "Then on Friday, we're all going dancing."

"Cowboy, can you do the Texas two-step?" Charise asked, shaking her backside like she was a twenty-something.

Before he could answer, Betty continued. "Saturday night we're all set for dinner theater."

So we are expected to attend. Every evening planned out, and he wasn't thrilled about it. The only plan that was acceptable was the one where he could spend more time with Paige. Preferably alone! But she nodded at each item Betty listed and acted as if she were all-in. So he did the only thing he could. "Sounds good." He would just have to make the most of the moments the two of them would have to themselves.

The next several days and evenings flew by with him working mornings in the booth. The afternoons, he and Paige walked the quilt show, talking, holding hands, growing closer together. The next few evenings they spent with his sister, CeeCee, and the three sisters. Ruth Ann and CeeCee had taken to the Hanahan sisters and were scheming to partner up with the Circle J quilt shop and the Sisters Three quilt retreat center in North Texas. All the while, Holt tried not to think on how Paige had to head back to Alaska soon.

As they all exited the dinner theater on Saturday night, Betty pulled out her darned calendar again. He'd come to despise that thing. "I took the liberty of booking us for brunch tomorrow morning. I hope that works for everyone?"

"Sorry," Holt jumped in. "I've already made other plans for Paige and me."

"Really?" Ruth Ann said.

Paige looked just as shocked, but she recovered quickly when he gave her a knowing glance. "Oh, yes, Holt has planned a special morning for us before he has to be back in the booth."

"Oooh, what are you two going to do?" Charise cooed.

Lila Mae shot her a stern look. "Never mind. Leave the lovebirds alone."

"I'd like to know," Betty said very practically, as if she and her itinerary had been affronted.

Paige turned to him with lifted eyebrows. "Go on, Holt. Tell them."

He didn't miss a beat. "We were going to watch the sunrise on the beach in Galveston and then have breakfast at one of the cafés." He'd been thinking about the beach, walking along the surf with Paige, and that kiss that kind of sealed the deal for him.

"You'll have to get up mighty early. An hour drive there and an hour drive back," said CeeCee.

"No earlier than if I was at the ranch," Holt said.

Paige gazed up at him and smiled. "I don't mind the early hour. I'm looking forward to it."

Her smile was like warm sunshine to him.

Holt and Paige said good night and headed back to their hotel. Holt kissed her at the door, gave her a hug, and said, "Sleep well."

He went to his room before he lingered too long. The morning would be here soon enough.

It was still dark out when he rolled out of bed and dressed. When he knocked on Paige's door, she immediately opened it with a curling iron in her hand, the wand end wrapped in her hair, the unplugged cord dangling at her side.

"Come on in. I'm almost ready. I've made coffee, if you'd like to have some."

"Thanks."

She rushed back to the bathroom and closed the door as he ambled into the room. He forewent the coffee and walked to the window to look out. On the table, he spied the sketchbook that Paige was working in all the time. He looked closer. He hadn't seen this drawing before. It wasn't a quilt but a landscape that included a snow-capped mountain with animals scattered about and a cabin off to one side. He flipped to a page with pink and blue flowers. He turned the page again to see three different colors of a buffalo plaid. Page after page held new images. She'd mentioned her dream of designing fabrics, so these must be it. He thought they were great! He wondered if Ruth Ann's old college roommate, Tiffany, would think so, too.

He pulled out his phone and took pictures of all of Paige's fabric designs. He wouldn't tell her what he was doing in case it didn't work out. Besides, if it did, he wanted to surprise her. He sent all the pictures to Ruth Ann with a note, asking if she thought they were good enough to pass along to Tiffany, who now worked at QT Fabrics.

When Paige came out of the bathroom, she looked really cute in her blue jeans, western shirt, and a bandanna holding back her long black hair.

"You look nice," he said, taking her in, thinking, *She's the perfect cowgirl for this cowboy.*

"Ready to go?" She picked up her backpack and looked around, her eyes landing on her sketchbook in front of him. She smiled and walked over and grabbed it, and then leaned up to kiss him.

"Thank you," he said.

"For what?"

"That kiss. It's a great way to start the morning." He could get used to starting his days this way. He put his hand to her back and guided her out.

When he pulled onto the highway, he reached over and took her hand again as they drove to Galveston. They arrived in plenty of time to grab a coffee and pastry to take to the beach before the sun rose at seven thirty; probably the most romantic thing he'd ever come up with in his life. He was glad he was doing it with Paige.

The next few hours passed quicker than he wanted, but he'd promised his sister he'd be back in time. "Ruth

Ann and CeeCee will be expecting me." He wished he'd begged off.

"Then we better head back," Paige said.

"How about lunch today? Just you and me?" Maybe he should've told her earlier of all the practical things he'd been thinking about. Things about the two of them. But this morning had been reserved for romance, while lunch would be about real plans and strategies, and would give him a chance to tell her how he saw their future unfolding. A lifetime together. How he planned to build her a quilting studio of her own, if his mother's studio wasn't big enough. How he'd called Marsha, who lived down the road from the ranch and who owned a plane, and who had agreed to fly Paige to the airport when she needed to get to her quilting workshops and engagements.

"Sure. I can do lunch," Paige said. "I'll be at the booth at noon. I have a demo to go to first." He said goodbye to her at the authors' book signing booth but it wasn't really goodbye. He was feeling confident that they were just getting started.

Chapter 7

Paige spent her morning going to all the booths that she planned to see, but hadn't been able to stop herself from feeling jumpy, nervous that she was leaving soon and Holt had said nothing more about his feelings for her. Nothing about the future. He certainly did like to hold her hand, and he certainly kissed her all the time, which made her dizzy and happy and quelled her worries for that particular moment. But right afterward, the ugly head of her insecurity rose again.

At five minutes to twelve, she made her way to the Circle J booth, but Holt wasn't there.

Ruth Ann hurried over. "Holt will be right back. He's taking a large roll of batting to one of the other vendors' van."

"Thanks."

Ruth Ann looked expectant. "I was hoping you could stay a few extra days in Texas."

Paige had been waiting for an invitation but the wrong Champion sibling was making the invite.

"My flight is tonight."

Ruth Ann pulled out her phone and scrolled through her pictures. "I'm trying to get ahold of my friend about your designs."

"Designs? What designs?" The cold shiver of déjà vu slid up Paige's spine. A moment ago she'd been happy, but instantly, she was reliving her last horrifying visit to Houston and feeling she'd been suspended once again over the precipice of betrayal.

Ruth Ann held up her phone and confirmed Paige's worst fear: the image was the *Once Upon a Cabin* scene, Paige's sketch. "I think these are great. Inspired. I'm blown away and a bit jealous, enough so that I'd like to steal them." She had the audacity to laugh. But it was no joke to Paige!

She was drowning in another nightmare, much worse than when Malcolm had stolen her designs, as Ruth Ann was outright telling her what she meant to do.

There was a buzzing in Paige's ears but she managed to say, "H-how did you get those?"

"Holt sent them to me," Ruth Ann said. "I—"

"Fine. Just keep them. Do whatever you want." Paige's voice was hoarse, harsh. She was completely stunned and heartbroken. She bolted from the booth as tears blinded her eyes.

She couldn't believe she'd been a chump again! Holt hadn't talked to her about a future because he'd only been buttering Paige up to steal her designs for his sister.

At the same time, her heart disagreed, telling her that Holt would never deceive her. But her heart was renowned for being dead wrong when it came to good-looking men. Once again, her mother and grand-mother's DNA had won out and let a con man into Paige's life. How could she have let herself be duped again?

Her cell phone rang. One look at the sender and she declined the call. She kept rushing to the ballroom doors. Her phone dinged again with a voicemail. She deleted it without listening first.

She made it out of the ballroom to the large outer hallway and was running past registration toward the exit when she heard her name called out.

"Paige. Yoo-hoo, Paige!" It was Charise and the other two sisters.

For a moment, Paige thought about ignoring them but she couldn't. She quickly wiped the tears from her face before turning around to see the three Hanahans rushing toward her.

Their smiles turned to worry as they searched her face.

Lila Mae's normally stern expression now held concern, as she gently brushed Paige's hair away from her eyes. "What's wrong, dearest?" She glanced around as if the bully who'd brought Paige to tears might be nearby.

"Nothing's wrong," Paige said, trying to smile but she couldn't exactly pull it off.

"You can tell us," Betty said wrapping her arm around Paige while Charise took her hand and squeezed.

Because these three felt as comfortable to her as her quilting group back home, she couldn't help but tell them the truth. "Holt isn't the man I thought he was."

Lila Mae's face turned to stone. "Did he take advantage of you this morning? I knew letting you go off on your own on this sunrise business was a bad idea."

The answer was yes, he had taken advantage of Paige, but not in the way that the older woman meant. "No. I just want to head back to the hotel."

"We want to help," Betty said.

"Yes!" Charise piped in.

"There's nothing to be done."

"We'll see about that. Let's get coffee and talk. No argument." Lila Mae pointed to the elevator. "Upstairs to the coffee shop."

"Sure," Paige said, knowing the eldest sister meant business. But Paige didn't have to tell them anything. Soon she'd be back in her hotel room alone. This was just another trip to Houston that had gone wrong.

Her phone rang again.

"Aren't you going to answer it?" Betty asked.

"No. It's nothing important." Paige silenced her phone.

As soon as they sat with their coffees and pastries, Lila Mae prompted her. "Tell us what your cowboy did."

"He's not my cowboy," Paige protested as the tears welled up again. "I thought he was . . ." And then, because she couldn't stop herself, she told them the whole dreadful story, starting with what happened the last time she was in Houston and ending with Holt giving Ruth Ann her designs.

"Are you sure?" Betty said.

"He seems like such a lovely man," Charise added.

Lila Mae took her hand. "I'm truly sorry, Paige." But a determined look came over her face and she stood. "We should get downstairs and finish visiting the booths."

"Yes, and I need to get to the hotel and pack." Paige couldn't wait to get on the plane and put Texas behind her. She tossed her uneaten Danish in the trash and followed the sisters downstairs. She gave them each a hug at the exit. "I'll see you in the spring at Sisters Three."

"We have your dates all set for next year," Betty reminded her.

"Yes. They're in my calendar," Paige said. "Goodbye."

She walked to the door and pushed it open, finally outside, finally escaping where Holt was. But the problem remained; she couldn't outrun the ache in her heart.

Her ride back to the hotel was with a woman, thank goodness. And she was grateful for her late checkout. Paige packed the rest of her things, splashed water on her tearstained, blotchy face, and pulled out her phone to call Lolly to report what had happened . . . again. But instead, Paige just settled in for a long cry to get Holt out of her system—as if that would work!

When she got up to get more tissues from the bathroom, her cell dinged with a text message. It was from Lila Mae: **Come back to the convention center. We need you in our group picture, standing beside your quilt.**

Paige stared at her phone in disbelief. Why couldn't they leave her in peace to grieve how stupid and naïve she'd been?

A second text came in. This one from Betty: **Please**

hurry. We have a lot more ground to cover today at the quilt show.

Paige started to ignore the text. But she owed a lot to the Hanahans. They had booked her workshop when she was just starting out and then had her back at their retreat center over and over again.

She pushed herself off the bed and went into the bathroom to survey the damage from her crying jag. More foundation and blush did nothing to hide how she was feeling. She ordered another Uber and headed downstairs to wait. When she returned to the convention center, Lila Mae was waiting for her at the door.

"I thought we might have to send out the cavalry to get you." Lila Mae looped her arm in Paige's and began dragging her to where the quilts hung in the other side of the ballroom.

Paige just wanted to get this over with. But when her quilt came into sight, she didn't like what else she saw . . . *who else*! Paige stopped and dug her heels in to keep Lila Mae from pulling her farther.

Holt and Ruth Ann were talking to Charise and Betty. There was another woman there, too.

Lila Mae tugged. "Come along, dearest. You need to hear their side of the story."

"What side would that be? Where the Champions had planned to con me out of my designs?"

Holt and Ruth Ann had stopped and stared at her, and Paige had a decision to make. She could either put her head in the sand like she'd done when Malcolm had stolen her designs or she could do things differently, take this chance to stand up for herself and not let it happen again. She ignored Holt's eyes—ignored him—as she walked up to them.

Ruth Ann pointed to her companion. "Paige, this is Tiffany, the creative manager at QT Fabrics. We were roommates in college."

The introduction took Paige off guard and knocked some of the fight from her. She stared at them for a long moment but then finally said, "I don't understand." If Ruth Ann was going to claim Paige's drawings as her own, why was Ruth Ann introducing her to this woman?

"Can we go somewhere and talk?" Tiffany pointed to where there was a lounge area setup, out of sight in the corner of the building.

"Yes." But Paige was clueless as to what was going on.

Holt walked back to the booth, feeling like he'd lost Paige. He couldn't believe that she wouldn't even look at him before she walked away. He wasn't naïve enough to believe that Tiffany being here, or even if she signed Paige on, that that would fix things between them. He'd been stupid to share her artwork with Ruth Ann without asking permission first. He was kicking himself for such a bonehead move.

Most of all, he should've told Paige how he felt about her and what she'd come to mean to him. For the first time in his life, he was really in love. The same kind of deep love that his parents had. He should've told Paige what he'd been thinking and the arrangements he'd made. Things to make Paige's life easier when she said yes to marrying him and living on the ranch between her quilting gigs. Yes, he should've let her know he'd been planning—*heck, made her part of the conversation!*—but instead, he'd been stubborn and kept it all to himself, once again acting like he had no sense at all.

Tiffany returned to the booth alone, gave Ruth Ann a quick hug, and waved to CeeCee. "I gotta run. Dinner date with my aunt. We'll be in touch."

If Holt's arms hadn't been loaded down with containers from packing up the booth, he would've run after her to find out what happened with Paige. But he knew. Paige would be heading to the airport soon for her flight back to Alaska.

He took the first load to the truck, wishing once again that he'd done things differently. While he was outside in the vendors' parking lot, he helped an older woman maneuver her cart to her vehicle and unload it into her SUV, as if doing penance would make him feel better. It didn't. If he hadn't been expected to finish taking down the Circle J booth, he would've stayed in the parking lot and helped every last person, thinking to atone for what he'd done. But he couldn't and he doubted that would even be enough.

When he returned to the booth, he couldn't believe what he was seeing. Paige was hugging Ruth Ann and they both were laughing. He had to stop for a second to settle the pounding in his chest before he sidled into the booth.

She turned around.

But he spoke first. "Is all forgiven with me, too?" He held his breath, waiting for an answer.

"I'm not sure it's that easy. We'll have to discuss boundaries first."

"Yeah. I know. I really overstepped," he admitted.

"You Lower Forty-Eight folks could learn a thing or two from us Alaskans about privacy."

"Paige, I'm so sorry. I was an idiot."

Ruth Ann piped in. "An idiot that meant well. Paige, you'll have to tell him what happened with Malcolm Landis."

"How do you know about Malcolm?"

Lila Mae cleared her throat. "You never expected us to keep quiet about such a horrible thing, now did you?"

CeeCee shook her head with disgust. "The sisters explained everything that happened the last time Paige was in Houston, and what Malcolm Landis did to her. Despicable man! She has every right to be upset. And to not trust people. I'm thinking I'll let the quilt guild know what he did, and you can be sure that I'll never buy his books again for the shop."

Holt was red-hot with anger and glared at his sister. "Tell me what he did."

Ruth Ann took his arm. "He didn't physically hurt her but he did wound her spirit and taught her to distrust others." She gave Paige a sympathetic nod but then put her attention back on him. "So calm down, big brother, and have a private chat with Paige, will you?" She let go and gave him a sisterly shove toward the woman he loved.

He complied and walked with Paige from the booth, away from the earshot of others. "Are you okay?"

"Yes. I'm okay."

"What about this Malcolm Landis? Do I need to find him and teach him some manners?"

"I don't want to talk about him now, but I promise I'll tell you all about him later."

Her words, especially the promise of *later* lifted some of the weight from his chest.

Holt reached up and ran his knuckles over her cheek. Yes, it was a bold move, considering he didn't know where he stood with her yet, but he just couldn't keep from touching her any longer. "About the boundaries I crossed. I know you won't be able to forgive me right away, but would it help if I told you that I've fallen completely and helplessly in love with you?"

Paige gave him a Mona Lisa smile. "Perhaps."

That one word allowed him to breathe easier but . . .

"Do you think you can ever love me back?" he asked.

"It depends." She moved closer and took his hand, intertwining her fingers with his. "Can I get another look at that ranch of yours?"

His heart took flight, making it feel as if he were riding Thunder full tilt across the pasture with the wind in his hair and the sun shining down on his back. "And here I thought you could only love me for my truck." He was grinning at her like a goofy teenager but he didn't care. He was so very happy. "I do want to talk to you about the ranch and other things."

"Like what?"

"When you finally forgive me and agree to marry me, I would like for us to get hitched in Texas, if that's okay. Either at the ranch, in the barn with twinkly lights; or at the country church where my grandparents were married. Or under the old oak tree where my dad proposed to my mom." He loved the way Paige was beaming at him. "No rush or anything, I just wanted you to know your options. Of course, if you have your heart set on getting married in Alaska, that'll be fine, too. You name the time and the place and I'll be there."

"It's something we can definitely talk about." She leaned up and gave him a quick kiss on the chin.

He took it from there and wrapped her in his arms, giving her a long tender kiss, until he heard catcalls coming from the Hanahan sisters.

They broke away from each other, laughing.

"Are we invited to the wedding?" Charise hollered.

"Absolutely," Paige said.

That was precisely what he wanted to hear.

Epilogue

Paige stood in the back of the church where Holt had been baptized. The bows attached to the pews were fashioned out of her newly released fabrics, the modified buffalo plaids in multiple colors and the Fireweed and Forget-me-not florals. Different elements of her designer fabric were incorporated in other aspects of the wedding and reception, too, like the tablecloths and the wedding quilt that the Sisterhood of the Quilt and her new Texas family had collaborated on together.

Tiffany from QT Fabrics had become a close friend and had helped Paige, Ruth Ann, and CeeCee decorate the church yesterday. Last night, Selma and Louise and the Hanahan sisters had come to the ranch to take over preparations for the reception today, bringing chaos, love, and laughter to Holt's home, now to be Paige's home, too.

Paige gazed down the aisle. Ahead of her stood her future—her community and the man she loved. Others filling the pews were from her past. It felt like all of Alaska had flown to Texas to witness the ceremony—Lolly, Hope, and all of the Sisterhood of the Quilt were here. From the altar, Lolly beamed back at Paige, wearing her country blue plaid dress and matching cowboy boots. Paige was having an honest-to-goodness Texas country wedding. Her heart swelled with love. She gazed at the easel near the altar, which displayed her newly framed Wishing Quilt. Holt's idea. He thought it would be like having her grandmother standing with them during the ceremony. He promised to hang it, first thing, in their living room when they got home from their honeymoon.

Paige looked over at her mother, who reached out and took her hand. She'd arrived a week ago to help with the preparations. Being at the ranch had turned Mom into a new woman—from negative to positive with a constant smile on her face. Paige still couldn't believe the transformation.

Mom squeezed her hand. "I'm so happy for you." She was waiting to be ushered to her seat as mother of the bride. It had been Mom's idea for Ruth Ann to walk Paige down the aisle instead of her. Mom thought that being the mother of the bride suited her much better than standing in for the father Paige had never known.

Mom leaned closer. "You know, Paigey," she whispered and nodded toward Holt, "you've got yourself a good one and it gives me hope. Maybe one day, I'll find a man as upstanding as yours. Perhaps there's a cowboy on a neighboring ranch who might be interested in a mature woman?" Mom beamed at Paige then put her attention on the usher, one of Holt's tall, sturdy ranch hands, as he walked toward her.

Mom looped her arm in his. "I love you, Paigey."

"I love you, too, Mom." Paige leaned over and kissed her. Mom left with the usher to make her way to the front, looking happier than Paige had ever seen her.

Only Ruth Ann and Paige remained at the back of the church. "Are you ready for me to walk you down the aisle?" Ruth Ann asked.

Paige nodded toward the front, where Rodger stood next to the groom. "Ruth Ann, you've got to know that man loves you. When are you going to say yes and put him out of his misery?"

"Soon. Very soon. First, though, Holt has to have his happily-ever-after."

Which would be Paige's happily-ever-after, too! A strange mixture of love, contentment, and excited energy overtook her.

When she gazed upon Holt and saw that he was looking back at her with love in his eyes, she calmed. He always seemed to bring her back to center. The man of her dreams. Steady, strong, honest, and trustworthy. She didn't know how she'd gotten so lucky. Maybe the Wishing Quilt had done its magic after all. *Better late than never*, Paige thought. If Grandma Doris were here today, she would be so very proud and happy for her.

Grandma would also remind Paige that she had been on a journey from the beginning and that everything happened for a reason. Life was funny that way. Paige never would've guessed that her biggest trials and heartaches were only stepping-stones to her purpose, her career, and ultimately to the man she was marrying today.

The wedding march began to play. Her cue. Paige smiled brightly and eagerly took her first steps down the aisle toward Holt and their new life together.

Don't miss Jodi Thomas's heartwarming
STRAWBERRY LANE. . . .

Set in Someday Valley, surrounding the charming small town of Honey Creek, Texas, *New York Times* bestselling author Jodi Thomas's latest novel tells the heartwarming, tenderly romantic tale of a man who drives his car off a cliff—straight into a life he never imagined . . .

Starri Knight is a big believer in fate. How else to explain the compelling connection she feels to the stranger she pulls out of a wrecked car on the very same road where her parents died twenty years earlier? Alongside Auntie Ona-May, the only mother she's ever known, Starri saves Rusty O'Sullivan's life—just as Ona-May once did when Starri was an orphaned babe. But convincing Rusty he has something to live for is going to take all of Starri's faith in miracles . . .

Like a wish he hadn't even known to make, Starri landed in Rusty's life, filling him with a longing for a family. Then Jackson Landry, a new lawyer, turns up to present a surprise that will change the direction of his life: an inheritance from the father Rusty never knew—and the promise of the family he'd never had. It's a lot for the hard-bitten loner to accept as love from an unexpected direction rushes into his life . . .

A sense of duty has Rusty heading to Honey Creek to deal with his father's estate—and find his lost siblings. But having family is one thing, learning to love them is another. Good thing new friends are by his side to help him along the way.

Read on for an excerpt . . .

Prologue

The Will

"The bed is too hard. I thought hospital beds were supposed to be comfortable," Joey Morrell complained to Jackson Landry in a half-drunk whine.

"Mr. Morrell, I'm not involved in hospital furnishing. I'm your lawyer." Jackson lifted his briefcase as if showing proof of his new title. "Now, we need to get down to the topic of your will. You may not have much time left."

Jackson kept his voice low, hoping to sound older.

Joey reached for his cigarettes. Camels, no filter.

"I didn't know they still made Camels. Never mind. Irrelevant. You can't smoke in here, Mr. Morrell. I don't think Dr. Henton would approve and I saw the no smoking sign when I ran through the emergency entrance."

"Jackson, you're no more fun than your dad. The SOB up and died on me before I got my affairs organized. I'd just finished listing my heirs from a few of those affairs years ago, when they tossed me in the ambulance, and now I find out I've got a wet-behind-the-ears lawyer."

"You were having a heart attack, Mr. Morrell. The bartender called 911, then you told him to call me." Jackson noticed the old guy wasn't listening. If sins showed on a man's face, Joey Morrell was the bad side of Dorian Gray.

Joey coughed. "I did love those women I found in my younger days, but I never wanted to do the paperwork. Every darling I slept with cussed me out for not marrying her. They all said I didn't have a heart, so that's proof I can't die of a heart attack. But you, being my lawyer, are going to make it right, Jackson, just in case? I'm keeping my word to your old man to sign a will. I plan to pay for my folly."

"I'll do my best to help you, sir." Jackson thought of cussing. He should have been an accountant. His dad left him every crazy old goat in the valley to deal with. Joey Morrell was as bad as the lady who came in every Monday to change her will. Every time one of her cats died or peed on the rug, the feline was disinherited.

"Good. Make it fast, boy. I'm not feeling so good." Morrell coughed again. "About time to roll the dice on whether I walk out of this place one more time. The women I attract now-days are drunks, mean and ugly even with my glasses off. Might as well head down to Hell. The pickings couldn't be much worse."

Jackson leaned over the bed. "That why you're refusing the heart surgery, Morrell? You want to leave it to chance?"

Joey smiled. "I may have done a hell of a lot of bad things, but I swear I'm not a liar. I've spent sixty years gambling and I ain't stopping now. I like women, but I wasn't born with enough heart to love one. Strange little creatures if you ask me. Nesters. And me, I was born to ride the open roads." He stopped long enough to push the call button again.

"I've already cheated death three times. I got out of that hospital in New Orleans after I was left for dead in an alley for two days. Ten years ago, I was in a bad wreck they said no one could walk away from, and at twenty a medic took four bullets out of my chest.

"Jackson, it'll be another thirty years and another dozen women before I wear out, but I promised your daddy I'd make a will if I ever ended up in a hospital again."

"Then, let's get started. How about we begin with your assets, Mr. Morrell. I know you have an old Camaro, a little piece of land along the north rim, and an eighteen-wheeler truck. You never married. No living relatives."

Waving the lawyer away, Joey leaned back on a stack of pillows. "I'm tired, boy, and I'll miss the news if you stay any longer. I wrote down all you need to know." Joey handed him a folded piece of paper. "Draw it up all legal like. Don't come back until after breakfast. The nurse said she has to spoon-feed me if I'm weak come morning." A wicked smiled crossed his pasty face. "There ain't nothing nicer that a big-busted woman with short arms feeding a man."

Jackson had enough of Joey Morrell. The drunk was

as worthless as his father used to say he was. "I'll take care of everything, Mr. Morrell." Just for spite, he added, "Anyone you want to notify to come to your funeral?"

"No. I'll go it alone. Cremate my body and spread my ashes out on Eagle's Peak."

Jackson put the folded paper in his empty briefcase and walked out of Joey's room. As he passed Dr. Paul Henton, Jackson shook his head. "The old man thinks you're too young to be a doc and I'm too dumb to be his lawyer."

Paul took the time to look up from a chart. The doc nodded. "He won't let me operate or move him to a big hospital for surgery. Claimed he'd chosen option number three. Get over it. He told me he plans to be out of this place before happy hour tomorrow."

"What are his chances?" Jackson asked.

The doctor whom Jackson had played football with throughout high school was honest as always. "Not good. You might want to get that will done."

"I'm heading home before the rain gets worse. I'll work on it tonight and have it ready by morning." Jackson hesitated and added, "Call if you need me."

The doctor turned back to his charts as he added, "I will. Same for you."

Jackson turned his collar up and ran for his pickup thinking if he ever made any money in this small town, he'd buy a proper car. Maybe a Lincoln, or a BMW. Lawyers should drive something better than a twenty-year-old, handed-down beat-up farm truck.

Half an hour later Jackson was holding in his hand

the square of paper Joey had given him, when the hospital called. As the nurse explained how Mr. Morrell died yelling for his supper, the lawyer read the note below four names with birthdays beside each. It read: *Give it all to my offspring.*

Morrell's signature was clear. Dated an hour ago. Witnessed by a nurse and some guy who wrote "janitor" under his name.

"Damn," Jackson said as he stared at the names. "The old guy knew he was dying. Probably didn't mention it just to irritate the hell out of me."

Joey died leaving all he owned to four names on a piece of paper.

Four sons he'd probably never met. All with different last names and none of them Morrell.

ANDY DELANE—30—FORT SILL
RUSTY MACAMISH—34—SOMEDAY
    VALLEY
ZACHARY HOLMES—25—AUSTIN
GRIFFITH LAURENT—27—FRENCH
    QUARTER NEW ORLEANS

Joey lived within a day's drive of one of his sons. Another son lived thirty miles away on the other side of the valley, but Jackson would bet not one of them had ever seen Joey. That could be a good thing. Joey wasn't much of a man or a father. That not one carried his name was proof.

Jackson had taken over his father's practice in

Honey Creek two months ago and his first client left this world without paying.

But Jackson would do his duty and hope none of Joey's boys took after their sperm donor. He'd find the boys, now men, but he doubted they'd be glad to see him.

Chapter 1
Someday Valley

Midnight

Rusty MacAmish gunned the old Ford's engine just before he swung left and headed up the hill toward Someday Valley. There was always a chance the car wouldn't make the incline on the dirt road, but he'd had a hell of a day and figured bad luck had to run out sometime.

Mud moving downhill like lava on his left. A ten-feet drop was on his right. Bald tires didn't put up much of a fight to hold on to the two-lane road.

In the midnight rain Rusty felt the Fairlane begin to slide sideways. Then like a slow rerun, the Ford tilted left as the road disappeared and three thousand pounds of steel began to roll. Rusty tightened his grip on the steering wheel as if he still had some control of the car . . . or his life.

He didn't bother to scream or cuss. He simply braced for a crash.

The ground slammed into the passenger side, shattering glass and metal. Then, as the roof hit the incline, he felt the cut of his seat belt and it seemed to be snowing glass.

The Ford rolled again and the driver's door pushed against Rusty's shoulder. He clenched as it rolled again and the inside of what had once been a car was now a coffin of flying glass and metal.

Something hit his head and the night went completely black but, for a moment, the sounds remained in his head as if echoing what had been his life.

One last echo whispered through the bedlam. One word he'd heard for as long as he could remember.

Worthless.

Chapter 2

Starri Knight lay on the hardwood floor of her aunt's hundred-year-old cabin as she watched rain slide down the huge picture window. If she didn't move, maybe she'd feel closer to nature as she had when she was a child. Maybe the moon would play peek-a-boo with her in the storm clouds. She was almost positive the man in the moon had, once when she was small.

When she was a kid, stars winked at her and the moon smiled. She'd tell her Aunt Ona-May and they'd laugh.

But tonight, all Starri saw were car lights making their way up the hill and lightning running across the sky like a tidal wave igniting.

All her life, pretty much everyone who took the back trail in rain got stuck. Her Aunt Ona-May would wait until morning to back the tractor out of the barn and go pull them out of the mud. For thirty bucks, of course.

Starri watched the rain as she remembered the story of the night her aunt took her in as if she were really kin. Her aunt said one dark night a young couple, not out of their teens, took the road to Someday Valley way too fast. They collided with a pickup coming down hauling hay. The crash killed both the teenagers instantly, but the baby in the back didn't have a scratch.

While the two farmers to the north heard the crash and came running to help the driver pinned inside his truck, Ona-May crawled in the window and pulled out a baby in the back seat of the young couple's car. She said the minute she pushed the blanket away the baby reached up trying to touch the stars.

No one came to take the baby that night. Ona-May decided to call the tiny child Starri until kin came. But, no one came. No one wanted the tiny baby.

Since Ona-May Jones was a nurse in her younger days, the county let her foster the child.

Starri smiled, remembering the beginning of her story. She couldn't miss parents she'd never known, but she was thankful Aunt Ona-May found her. Auntie might never have a family of her own, but she poured all her love on a tiny baby.

Starri watched as the car on the incline began to roll sideways down the hill. For a moment it seemed no more than an awkward falling star.

Then the sounds of glass and metal snapping blended with the rain and Starri screamed.

Someone was dying in the same spot her parents had twenty years ago. She closed her eyes, reliving a memory that had formed before words.

As always Auntie's arms surrounded her. "Starri, it's all right." As the old woman saw the car rolling, she added calmly, "Get on your boots. We've work to do."

Auntie's old body straightened into the nurse she'd been in Vietnam, fifty years ago.

As she collected supplies, Starri dialed 911 and was told the road between Honey Creek and Someday Valley was closed. One of the bridges was out. The only ambulance in the valley was on the other side of the bridge.

"We'll take care of it, Starri. Don't worry. Doctoring humans is pretty much like doctoring the other animals around here."

Starri nodded but she wasn't sure she believed her aunt.

As they marched up the hill, the lights on the car went out but the rattling continued as if the auto was dying a slow death. The engine was still sputtering when they reached the wreck. Their flashlights swept the ground like lightning bugs hopping in the night.

"Here," Ona-May yelled as she moved a few feet below the car.

Starri ventured closer, making out the outline of a body. A tall man dressed all in black. Rain seemed to be pounding on the body as if determined to push him in the ground.

Auntie pulled off her raincoat and covered him. "I can't see where he's hurt, but he's breathing. We'll roll him on your raincoat and pull him to the cabin. If he makes the journey back to the house, I'd say he's got a chance."

Starri followed orders. She'd seen her aunt set a broken leg and stitch up a cowboy who refused to go to the doctor. Auntie delivered babies before the doctor could come out. The people in the valley were mostly poor and didn't go to a doctor unless they had to. They knew Ona-May would take care of what she could and often loan them money if she recommended the doctor.

As they pulled the unconscious stranger over the wet grass, Starri thought of another talent her aunt had. She loved people. Not just the good ones or the righteous ones like the preacher counted. She loved them all, even the sinners and the drunks.

Starri figured Ona-May overlooked folks' shortcomings because she had a few herself. She wasn't beyond stealing the neighbor's apples or corn and she cussed when she was frustrated. And, every New Year's Eve, she'd drink and tell stories of her days in the Army.

As they reached the cabin, her aunt started issuing orders as if she had troops and not just Starri.

"We'll put him on the floor by the fireplace. Get me towels and warm water. Start cleaning him up while I collect supplies and call the doctor over in Honey Creek. I can already see our patient has an arm broke, so cut off his shirt. I'm guessing he's got internal injuries. Oh, add logs to the fire, girl."

Starri stared down at the muddy man with hard times showing in worry lines. "You'll have to help me, mister. I can't even remember all the orders. Ona-May gets like that sometimes when she's excited, but my ears still listen slow. She was an emergency nurse for thirty years. You're in good hands."

"Starri, get moving," Ona-May yelled from the kitchen. "We got to keep him alive until the ambulance gets here."

She handed her aunt the phone as she ran for towels and a pan of hot water. When she returned, the stranger's eyes were open. She saw pain, but not fear.

"You an angel, sweetheart?" he whispered.

"No," she answered. "I'm a star that fell out of the sky twenty years ago. Kids at school said I'm as strange as they come, but I'm not. I'm just different."

"Me too," he said. "I'm Rusty MacAmish. Folks say I'm worthless. You're wasting your time fixing me up. I'll just scatter again."

He closed his eyes as she gently washed his face. She didn't know if he fell asleep or passed out, but the worry lines faded on his face. She barely heard him whisper, "Watch over me, little star."

"I will. You just rest. Don't worry about that wind-shield wiper sticking out of your side. My aunt can fix that."

Chapter 3

Jackson ran through his parents' house stripping off his clothes as fast as he could with one hand as he held his cell in the other.

"Slow down, Paul. I can meet you at the bridge with two mounts. I've got Raymond saddling two horses and loading them in the trailer now. I can be there by the time you can drive from the hospital to that old bridge heading into Someday Valley." Jackson hit speaker as he pulled on jeans. "Any idea who the injured man is?"

"Yeah," Paul answered. "He's your client's son. He's Joey Morrell's oldest son."

**Don't miss the prequel to *Ransom Canyon*, soon to
be a Netflix series
starring Josh Duhamel and Minka Kelly!**

SILVERLEAF
RAPIDS

by
Jodi Thomas

From the *New York Times* bestselling Jodi Thomas
comes the origin story of rancher Staten Kirkland, the
last descendant of Ransom Canyon's founding father,
and the unforgettable patriarch of the nationally bestselling series.

Available from Kensington Books